PROJEC

By
Jobic Chakalisa

Contents

1.Rooftop Telescope Rules

2.Blue Tape Briefing

3.Pallets at Pier 22

4.Three-Check Rule

5.No Glass After Dark

6.Pelican Case Silence

7.Badge Stays Visible

8.Cinder Coffee Newsroom

9.Binary Nucleus Printout

10.Red Wristband Line

11.Pad 39A Gate

12.Bunker Brunch Etiquette

13.Storm Net at Starbase

14.I-10 Contraflow Mile

15.Don't Take the Bridge

16.Hand-Crank Radio Hour

17.Warheads in the Stratosphere

18.Concrete Air and Lullabies

Chapter 1 - Rooftop Telescope Rules

Lila's phone vibrated against her palm on the third flight, right where the concrete stairs narrowed and the building's old paint sweated in the heat.

RAN IT BY LEGAL.

NO CONFIRMATION, NO STORY.

YOU PUBLISH VIBES, WE GET SUED.

Three lines. Her editor never wasted a fourth.

Lila kept climbing anyway.

The cheap telescope case banged her knee with every step. The strap cut into her shoulder. The stairwell smelled like hot dust and the chemical bite of somebody's too-strong cleaner. A mosquito whined at her ear, drunk on the damp air rising from the ground floor.

Above her, the rooftop access light flickered as if it couldn't decide whether to stay awake.

Her friend waited at the landing by the metal door, bent over a phone screen, knuckles white around the handle of a second bag—tripod, she guessed, because nothing else unfolded into that many sharp angles.

"You brought it?" he asked the second she cleared the last step.

Lila lifted the telescope case like evidence and let it drop against her thigh. "I brought it. I didn't bring a court order, a NASA badge, or a miracle."

"You brought the only thing that matters."

"Flattery won't stabilize your tripod."

He didn't laugh. He had that look he got when he'd spent all day staring at numbers and light curves and had come out the other side convinced the universe had whispered his name. Lila had seen

2

it a dozen times and spent years turning it into copy without getting burned.

Tonight, he looked like he'd been burned already.

He leaned close to the door and pressed his ear to it, like the roof might talk back. Then he tapped the push bar, testing.

"Try it," he said.

Lila pushed. The metal gave with a stiff complaint, and warm air rolled through the crack as if the roof exhaled.

Heat hit her face. Houston didn't cool down at night. It just changed flavors. This was tar and exhaust and the faint rot of standing water in gutters that never drained right.

Her friend held the door while she squeezed past. The handle was warm enough to sting.

"Rule one," Lila said, because her mouth did that when pressure climbed—made jokes, pretended she didn't care. "If a raccoon attacks, you're the shield."

He hauled the second bag through. "Rule one is don't talk."

"Rule two is don't tell me what to do."

"Rule two is *don't turn on your flashlight*," he snapped, and his tone cracked the humor clean off the moment.

Lila stopped with one foot on the roof and one still in the stairwell. A building groan carried through the doorframe, old steel settling.

She tucked her phone in her pocket without turning the screen back on. "Okay."

He shut the door behind them with a careful pull, not a slam. The latch clicked anyway, loud in the open air.

Both of them flinched.

"Jesus," Lila muttered.

"Sorry," he whispered.

"Don't apologize like you did something wrong. Apologize like you did something dumb."

He gave her a look that would've been an argument on any other night. Tonight, he just shouldered the gear and walked.

The roof spread out under the orange dome of city light—flat tar, patches of gravel, white paint lines around HVAC units and utility boxes. Wind moved warm across it, not enough to cool, enough to shake anything you tried to keep still.

Lila's sneakers stuck a little with each step. The tar had held the day's heat like a grudge.

He led her toward the HVAC units, the ones that clanked in a steady rhythm and created a pocket of broken wind. Not quiet, not hidden, but less exposed than the roof's edge.

"Here," he said.

"You picked a romantic spot," Lila whispered, kneeling. "Nothing says intimacy like industrial humming."

He dropped to his knees and unzipped the tripod bag with hands that didn't tremble. That scared her more than shaking would have.

Lila set the telescope case down and unlatched it. Foam creaked. The telescope itself looked like a toy next to the seriousness in his posture. Cheap black tube, scratched in places, a brand sticker peeling at one corner. The kind of telescope you bought online at midnight because you needed something to point at the sky and convince yourself you belonged under it.

Her editor's message burned in her pocket like a live coal.

No confirmation, no story.

Her friend extended the tripod legs and planted them, hard, as if he could punch stability into the tar.

"You're sure it's not just—" Lila began.

"Don't," he said, still quiet, and now she heard a tremor under the control. "Please don't."

That stopped her. Not the word. The please.

Lila slid her fingers over the eyepiece and then wiped it with the hem of her shirt anyway, a quick, familiar swipe. Her ritual. Her superstition. Clean lens, clean truth.

Her friend's eyes tracked the motion. He didn't comment. He just tightened a knob, then another, jaw clenched.

"Tell me what you saw," she said. "One more time. But in English."

He adjusted the telescope's mount with precise movements. "It's not in the catalog."

"Nothing is in the catalog if you don't look in the right one."

"I looked in all of them."

Lila set her notebook down on the tar. The cover was already soft from being jammed into bags and back pockets, bent around her life. She flipped it open and clicked her pen.

"What's the object?" she asked.

He nodded toward the sky, like he could point to a specific slice of black through the light dome. "It's moving wrong."

"That's not English. That's panic."

His mouth tightened. "It's bright enough to show up. It has a tail. Barely. But it has one."

"Comet?"

He shook his head once, fast. "Not cataloged. Not announced. The line of travel doesn't match expected. If it's what I think—"

"If it's what you think, you send it to an observatory," Lila said.

"I did."

"And?"

He pulled his phone from his pocket, screen dim, brightness cranked low. He turned it toward her. An email thread. Names she didn't recognize. The kind of polite professional language that took a request and buried it under process.

Lila scanned the subject line: **RE: Observation Request — Urgent**.

A reply sat under it with a single sentence: **We cannot comment on unverified observations.**

No signature. No help.

Her friend's thumb hovered over the screen, as if he wanted to tap hard enough to break through it.

"You tried," Lila whispered.

"They told me to stop," he said.

Lila looked up from the phone. "They told you to stop looking at the sky."

He didn't answer right away. A gust of wind rattled the HVAC grates, lifted grit across the tar. Somewhere down on the street, a car alarm chirped once and died.

"He didn't say 'sky,'" her friend said finally. "He said 'this.'"

Lila's stomach tightened in a small, quiet way. The kind of tightening that came before a real decision.

She put her pen between her teeth for a second, thinking, then pulled it out and wrote the sentence down anyway: **TOLD TO STOP.**

"What did you do?" she asked.

"I kept watching."

Lila closed her notebook and shoved it under her thigh like a weight. "Okay. Then we do this clean. You promised me clean."

"I promised you proof," he said.

"Same thing. If I can't run it past legal, it's not proof, it's suicide."

He lowered his gaze. "Satellite imagery is behind paywalls. They lock the good stuff behind NDAs."

"You don't need to explain that to me," Lila said. "My editor just reminded me with three texts."

Her friend tightened the mount again. "Phones," he murmured.

"What?"

"Put yours on airplane mode. No Bluetooth. Nothing."

Lila stared at him. "You think my phone's going to—what, betray me?"

"I think you're standing on a roof in the middle of a city pointing glass at something somebody told me not to look at," he said, and his voice stayed controlled, but something in it scraped. "Just do it."

Lila's instinct rose, sharp and proud: don't take orders. Don't act scared. Don't turn this into a thriller because your friend had watched too many late-night documentaries.

Then she thought about her editor's message. Legal. Lawsuit. Disposable.

She slid her phone out and killed everything but the clock and the camera. Airplane mode. Then she looked at her friend.

"You happy?" she whispered.

"No," he said. "I'm not."

He nodded to the telescope. "Get down."

Lila dropped to her knees beside him. The tar pressed heat through her jeans. She leaned in and pressed her eye to the eyepiece.

Cold glass kissed her eyelid. The contrast hit her—hot air, cold lens. The sky through the scope looked darker than it should have, like the telescope cut through the orange haze and revealed the bruise under it.

"Okay," her friend murmured. "Left. A touch. Now up."

Lila adjusted with careful fingers. The mount resisted, then gave. Stars slid. Not points, not pretty—blurred by humidity, winking in and out through the city's light dome. It took work to make them stand still.

Her friend's breath held beside her. She heard it, then the tiny release, like he'd been saving oxygen for this.

"Do you see it?" he asked.

"Hold on."

She hated how much she wanted to see it. Not because she believed him—because she wanted to be the one who found the crack in the official story first. Because the newsroom ran on a simple fuel: being right before anyone else.

And because being wrong made you a joke.

She nudged the scope again. The field shifted. A brighter point entered at the edge, then slipped away. She cursed softly and steadied her hands.

"Count," she whispered to herself, and she didn't know why. One. Two. Three.

On three, she hit record on her phone, positioned behind the eyepiece with the clamp her friend had rigged—cheap plastic, tightened so hard it creaked. The phone's red record dot glowed like an accusation.

"Now," her friend said. "Stay on it."

Lila froze her body into a tripod. She locked her elbows. She slowed her breathing. She stopped being Lila Reyes, journalist, and became Lila Reyes, person trying not to shake.

For a second, the view held.

Then she saw it.

Not a comet streak. Not Hollywood. Not a clean, bright tail drawn with a confident hand.

A smear.

A pale, thin smear that shouldn't have been there, angled wrong against the black, like someone had dragged a fingertip through chalk and then tried to erase it.

It hovered at the edge of visibility, the kind of thing your mind wanted to invent and then your mind wanted to deny.

Lila pulled her eye away and blinked hard. Sweat cooled on her spine and then warmed again.

"Again," she whispered.

Her friend didn't move. "Keep it in frame."

Lila leaned back into the eyepiece and forced herself not to squint. Squinting made lies. She relaxed her face, widened her eye, let the image settle.

The smear remained.

It didn't belong to any star. It didn't belong to any known satellite track. It sat there with quiet insult, barely visible against the light dome, as if the city's glow tried to bury it and failed.

Her throat tightened.

"Okay," she breathed. Not loud. Not triumphant. Just the word. A surrender.

"You see it," her friend whispered.

"Yes."

"Tell me what you see."

"A point with a dirty line behind it," she said, and the words came out sharper than she meant. "A tail."

"A tail," he echoed, like the sound might anchor it in the world.

Lila kept the phone recording. Her hands started to sweat against the mount. She adjusted one millimeter and watched the smear shift—still there. Still wrong. Still real.

Her heart beat so loudly she worried the scope would pick it up and turn it into wobble.

She pulled her eye away again and stared at the real sky with naked vision. Nothing. Just the orange dome and the suggestion of stars too tired to fight through it.

Through the telescope, the sky changed.

Truth barely visible through glare.

Her friend exhaled like he'd been underwater.

"We have it," he whispered.

Lila didn't answer. She watched the record timer climb on her screen. Twenty seconds. Thirty. Forty.

Something in her mind shifted. Not from skepticism to belief. From belief to calculation.

If this footage held, it mattered. If it mattered, someone already knew. If someone already knew, the silence wasn't empty. It was enforced.

She reached for her notebook with her free hand and wrote with small, careful strokes, bending over the page to block wind.

Tail visible. Raw footage. Phone clamp. Time: 11:47 PM.

She didn't know why she wrote the time. She just knew she would need it later, in a room with fluorescent lights where someone would question her memory like it was a stain.

A distant clang cut through the HVAC hum.

Lila jerked her head up.

Her friend froze beside her, eyes wide in the dim.

Another sound followed—metal on metal, sharper, purposeful. Not roof settling. Not a loose vent cover. Footsteps, heavy enough to carry through wind.

Lila's hand tightened on the telescope tube.

"Did you hear that?" she mouthed.

Her friend nodded once, slow. He angled his head toward the neighboring building, the one across a narrow gap—close enough to see windows, too far to hear voices unless someone shouted.

Lila crawled on her knees toward the roof edge, careful not to let gravel scrape loud. She kept low behind an HVAC unit and peered over.

At first, she saw nothing but the city's glow reflecting off glass and the pale lines of another rooftop. Then a beam of light swept across concrete like a blade.

A figure moved through it. Then another. Then three.

Not maintenance. Not some guy with a toolbox.

They moved in a line, coordinated, spaced out, their steps measured. Dark uniforms. Hard cases carried with two hands. Radios clipped high on shoulders. No frantic gestures, no confusion. The kind of calm you only got from practice.

Lila's mouth went dry.

One of them lifted a hand. The others stopped without talking.

They stood for a moment at the edge of their roof, scanning.

The flashlight beam swung toward Lila's building.

She ducked down so fast her knee hit gravel and pain shot up her leg.

Her friend grabbed her elbow, hard, and pulled her deeper into the shadow of the HVAC unit.

"Who is that?" he whispered, and his voice almost broke.

Lila swallowed. Her tongue stuck to her teeth. "Security."

"That building's empty."

"It was empty," Lila whispered back.

The flashlight beam drifted away. She risked lifting her head again, slower this time, inch by inch.

On the neighboring roof, the team moved again. One knelt near a roof hatch. Another set a hard case down and opened it with quick fingers. Foam inside. Equipment that didn't belong in a casual world.

Lila's journalist brain tried to label it. Thermal camera? Antenna? Some kind of portable array?

Her other brain—the one that kept her alive in bars at closing time, in interviews with men who smiled too wide—said: *They're not here for the view.*

A radio hissed, faint but present on the wind. A clipped voice answered. Words lost in distance, but the cadence carried: brief, coded, practiced.

Lila slid her phone from behind the telescope mount. The record still ran, capturing the pale smear in the sky.

She hesitated.

If she stopped recording, she lost evidence. If she kept it running, she risked missing whatever was happening next door.

Truth vs timing.

Her editor's message flickered through her mind. Legal. Lawsuit. Disposable.

Then Lila saw one of the security team members glance up at the sky, not like a man admiring stars but like a man checking a clock.

Her hand moved without asking permission.

She angled her phone away from the telescope and toward the neighboring roof, still keeping low. The camera adjusted to darkness, struggled, then found enough light from the sweeping flashlight to show silhouettes and movement.

Her friend's hand slid to her shoulder, a silent question.

Lila put a finger to her lips and kept filming.

The flashlight beam swept again, closer this time, wider. It flashed across Lila's roof edge and painted the HVAC unit in brief white glare.

Lila pressed her back flat against the tar. The warmth of it soaked through her shirt. Her phone hovered just above the roof surface, lens tilted toward the edge without exposing her face.

The beam passed.

Her lungs burned. She hadn't breathed in seconds.

Her friend's whisper came, barely air. "They can't see us."

"You don't know that," Lila whispered.

"We're in the dark."

"Dark doesn't mean invisible."

On the neighboring roof, the team set something up—tripod, maybe, or a stand. Two men worked the same piece with synchronized hands while a third watched the roof hatch like he expected company.

Lila's stomach tightened again, different now. Less fear of being caught doing something illegal. More fear of being caught doing something they didn't want anyone doing at all.

Her friend leaned toward her ear. "This is because of it."

"Maybe," Lila breathed.

"It's because of it."

Lila kept her phone steady and counted silently, the same superstition she used for the telescope, as if numbers could hold the frame still. One. Two. Three.

She stopped herself from zooming. Zoom made shakiness. Shakiness made doubt. Doubt made lawsuits.

She forced her hands to stay calm, wrists anchored against the roof. The video captured dark shapes, flashlights, hard cases. It captured enough to show one undeniable fact: professionals in coordinated gear moved on an empty building's roof at midnight.

A man near the roof hatch lifted his head and turned, slow, as if he sensed movement.

Lila froze. Her finger hovered above the stop button, not pressing, not lifting.

His flashlight beam tilted—swept her direction—paused.

Lila held her breath until her chest ached.

The beam moved on. The man looked away.

Her friend's grip on her shoulder loosened a fraction. He whispered, "We should go."

Yes, Lila thought. Yes, get out, take the footage, go downstairs, lock the door, pretend you didn't see anything.

Then she looked at the telescope still pointed at the sky, phone clamped to it, recording the pale smear. She looked at the neighboring roof, at the hard cases and the radios and the practiced calm.

Someone had already decided this mattered.

Which meant she had stepped into a story that didn't want her.

Lila's pulse hit her throat. She tasted metal.

"We leave," she whispered. "But we take everything."

Her friend didn't argue. He moved with an urgency that tried to stay quiet. He reached for the telescope clamp.

"Wait," Lila breathed. She slid back to the telescope, keeping low, and grabbed her phone off the mount without shaking the scope too much. The video timer kept climbing. She hit stop. The red dot disappeared, replaced by a thumbnail that showed a dark sky and a pale, wrong smear.

Her stomach flipped.

She shoved the phone into her pocket like it could burn through fabric.

Her friend folded the tripod with hands that moved too fast. Metal clicked. A sound too loud. Both of them paused, eyes on the neighboring roof.

No immediate reaction. No shout. No flashlight swinging their way.

Lila snapped the telescope case shut and latched it with a careful push.

"We can't take the stairs too slow," her friend whispered.

"And we can't take them too fast," Lila whispered back.

They crawled toward the rooftop access door in the shadow of the HVAC units, keeping their bodies low and their gear close. The wind shifted and carried another burst of radio static from next door. The sound raised the hair on Lila's arms.

Her friend reached the door first and put his hand on the handle.

He looked at her, question in his eyes: now?

Lila nodded once.

He pressed down, slow. The hinge complained anyway, a thin squeal that sliced the night.

Lila's shoulders tightened. She waited for a flashlight beam to swing and pin them.

Nothing.

They slipped into the stairwell. The air inside hit cooler, stale, smelling of old concrete and somebody's laundry soap.

The door clicked shut behind them with the same loud finality as a verdict.

Lila stood still for one beat, listening.

Above, the roof held its own noises: HVAC hum, wind, far-off traffic.

Below, the stairwell held breath and distance.

Then she heard it.

Footsteps. Not theirs. Lower down. Slow, deliberate, climbing.

Her friend's eyes widened. He tightened his grip on the tripod bag.

Lila lifted a hand, palm down: stop.

She leaned her ear toward the stairwell void. The footsteps climbed one flight, paused, then continued. Heavy soles. Not a resident in flip-flops. Not a delivery guy.

Lila's mouth dried again.

Her friend mouthed: *Security?*

Lila shook her head. She didn't know. She knew only that someone moved in the same building as them, at the same time contract security moved next door, and the coincidence tasted bitter.

She took her phone out, screen still dark, and resisted the urge to check the video. She didn't need proof of what she'd already seen. She needed to get downstairs without becoming a shadow in someone else's report.

She tipped her head toward the next landing and started down, slow, placing her feet near the wall where the stairs creaked less. Her friend followed, gear hugged to his chest.

The footsteps below paused again, as if listening too.

Lila held her breath and took another step.

A door opened somewhere beneath them. A metal click. A whisper of air.

Lila's skin prickled.

She forced herself to keep moving. One step. Then another. She reached the landing and turned the corner.

The stairwell light overhead buzzed and flickered, throwing shadows that jumped with each flash.

Her friend stayed close, not touching her, but near enough that his fear warmed the space between them.

They descended two flights like that—quiet, measured—until the footsteps below shifted direction.

Not up toward them.

Away.

Lila didn't relax. She didn't speed up. She held her pace like a line on a graph, steady enough to not draw attention.

At the bottom, the stairwell opened into a service corridor that ran behind the building's main elevator bank. A smell of adhesive and cardboard hung in the air, mixed with the sour tang of old trash.

The service elevator sat at the end, its doors closed. A fluorescent light above it flickered the same way the stairwell light did, as if the building couldn't decide whether to keep the night lit.

"Go," her friend whispered, pointing toward the hallway that would lead back to their apartments.

Lila took one step, then stopped.

Something sat beside the service elevator, half in shadow, half in the sick light.

A shipping crate. Cardboard reinforced with wood slats. Discarded like packaging, left at an angle against the wall. Nothing about it should have mattered.

Except for the strip of tape sealing one corner.

Blue.

Not the cheap clear tape maintenance used. Not the brown packing tape landlords slapped on everything. This was a bright, almost electric blue that caught the flickering fluorescent light and threw it back like a signal.

Lila's pulse jumped.

Her friend hissed, "Lila."

She didn't move.

The tape had a handwritten label on it—black marker, letters pressed hard enough to dent the surface. The words didn't make sense at first glance because her brain still held the roof, the smear, the flashlights.

She stepped closer. The air smelled stronger here—fresh adhesive, dust, the faint chemical sweetness of new cardboard.

Her friend grabbed her sleeve. "We need to go."

"One second," Lila whispered.

She knelt beside the crate. The cardboard felt dry under her fingertips, gritty with construction dust. The blue tape edge had started to peel, curling away like a tongue.

Without thinking, she touched it.

The tape was warmer than it should have been, as if it had been handled recently.

Lila snatched her hand back fast, as if the tape could bite.

Her friend's face tightened. "What are you doing?"

"Getting one tangible detail," Lila whispered. Her own words came back to her like a warning. Compulsion to solve it immediately. "Something I can track."

She pulled her notebook from her back pocket. The cover bent where her grip tightened too hard. She flipped it open and held it under the flickering light.

Her pen hovered for half a beat. Her fingers steadied over the page with a calm that didn't match her heartbeat.

She wrote: **BLUE TAPE. SERVICE ELEVATOR CRATE. LABEL**— and then she leaned in closer, eyes narrowed, reading the black marker dents in the tape.

Her friend hovered above her, breathing shallow.

Lila copied the letters exactly, even the weird spacing, even the way the marker dragged.

Then the fluorescent light flickered hard—off, on—off, on—like a nervous blink.

Lila snapped the notebook shut and stood.

The building's silence pressed around them. The footsteps from below didn't return. The service elevator stayed closed, indifferent.

Lila looked at the blue tape one more time, and the roof returned in her mind: the pale smear, barely visible through the glare; the hard cases; the radio cadence; the flashlight beam pausing as if it had noticed her.

The sky didn't look empty anymore.

Her friend whispered her name again, urgent now. "Lila."

She shoved the notebook into her pocket and lifted the telescope case, muscles protesting. Her friend turned first, walking, not running, toward the hallway.

Lila followed, keeping her steps quiet, her posture ordinary.

Inside her pocket, her phone pressed against her thigh like a secret with weight.

Behind her, the blue tape caught the flickering light and held it for a breath, bright as a bruise.

Chapter 2 - Blue Tape Briefing

Naomi's badge hit the scanner and came back with a flat, indifferent beep that didn't open the turnstile.

She tried again, slower, as if pace could persuade a machine.

Beep.

The predawn air outside JPL bit at her knuckles and made her eyes water. She blinked hard, not from cold but from a sleep debt that felt older than her own body. The parking lot lights buzzed overhead. In the distance, the San Gabriels sat as a darker shape against a sky that refused to brighten.

Behind her, a contractor in a reflective vest cleared his throat.

Naomi slid half a step to the side to let him reach another scanner lane. He didn't. He hovered too close, a polite pressure that still took up space.

"Try the other reader," the guard said through the glass. He didn't look up from his screen.

Naomi kept her face neutral. She angled her badge toward the second scanner. Her hand didn't shake. It wanted to.

Beep.

The guard finally raised his eyes. His gaze traveled from her face to the satchel on her shoulder, then to the hard-sided case in her left hand.

"You Naomi Park?" he asked, like the question was new information.

"Yes."

He pressed a button, and the window slot in the glass clicked open. "Slide it in."

Naomi did. The badge scraped plastic.

He held it up under a smaller light and watched the tiny holographic strip. "You're on the list."

Naomi swallowed. "I have a briefing in"—she checked her watch without lifting her wrist too high, as if sudden movement could trigger suspicion—"twelve minutes."

The guard's mouth stayed flat. "Secondary."

The word landed with weight. Secondary meant delay. Secondary meant eyes. Secondary meant the kind of attention she'd spent her career avoiding.

Naomi shifted her grip on the hard case. The handle had a rough spot that caught her thumb in the same place every morning. She'd told herself she should sand it down. She never did. It reminded her she was still holding something.

"I've been coming in this gate for seven years," she said, and hated how defensive it sounded.

"Things change," the guard replied.

Behind him, a poster about workplace safety curled at one corner. A second poster warned about badge tailgating in cheerful colors that didn't match any human mood at five in the morning. The guard tapped a line on his screen, then pointed with two fingers toward a side door.

Naomi didn't argue. Arguing burned time and marked you as difficult. She turned toward the side door and kept her stride steady.

A second guard waited in a small vestibule that smelled like disinfectant and tired coffee. He wore a uniform that fit too well, as if he'd been measured for it. His eyes held the empty calm of a man trained to watch without reacting.

"Bag," he said.

Naomi set her satchel on the table and unzipped it. Her laptop, a spiral notebook, a pen case, a folded sweatshirt she hadn't worn. The guard pushed her things around with gloved hands, not searching for contraband so much as searching for her.

The hard case stayed in Naomi's grip.

"That too," the guard said.

Naomi placed it down and popped the latches. Foam inside, cut to fit paper stacks and a small binder. Everything printed. Everything tangible. Not because she loved paper—she didn't—but because paper left a trail that couldn't be edited after the fact without visible scars.

The guard lifted the binder. Its cover bore a plain typed label and a strip of blue tape sealed across the edge like a promise you couldn't open without breaking.

He looked at the blue tape, then at Naomi.

"You made it?" he asked.

"I received it," Naomi said. "I made the contents."

That wasn't precisely true. She had made the numbers. Others had added their own language around them, shaving edges, rounding phrases, sanding down uncertainty until it sounded like competence.

The guard turned the binder in his hands, then set it back in the foam. He closed the hard case with a careful snap, as if the case contained something fragile.

"You're clear," he said.

Naomi picked up her things. Her badge waited on the table like a small verdict. She slipped it back onto her lanyard and walked through the final door.

Inside, the hall lights ran a dimmed version of daylight. The building hummed with air systems and distant machines. JPL at predawn always felt like the inside of a throat—quiet, controlled, lined with rules that existed to keep something from spilling out.

Naomi moved faster now, shoes whispering over polished floors. She took the shortest route, the one past labs where night-shift engineers slept in chairs, and past a windowed room where a cluster of people stood around a table too early for any ordinary meeting.

They didn't look up as she passed. That should have reassured her.

It didn't.

Her conference room sat in a corridor with no windows. She swiped her badge. This time the door opened without protest, like it had only wanted to remind her who owned the lock.

Inside, the projector already ran. Its fan pushed out hot air. The light threw a rectangle onto the screen where error bars widened and narrowed like a pulse.

Burnt coffee clung to the room in layers. Someone had left a box of powdered creamer on the counter and never replaced it. A stack of white paper cups waited beside a drip carafe that had cooked itself into bitterness hours ago.

Naomi set her hard case on the table and flipped it open.

Printed handouts, neatly stacked. A laser pointer. A handful of paperclips she'd stolen from her own desk because procurement moved slower than fear. She lined the printouts by page number, squared the edges, and forced her fingers to stop fussing.

She straightened things because alignment gave her the illusion of control.

Chairs scraped outside. Voices murmured through the door seal. Naomi checked her watch again. Six minutes. She took one sip of coffee from the cup she'd poured and immediately regretted it. The taste was ash and old heat.

The door opened. People filed in with the practiced neutrality of those who understood the room belonged to nobody and to everyone.

Leadership first—JPL director-level, a program manager Naomi barely knew, a liaison from NASA who smiled without warmth.

Then interagency observers: a woman in a tailored suit with a Homeland Security badge clipped low, a man with the posture of military and the face of a politician, another who carried nothing at all, as if paperwork couldn't touch him.

Naomi watched their hands. People told the truth with their hands.

The military man's fingers tapped twice against his folder, then stilled. The woman in the suit adjusted her cuff and glanced at the corners of the room. The man with nothing sat and folded his hands on the table like prayer.

Naomi sat last. Not as a show of deference—she had to remain standing for the briefing—but because she needed one more breath with her own body before the room claimed it.

"Dr. Park," the program manager said, voice clipped, "thank you for getting here."

Naomi nodded once. She didn't offer small talk. Small talk wasted oxygen.

She slid the handouts down the table. Paper moved like a wave, soft friction against wood.

A skeptical official—NASA, she thought, but the badge was turned away—picked up his copy and flipped through without reading. He let the pages flutter as if the motion itself conveyed judgment.

Naomi kept her eyes on the screen.

She held the laser pointer in her right hand. It felt too light for what it had to carry.

"Current object designation remains provisional," Naomi began. Her voice came out level. She could hear the faint shake under it anyway, like a held note that wanted to break. "We've been tracking observational data from multiple sources and refining the orbital solution."

The word *multiple* hung there. It wasn't a lie. It was also an exclusion.

She clicked to the next slide—another printed plot mirrored on the screen. No fancy graphics, no logo. Just lines, bands, and dates.

A man near the end of the table raised a hand before Naomi finished the first sentence. His suit jacket didn't crease when he moved, which meant it cost more than Naomi's monthly rent.

"Before you continue," he said, "we need a simple answer. Are we talking about a public crisis or an internal planning exercise?"

Naomi looked at him. She didn't smile. "You're asking for a binary."

"I'm asking for clarity," he replied.

Naomi's knee bounced once under the table. She stopped it with a deliberate press of her heel into the carpet.

"Clarity is what we're trying to earn," she said.

The woman in the suit made a sound that wasn't quite a laugh.

Naomi clicked again. The screen showed the probability curve, a line that had climbed over weeks and now sat higher than anyone in this room wanted it to sit.

"Based on the latest observation set," Naomi said, "impact probability increased."

"How much?" the skeptical official asked.

Naomi tapped the laser pointer against the printed number on her handout, then aimed it at the screen.

"Significantly," she said. "We crossed a threshold."

She heard her own words and hated them. *Crossed a threshold* sounded like a metaphor, like drama. But the math didn't care about her preferences. The curve had moved. The world had changed in a way you couldn't feel yet.

The military man leaned forward. "Give me the percent."

Naomi held his gaze. "It depends on the model confidence interval and assumptions about non-gravitational forces."

The man with nothing spoke for the first time. "That's not an answer."

Naomi inhaled, slow. "It's the truth."

A silence settled, heavy and close. The projector's fan kept spinning, a quiet insistence.

Naomi slid her own copy of the plot forward, the one with her handwritten notes along the margin. She didn't hand it to anyone. She just made it visible.

"Here," she said, tapping the top of the chart with her fingertip. "This is the current solution. The band shows uncertainty. I can give you a single number, but I will be lying by omission."

The skeptical official flipped his pages again, this time with sharper movements.

"Dr. Park," the program manager said, soft as caution, "we're not here for philosophy."

Naomi turned toward him. "I'm not giving you philosophy. I'm giving you the only kind of certainty that exists in this problem."

Her voice stayed even. Her throat tightened anyway. She could taste that burnt coffee rising back up.

The man with nothing leaned back. He didn't look at the screen. He looked at Naomi like she was a malfunctioning component.

The military man's finger tapped his folder again. Twice. Stop.

Naomi's gaze caught the blue tape on a folder near the program manager's elbow. A strip sealing the edge. A bright line marking what could and could not be opened in front of whom.

"Let's say we accept uncertainty," the woman in the suit said. "What are you asking for?"

Naomi exhaled. This, at least, was a question she could answer.

"We need resources," Naomi said. "Time, personnel, hardware access. We need to increase observation cadence. We need modeling support outside our current compartment."

The skeptical official snorted. "Outside the compartment. You want to widen the circle."

"Yes."

He leaned forward. "And you want to do that without leaks."

Naomi didn't flinch. "Leaks happen when people don't have a plan and panic fills the space."

The man with nothing's eyes narrowed. The program manager's jaw tightened. Naomi saw it—the slight recoil at the implication that their containment strategy created its own poison.

"Leaks happen when someone wants attention," the skeptical official said. His gaze moved over Naomi's face, then down, then back up again in a way that made her skin prickle. "Or when someone doesn't understand the stakes."

Naomi felt heat rise behind her eyes. She forced it down. Emotion didn't persuade in this room. Numbers did. Or at least, numbers decorated with the right words did.

She clicked to the next slide. Another plot, this one showing possible impact corridor projections. The lines overlapped and diverged, converging on Earth's orbit like a hand reaching.

"We're not in a position to discuss impact corridor publicly," Naomi said. "We are in a position to plan mitigation."

The military man's gaze sharpened. "Mitigation."

Naomi nodded once. "Deflection options are limited by time. We're past the point where we can pretend a single answer exists. We can still reduce risk if we act now."

The program manager interlaced his fingers. "And your confidence level that we have enough time?"

Naomi didn't look down at her notes. She'd memorized the numbers. She'd memorized the cost.

"My confidence," Naomi said slowly, "is that if we wait for a clean story, the story will write itself and we won't like the ending."

The room held its breath.

The man with nothing turned his head toward the program manager. A small shift, like the transfer of permission.

The program manager cleared his throat. "We are elevating this," he said. "There will be a formal structure."

Naomi's pulse spiked. Formal structure meant oversight. It meant committees. It meant meetings that replaced work.

It also meant money.

The woman in the suit straightened. "What are we calling it?"

Naomi watched the program manager's hands. He slid the blue-taped folder open with a practiced motion, breaking the seal as if breaking didn't matter in here.

He pulled out a single sheet, typed, stamped, and already decided.

He didn't look at Naomi when he spoke.

"Project Hail Mary," he said.

For a second, Naomi didn't understand the words as meaning. They hit her like sound first. Two syllables, then two, then three. A religious phrase in a room of engineers.

Hail Mary: a prayer you threw when you ran out of options. A last play. Desperation rebranded as strategy.

Naomi felt something cold settle low in her body.

The military man nodded, satisfied by the neatness of a name.

The skeptical official's mouth twitched as if he wanted to smile but remembered cameras existed somewhere outside this room.

The woman in the suit wrote it down without emotion.

Naomi tasted nausea. She kept her face still.

"We're naming it now?" she asked. The question came out calmer than she felt.

"We're organizing it now," the program manager corrected. "Naming is part of organizing."

Naomi stared at the stamped sheet. The stamp mark sat heavy. An official mark that turned a celestial object into a budget line.

Project Hail Mary.

"Compartmentalization will increase," the program manager continued. "Communications will go through designated channels only. No direct contact with external analysts without approval."

Naomi's fingers tightened on the laser pointer. Plastic creaked softly.

"No direct contact?" she asked.

The man with nothing spoke again. "You understand why."

Naomi did. She understood too well. It wasn't about science. It was about narrative control. If people couldn't talk, people couldn't contradict the version that served the system.

"What about internal collaboration?" Naomi asked. "At least let me pull in—"

"Designated channels," the program manager repeated, slower, like she was a student pushing against a syllabus.

The skeptical official leaned back. "You're the technical lead, Dr. Park. That comes with trust."

Trust. In this room, trust meant leash.

Naomi looked at her handouts, at the clean edges of paper that didn't show the nights she'd spent running simulations and rereading observation logs until her eyes stung.

"You're asking me to deliver certainty," she said quietly, "and then you're asking me to do it with fewer minds."

The program manager's face softened in the way people's faces did when they were about to do something harmful and wanted to appear kind. "We're asking you to do it with controlled minds."

Naomi forced her shoulders to relax. Tension read as instability. Instability made you easier to manage.

"What about public preparedness?" Naomi asked. "Even basic coordination—"

The woman in the suit cut in. "Public preparedness is not our lane at this stage."

"It becomes your lane when hospitals run out of oxygen," Naomi said before she could stop herself.

Silence snapped tight.

The skeptical official's eyes widened a fraction. He recovered fast. "We are not discussing hospitals."

Naomi heard the message under his words: *We are not discussing people.*

She clicked off the projector, not because the data was done but because the room had decided it was.

The sudden dimness made the conference table seem smaller, more intimate. More dangerous.

The program manager gathered the blue-taped folder and resealed it with a fresh strip. The tape pulled taut with a soft rip. It sounded like a wound being covered.

"We appreciate your work," he said. "Proceed with the next steps. Your access will reflect your new role."

Naomi stood. She packed her hard case with neat, efficient movements. Her hands didn't tremble now. They felt too steady, as if her body had decided to become a machine to survive the morning.

As the room emptied, the man with nothing paused near the door.

He leaned in just far enough that Naomi caught the faint scent of expensive soap.

"You did well," he said.

Naomi looked at him. "Did I?"

He didn't answer her question. He offered a small smile, and it felt like a warning.

"Stay in your channels," he said, and left.

Naomi stood alone in the conference room for three full breaths. Then she moved.

The hallway outside buzzed with fluorescent lights and distant voices. People walked past her without seeing her, which was both relief and insult.

An administrator caught up to her before she reached her lab.

"Naomi," he said softly, matching her pace. He wore a badge that sat too high and a tie that wasn't quite straight, like he'd dressed in a hurry. "Quick word."

Naomi didn't slow. "I'm on a timeline."

"So is everyone," he replied, then angled his body toward a side alcove near a copier that hummed quietly.

Naomi stopped. Her patience was thin, but she kept it from showing.

The administrator lowered his voice. "You're being told to go through designated channels."

"Yes," Naomi said.

He glanced down the hallway, then back at her. "That's not a suggestion."

Naomi's eyes stayed on his face. "Do you want me to lie less loudly or lie more quietly?"

His mouth tightened. "Do not put it that way."

Naomi almost laughed. The humor rose fast and bitter, then died in her throat.

"What are you actually saying?" she asked.

He leaned closer. "There are political sensitivities. People above you are concerned about—"

"Leaks," Naomi finished.

"Panic," he corrected.

Naomi held his gaze. "Panic is what happens when the truth shows up late and hungry."

His eyes flicked away. That was his tell.

He didn't believe his own words. He just needed her to follow them.

"I need to bring in an outside modeling group," Naomi said. "Someone not trapped in our assumptions."

"Not possible," he replied.

Naomi's jaw clenched. "Not possible, or not permitted?"

He exhaled. "Not permitted."

Naomi nodded, once. "Then permit it."

He gave her a look that held both pity and frustration. "Naomi. This thing has a name now."

"As if naming makes it behave."

"It makes people behave," he said.

Naomi waited. She didn't speak. Silence forced people to fill it.

The administrator swallowed. "If you go around the channels," he said, "you won't just lose the project. You'll lose your clearance. Your career. Your ability to work anywhere in this field."

Naomi felt the threat land. Not as fear, exactly—more as a new constraint locking into place.

Truth required coordination. Coordination required permission. Permission required politics.

Politics required obedience.

Naomi pictured the error bars on the screen. Widening, narrowing. A pulse. A body trying to survive.

"I won't falsify confidence," she said.

"We're not asking you to falsify," he said quickly.

Naomi stared at him until he looked away again.

He softened his voice. "Be careful."

With that, he moved on, swallowed by the corridor's flow like he'd never existed.

Naomi walked the remaining distance to her workstation with her shoulders squared and her stomach hollow.

Her lab smelled faintly of solder and old air. Screens glowed with paused windows. A night-shift engineer sat slumped in a chair, mouth open, a spreadsheet printout crumpled under his elbow like a pillow. Naomi didn't wake him.

She set her hard case down and opened it.

The printed handouts were still warm from the conference room's projector heat.

Naomi slid them into a drawer. She didn't shred them. She didn't lock them away. She placed them where she could reach them.

Then she pulled out a thick packet of observation logs, printed on plain paper. Rows of timestamps. Coordinates. Not glamorous. Not cinematic. The kind of data that told the truth while everyone else argued about language.

Naomi flipped through until she found the line she'd seen weeks ago and then dismissed because it didn't fit.

A timestamp from an amateur observer. A small backyard setup, maybe, or a private rig. No official header. No agency stamp. Just a date and time that sat too early.

Predating "official" discovery.

Naomi stared at it.

Her body went still in a way that made her aware of every small sensation: the faint tremor in her forearm from too much caffeine, the tightness at the base of her skull, the dry ache behind her eyes.

She read the timestamp again.

Then again.

Her pen hovered over the page. She drew a single circle around the line with controlled pressure. One loop. Clean. She didn't doodle. She didn't scribble. She circled it like she was marking a wound on a chart.

A knock came at the lab door.

Naomi didn't look up immediately. She finished the circle. Then she slid the paper under a folder and turned.

A junior analyst stood in the doorway holding a cardboard tray with two coffees. His hair stuck up on one side, and his badge lanyard twisted as if he'd put it on in the dark.

"Dr. Park?" he asked, voice cautious. "They told me to bring you this."

Naomi's gaze went to the coffees. "Who told you?"

He hesitated. "Admin."

Naomi watched his fingers tighten on the tray. He didn't want to be here. He'd been sent.

She rose and took one cup. The cardboard sleeve had a logo from the café down the hall. Fresh coffee, not burnt. A small kindness. Or a small leash.

"Thank you," Naomi said.

The analyst's shoulders loosened with relief. He started to back away.

"Wait," Naomi said.

He stopped.

"What did they tell you?" Naomi asked, gentle on the surface.

His eyes darted to the hallway. "That you're... busy. That I shouldn't ask questions."

Naomi nodded. "Did they say why?"

"No."

Naomi held his gaze. The young had a way of believing silence meant safety.

"Questions aren't the problem," Naomi said. "Careless answers are."

The analyst blinked. He looked confused, then uneasy.

Naomi didn't push. She didn't recruit him into her dread. Not yet.

"Go get some sleep," she said instead.

He gave a grateful nod and left.

Naomi sat again. She sipped the fresh coffee. It tasted like heat and bitter bean, clean enough to feel almost real.

She pulled the observation log back out and stared at the circled amateur timestamp.

Someone had seen this earlier.

Someone had known earlier.

And now, this morning, a room full of adults had wrapped the threat in a name that sounded like a prayer and locked Naomi behind designated channels.

Naomi opened a new folder in her drawer, one she'd used for mundane paperwork—travel receipts, HR forms, the small administrative debris of a career.

She slid the page with the circled timestamp into it.

She didn't label the folder. Labels made things easier to find for other people.

Naomi closed the drawer.

Her badge rested against her chest, heavier than it had been an hour ago.

Project Hail Mary.

Naomi stared at her hands on the desk.

They looked normal. They looked like the hands of a person who would go home later, eat dinner, maybe sleep.

But the world outside her lab still turned under a sky that had shifted without asking permission.

Naomi leaned back and let her eyes close for one beat.

Not long enough to rest.

Long enough to decide.

When she opened them again, she pulled a fresh sheet of paper from the printer tray and wrote at the top, in small, careful letters:

What I can prove.

Then she wrote beneath it:

What they're hiding.

Her pen paused.

She didn't know yet.

But she had just watched a system turn scientific uncertainty into a containment strategy.

That was enough to begin.

Naomi set the paper under her keyboard like a private oath and turned back to the observation packet, eyes scanning, hunting for the next line that didn't fit.

Outside the lab door, the corridor lights buzzed on, one after another, as if morning could be switched into place.

And in Naomi's drawer, the circled timestamp waited, quiet and stubborn, older than the story they planned to tell.

Chapter 3 - Pallets at Pier 22

The forklift's backup alarm chopped the morning into ugly little pieces.

Malik kept one hand up, palm out, to hold the driver in place while a second forklift slipped past with a pallet wrapped so tight the plastic shone like wet skin. Heat already shimmered off the asphalt. It wasn't even nine. The air smelled like diesel, brackish water, and sun-warmed metal.

"Hold," Malik called.

The driver eased off, tires squealing against grit.

Malik pointed, two quick motions—left a foot, straighten, then lift. He didn't wave big. Big meant panic. Big meant people looked.

A port supervisor in a white hard hat walked beside him with a clipboard tucked under his arm like a shield.

"You're stacking these like we're prepping for a Category Five," the supervisor said.

"That's the cover," Malik replied, keeping his voice even.

The supervisor's eyes flicked toward the container stacks, then up, like the sky might answer questions the paperwork wouldn't. "We get hurricanes. We don't get... whatever this is."

Malik didn't bite. He let the machines talk. He watched the lane: pallets moving, straps intact, count marks visible. He'd taught himself to see supply like a living thing—healthy when it flowed, dying when it stalled.

A man in a longshore vest paused at the edge of the lane, one gloved hand resting on a container corner. Instead of watching the forklifts, he stared past them, face tilted toward the brightening sky. Like he expected to catch something falling.

Malik followed his gaze without turning his head too far. Nothing visible. Just blue, thin and indifferent.

"Hey," Malik called to him. "You good?"

The longshoreman's eyes dropped to Malik's badge, then to Malik's face, then away again. "Y'all moving a lot of bandages for a storm."

The words landed soft, but they carried a hook.

"Hurricane readiness surge," Malik said. "Funding cycle. You know how it is."

The man's mouth twitched. Not a smile. Something closer to disbelief.

"You tell me," the longshoreman said. "I just move what they tell me. That's what we all do."

He stepped back into the noise, swallowed by orange vests and steel.

Malik kept his posture loose. Inside, his mind did the math it tried not to do.

T–420 days.

A number you couldn't feel in your bones. Yet.

He checked his watch. The band rubbed a tender spot on his wrist, a small punishment for time passing. He adjusted it and forced his focus back to the lane.

"Carter," the supervisor said, dropping his voice, "we got a hold on Container JX-113. Customs says it needs secondary before it clears the stack."

Malik's shoulders stayed steady. His stomach didn't. "Secondary for what? It's medical and shelter inventory."

The supervisor lifted the clipboard, like paper could block consequences. "I don't get told. I get told what to tell you."

Malik stared past him at the container rows. Thousands of metal boxes. Each one a door. Each one controlled by someone who'd never sweat on this asphalt.

"Who put the hold?" Malik asked.

The supervisor's gaze slid sideways. "Not port. Federal."

Malik let the word settle. Federal meant more than inspection. It meant attention. It meant somebody had reached down into a normal system and tightened it.

He scanned the lane again, checking faces. People worked harder when they felt watched, but they also made mistakes. Mistakes became stories. Stories became rumors. Rumors became theft.

A security guard—private contract, not port police—walked the perimeter with a posture too squared to be casual. Malik hadn't seen him last week.

The guard's hand hovered near his belt. Not a weapon draw. Not a threat. A reminder.

"Fine," Malik said. "We go around it. We keep moving."

The supervisor exhaled like Malik had offered mercy. "We can reroute through Bay 3, but you'll need a release number."

"I'll get it," Malik said.

He turned toward the trailer office and felt the heat hit his back like a shove.

Inside the office trailer, the air fought itself. A cheap fan pushed hot breath from one corner to another. Paper stacks leaned like tired buildings. Malik's boots tracked dust across the floor. He didn't sit. Sitting slowed him down.

He dialed procurement on the desk phone because his personal cell stayed in his pocket unless he had no choice. He'd learned that early: phones made you sloppy. Phones made you reachable.

The line rang three times.

"Procurement," a woman answered, voice dry.

"Dana, it's Malik Carter," he said. "I need the release on JX-113. Federal put a hold."

A pause. Paper rustled on her end. "You want a release number for a held container."

"Yes."

"That's not how holds work," Dana said.

"It's how the day needs to work," Malik replied.

He heard her sigh. She had a family, he guessed. She had her own private panic she hadn't named yet.

"You're staging under hurricane readiness," she said, careful. "That cover gives you some wiggle, not miracles."

"I'm not asking for miracles. I'm asking for a signature."

"You don't get signatures for federal holds."

Malik leaned his hip against the desk. The edge dug into his side. Pain made things real.

"Who do I call?" he asked.

Dana lowered her voice. "You're not supposed to call anyone. You're supposed to wait."

Wait. The favorite word of systems that never ran out of time.

"I can't wait," Malik said.

"You can," she replied, and there it was—fear wearing a bureaucratic mask. "You just don't want to be the one holding the bag when something goes wrong."

Malik's jaw tightened. He pictured a warehouse after a storm: people lined up, the wrong boxes in the wrong place, someone sick because the right shipment got stuck behind paperwork.

"I'm already holding it," he said.

Dana didn't respond right away. When she spoke again, her voice sharpened. "Malik. This is bigger than a storm drill."

He felt his pulse pick up. "Who told you that?"

"Don't do that," she said. "Don't make me say what I didn't say."

The fan rattled against its cage, as if it wanted out.

Malik lowered his own voice. "Dana, I need to keep inventory from walking off this pier. I need to keep workers from thinking I'm lying to them. If federal holds containers with no explanation, we're going to have a problem."

"We already have a problem," Dana whispered.

A silence hung between them. He could hear her breathing. He could hear a printer in the background chewing through paper like it had teeth.

Then Dana said, "I can't get you a release number. But I can tell you which office put the hold in. Off the record."

Malik's throat tightened. "Tell me."

She gave him an extension. No names. No titles.

When he hung up, his fingers stayed on the receiver an extra beat, as if he could pull more truth through the plastic.

He wrote the extension down on a sticky note and pressed it under his keyboard. Not visible unless you knew where to look.

A knock hit the trailer door.

Malik straightened. "Yeah?"

The door opened without waiting. A union steward stepped in, hard hat scuffed, shirt darkened with sweat. He had the calm posture of a man used to negotiating with people who held power and pretended they didn't.

"Morning, Carter," the steward said. "You got a minute."

Malik nodded. "I've got thirty seconds."

The steward's eyes moved over the paper stacks, the clipboard, the port schedule pinned crooked on the wall. "Y'all are moving like you expect the docks to flood."

"Hurricane readiness surge," Malik said again, the phrase tasting like metal.

The steward's mouth flattened. "We get the cover story. We also get the questions. My people are hearing talk."

"Talk about what?"

The steward held Malik's gaze. "About why there's federal eyes on Pier 22."

Malik didn't blink. He couldn't afford tells.

"We rotate security on high-value shipments," Malik said.

"That's not what they're saying," the steward replied. "They're saying it's not about value. It's about who gets to live."

The sentence hit like a slap, not because it was true—Malik didn't know if it was—but because it lived in the air already. People didn't need proof to fear. They needed a shape.

Malik kept his hands on the edge of the desk where the steward could see them. "Your people don't have to guess. They can ask me."

The steward's eyebrows rose. "They did. You gave them hurricane."

Malik let out a slow breath. "Because if I give them anything else, I'm done. I lose clearance. I lose the ability to move anything through this port. Then what?"

The steward's gaze sharpened. "So you admit there's 'anything else.'"

Malik felt his spine go rigid. He softened it on purpose. "I admit there are decisions above my pay grade."

The steward stepped closer. Not aggressive. Intimate. A way to make a man feel cornered without touching him.

"I'm not here to blow up your day," the steward said. "I'm here to keep my people safe. When rumors turn into fists, they don't land on politicians. They land on forklift drivers."

Malik nodded once. "What do you need?"

The steward glanced toward the door, then back. "I need to know you're not setting them up. I need to know you're not moving supplies that'll disappear into some private warehouse while the rest of us get told to line up and pray."

Malik's chest tightened. He pictured the longshoreman staring at the sky. He pictured families on the other side of the Ship Channel who couldn't buy their way out of heat or hunger.

"I can't promise outcomes," Malik said. "I can promise process."

The steward's lips curled. "Process doesn't feed kids."

"No," Malik replied. "But process gets trucks out the gate instead of sitting in a yard with a hold nobody can explain."

The steward studied him. Malik held still and let the man look. People could sense when you were hiding something for yourself versus hiding something because the system demanded it. Malik didn't know which category he fell into anymore.

"What can you do right now," the steward said, "to keep this from turning ugly?"

Malik thought fast. Concrete. Not slogans.

"I can stagger breaks so your crews aren't standing around with nothing to do," he said. "Idle time breeds stories. I can add a second headcount check at the lane to catch missing pallets before they walk. And I can get you a safety walk with the new security team so your people know where the lines are."

The steward's gaze narrowed. "New security team."

Malik didn't answer. The omission spoke louder.

The steward nodded once, slow. "You do that, and I keep my folks working. For now."

"For now," Malik agreed.

The steward turned to leave, then paused with his hand on the door.

"One more thing," he said without looking back. "If you're lying, you better be lying for us too."

The door shut behind him.

Malik stared at the dented metal for a beat, feeling the trap tighten. If he lied to protect the system, labor would hate him. If he told labor the truth, the system would crush him. Either way, he became the face.

He grabbed his lanyard and smoothed it flat against his chest before he stepped outside. A habit. A shield.

Back on the pier, the heat had climbed. The sun bleached the lane until the shrink wrap looked almost white. Forklifts moved like insects, purposeful and small against container stacks that didn't care about urgency.

A security guard—same one from earlier—stood near the staging lane, watching.

Malik walked toward the cut-plastic smell before anyone could call him over. He saw the problem the moment he reached the pallet row: straps sliced clean, not torn. Boxes shifted. A gap where something had been.

A port worker stood nearby with his hands jammed into his pockets, eyes fixed on the ground like it had answers.

"What happened?" Malik asked.

The worker shrugged too fast. "Don't know."

The security guard lifted his chin toward the pallet. "Someone got curious."

Malik crouched and ran his fingers along the cut strap. It was a clean slice, made with a blade, not an accident. He didn't need an investigation to see intent.

He stood and looked at the worker. "You saw anything?"

The worker's gaze flicked toward the guard's belt, then back to Malik. "Nah."

Malik kept his voice low. "If something's missing, I can't replace it with good intentions."

The worker's mouth tightened. "People out there got nothing, man. Y'all stacking supplies like it's a game. Folks talk."

Malik's chest flared with a reflexive anger—how easy it was to make him the villain when he was the one sweating on the pier.

He forced the anger into focus. "Talking doesn't justify stealing from sick people."

The worker flinched at the word *sick*.

The guard stepped forward, posture hardening. "You want me to pull him aside?"

Malik looked at the guard and felt the crackle of power. The guard wanted permission. The guard wanted an enemy.

Malik pictured the steward's warning. Fists landing on forklift drivers.

"No," Malik said.

The guard's eyebrows lifted. "No?"

Malik held his gaze. "Not without facts."

The guard's jaw tightened, annoyed by restraint.

Malik turned back to the worker. "I'm not here to blame you for rumors," Malik said. "I'm here to keep this lane moving. If you know something, tell me, and I handle it without making you a target."

The worker swallowed. Sweat ran down his temple. "I didn't do it," he muttered.

"I didn't say you did," Malik replied.

A pause. Then the worker's eyes darted toward a container row.

"Some guys been talking about what's inside," he said, barely audible over the alarms and engines. "They said... they said it's not hurricane."

Malik's pulse hit his throat. "Who said that?"

The worker shook his head. "I don't know names. It's just talk."

Malik nodded once. He didn't press for names. Names turned talk into betrayal. Betrayal got people hurt.

He pointed to the pallet. "We strap this again. You help the crew lead. You see someone cut straps, you tell me. Not him."

He tilted his head toward the guard.

The worker nodded, eyes still low.

Malik glanced at the guard. "You tighten the perimeter," Malik said. "No hands on people unless they touch you first."

The guard's mouth tightened, but he nodded.

Malik walked away before he could feel the guard's resentment.

He passed the longshoreman again—the one who'd stared at the sky earlier. The man still watched upward, hand resting on steel like a grounding wire.

"Hey," Malik called, more gentle this time. "You got family?"

The longshoreman's gaze dropped. "Everybody got family."

Malik nodded. "Keep your head down."

The longshoreman's laugh came out dry. "You too."

Malik's phone buzzed in his pocket. He didn't pull it out yet. Vibrations happened all day. Half of them meant nothing. The other half meant you didn't get to go home the same way you'd come in.

He walked toward a shaded gap between trailers where the sun couldn't cook his thoughts. He leaned a shoulder against his car and finally checked the screen.

Unknown number.

He stared at it for one beat, then answered.

"Carter," he said.

A man's voice filled his ear, too calm, too controlled. "Mr. Carter. You're at Pier 22."

Malik's spine tightened. He didn't ask how the man knew. That question never got answered.

"Who is this?" Malik asked.

"A liaison," the voice said. "You don't need my name. You need to follow instructions."

Malik kept his tone neutral. "Instructions usually come with paperwork."

A pause. Then the voice softened, like a teacher correcting a child. "Not this time."

Malik watched a forklift pass in the distance, load lifted high. Machines did what they were told. People had to live with it.

"What do you want?" Malik asked.

"I need you to prepare high-risk evacuation protocols," the voice said.

Malik's throat went tight. High-risk meant what it sounded like. It meant moving people who couldn't move themselves. It meant security. It meant triage that would look like cruelty to anyone watching.

"What's the justification?" Malik asked.

"You don't need justification," the voice replied. "You need readiness."

Malik's hand clenched around the phone until his knuckles ached. "Readiness for what."

A small pause again. Not hesitation. Calculation.

"Contingency," the voice said. "If certain triggers occur, we need rapid movement."

"Triggers like what?" Malik pressed.

"Mr. Carter," the voice said, and the courtesy drained out of it. "You are not authorized to ask that."

Malik stared at the bright sky above the container stacks. It looked clean. It looked innocent.

His pulse hammered anyway.

"You're asking me to plan mass movement without written directive," Malik said. "You're asking me to make decisions that will get me arrested later."

The voice didn't rise. That was the worst part. "You will not be arrested if you follow instructions."

"And if I don't?"

A beat. Then, "Your access ends. Your position ends. Your ability to help ends. Choose."

Malik's mouth went dry. He thought of the union steward, the sliced straps, the hold on the container. He thought of the way systems made you complicit by starving you of options.

He pictured Darius—just the name, the weight of it. A person Malik couldn't fail.

"Say you understand," the voice demanded.

Malik swallowed. "I understand."

"Say you will comply," the voice said.

Malik didn't answer right away. He tasted blood where he'd bitten the inside of his cheek.

The voice stayed patient, like it knew time belonged to it.

Malik forced the words out. "I will comply."

"Good," the voice said. "No email. No memo. No messages. You speak of this only to those already involved."

"Who's already involved?" Malik asked before he could stop himself.

The line went silent for a second. Then the voice returned, colder. "If you have to ask, they aren't."

The call ended.

Malik stood there with his phone pressed to his ear, listening to nothing. The engine of his car ticked as it cooled. A container door slammed somewhere down the pier, a metallic boom that echoed like thunder.

He lowered the phone and stared at the screen until it went dark.

His hands felt too clean. Like he hadn't just agreed to something that could ruin him.

He reached into his pocket and pulled out a small notebook he kept for counts and schedule notes. Not official. Not hidden, either. The kind of thing nobody questioned until they needed someone to blame.

He wrote the time of the call and a few clipped phrases. Not a confession. Not a record for court. A private anchor so he couldn't pretend later that it hadn't happened.

He shoved the notebook back into his pocket and stared at the pier again.

Everything looked the same. Everything had changed.

He walked back into the sun and made himself move like he hadn't been punched in the chest by a voice.

At the break area, a vending machine hummed behind a bent picnic table. Malik found a spot in the shade and took a swallow from a bottle of water that had turned warm.

A man approached in a button-down shirt with rolled sleeves, no hard hat, the kind of person who didn't belong on a pier unless he owned something. He carried a paper cup of coffee and a smile that tried to be friendly.

"Malik Carter?" the man asked.

Malik looked him up and down. "Depends who's asking."

The man laughed like that was fair. "Ray Hsu. Gulf Coast Transit. We talked last month about hurricane evacuation contracts."

Malik stood, offering a hand. Ray's grip was firm, quick. Business-like. Nervous under the surface.

"You picked a hot day to come down here," Malik said.

Ray glanced around at the forklifts, the security presence, the container stacks. His smile thinned. "I could say the same."

Malik nodded toward the picnic table. "You got five minutes?"

Ray sat, set his coffee down, and rubbed his palm on his thigh like he'd wiped sweat there. "You said you wanted extra buses on standby."

"For storm season," Malik said, keeping the cover in the open.

Ray's eyes locked on Malik's face. "Storm season," he echoed, a question in the repetition.

Malik didn't answer. Silence did the work.

Ray leaned in. "Look, Malik, I'll be straight. I've been getting calls."

"From who?" Malik asked.

Ray lifted one shoulder. "People who don't leave voicemail. People who know my fleet numbers better than my dispatch does."

Malik's stomach tightened. "What do they want?"

Ray hesitated, then pushed it out fast, like ripping a bandage hurt less than dragging it. "They want exclusive contracts. Routes that don't show up on any public schedule. They want drivers willing to go without asking where they're headed."

Malik's jaw clenched. "And you told them no."

Ray's laugh came out sharp. "I told them my drivers aren't soldiers."

"And?"

Ray stared at his coffee. "And they offered numbers I can't compete with. I've got notes due. I've got insurance. I've got payroll. My drivers got kids."

Malik watched Ray's hands. The man's fingers shook slightly as he picked up his cup.

Ray met Malik's eyes again. "If this is real—whatever's coming—then the rich already bought the drivers."

The sentence hit Malik in the sternum. Not because it was clever. Because it sounded like the kind of truth you heard too late.

Malik didn't let it show. He kept his face calm. "You don't have to sell," he said.

Ray gave him a look that held both apology and anger. "You ever had to keep a business alive when the world decides rules don't apply anymore?"

Malik felt the sting. He had kept systems alive, not businesses. Different kind of hunger.

"What do you need?" Malik asked.

Ray's eyes flicked around again, landing on the security guard by the lane. "I need a reason to believe saying no won't get my people hurt."

Malik held his gaze. He didn't offer lies. He didn't offer comfort.

"I can't promise you safety," Malik said. "I can promise you I'm not asking you to do anything without thinking about the cost."

Ray's mouth twisted. "That's not a yes."

"It's honest," Malik replied.

Ray leaned back, exhaling through his nose. "Honest is expensive these days."

Malik nodded. "So is silence."

Ray stared at him for a long moment. Then he stood. "Put together what you need," he said. "Routes. Headcounts. Timing. I'll look at it."

Malik's pulse jumped. "You're saying you'll help."

"I'm saying I'm not selling my fleet without a fight," Ray replied. "Not yet."

He hesitated, then added, quieter, "And if somebody already bought the drivers, Malik... then the rest of us are going to be walking."

Ray left, swallowed by the movement of the pier.

Malik stood in the shade with sweat cooling on his forearms and felt the words echo.

Walking.

He looked toward the longshoreman again. The man still stared at the sky, face tilted up like prayer was the only language left.

Malik followed the gaze.

The morning sun burned clean. The blue stretched wide and harmless.

And still, Malik couldn't shake the sense that something out there moved toward them with patient speed, while people on the ground fought over release numbers and contracts.

His phone buzzed again in his pocket. He didn't check it.

He walked back into the lane and raised his hand, palm out, to stop a forklift that came in too fast.

The driver braked hard. The load rocked. For a second, Malik pictured it tipping, spilling boxes across the asphalt like a warning no one could ignore.

The pallet steadied.

Malik pointed the driver into a safer line.

No action without cost, he thought—not as a slogan, as a weight.

He turned his head and caught the port supervisor watching him from a distance, clipboard held tight, face strained. Malik didn't wave. He didn't reassure. He kept moving.

Container doors slammed somewhere down the pier, the sound rolling through steel and heat.

In the bright morning, a longshoreman kept staring upward.

Malik's pocket vibrated again, a quiet insistence against his thigh.

He pressed his fingers against the fabric over the phone, not answering, just feeling it there.

A small machine trying to pull him into the next trap.

Chapter 4 - Three-Check Rule

The crane's warning beep cut through the integration bay like a blunt instrument, steady and indifferent, ricocheting off concrete and steel until it lived inside Ben's teeth.

"Clear!" someone shouted.

Ben kept his eyes on the load as it swung in slow authority over the floor, a cylinder wrapped in protective foam and taped like it had secrets. Heat haze shimmered above the concrete pads outside the bay doors, turning the far end of the facility into a mirage. Inside, the air held the tang of coolant, hot electronics, sweat trapped under PPE.

A technician jogged backward with his hands up, guiding the crane operator with two fingers and a glare. Another tech barked numbers that echoed off the rafters like prayer.

Ben stood at the edge of the marked zone with a clipboard pressed flat against his thigh. The paper stuck there—humidity and friction—like the building didn't want him moving too fast either.

"Ben!" Floor lead, Ro, called from under the crane's shadow. "You signing the lift plan or you gonna watch it like it's a movie?"

Ben didn't smile. He didn't have the extra energy for it.

He glanced once at the lift sheet. Load weight. Sling angle. Clearance margins. The answers lived in the boxes and in his muscle memory, both. He still ran the ritual because rituals kept you alive when deadlines tried to talk you into skipping steps.

Three-check rule, he told himself.

He murmured it under his breath as his pen hovered.

Check the numbers. Check the people. Check the consequence.

He signed.

Ro snatched the clipboard with a grunt and turned back into the noise, satisfied for the moment.

Ben watched the crane set the load down onto the integration stand with a metallic clank that sounded like a door closing. A cheer rose from someone too young to have been burned by a schedule before. It died fast when another alarm chirped from across the bay—small, urgent, like a smoke detector finding an excuse.

He walked toward it, boots sticking slightly where spilled coolant had been half-mopped and abandoned. His phone vibrated once in his pocket. He ignored it. Everybody wanted something from him, and half of them wanted it yesterday.

A QA rep stood by a whiteboard station, arms folded. The rep's safety vest looked new. His face looked like it had been carved by meetings.

"Don't," the QA rep said before Ben even opened his mouth.

Ben stopped two feet away, the exact distance that kept him from doing something stupid like crowding.

"Don't what," Ben replied.

"Don't try to bulldoze a gate because you're high on your own timeline," the QA rep said.

Ben's jaw tightened. He didn't deny it. He just shifted his weight so the irritation didn't turn into movement.

"You see the range calendar," Ben said. "We lose the slot, we lose three weeks. FAA doesn't care that the sky doesn't wait."

The QA rep flicked his gaze to the bay. "And the sky doesn't care if you cut corners. One failure and you don't just lose three weeks. You lose the whole program. You lose public tolerance. You lose funding. You lose people."

Ben wanted to snap back that public tolerance wasn't the bottleneck, paperwork was. He wanted to say the real enemy wasn't physics, it was committees. He wanted to say they were past the point where caution could save them.

He didn't. He had learned the hard way that saying the quiet part out loud turned you into a liability.

He tapped his pen against the clipboard, once. A metronome. A leash.

"What's the hold?" Ben asked.

The QA rep grabbed a marker and wrote a single line on the whiteboard: FASTENER TRACEABILITY.

Ben stared at it, feeling his pulse in his jaw.

"We have traceability," Ben said.

"You have a spreadsheet that says you have traceability," the rep replied. "I need physical batch certs on the last shipment. The ones that came in after midnight. The ones that weren't supposed to exist."

Ben's eyes narrowed. "You saying someone snuck parts in?"

"I'm saying I didn't sign off on them," the rep said. "And you don't get to integrate them until I do."

Ro's voice cut through the bay again, sharp. "Ben! We need a go/no-go on bay door closure in fifteen!"

Ben didn't turn. He kept his eyes on the QA rep.

"Where are the certs?" Ben asked.

"Shipping desk," the rep said. "If they exist."

Ben inhaled through his nose and tasted metal. He tightened the strap on his glove instead of cursing. The gesture looked practical. It wasn't. It was restraint made visible.

"Fine," Ben said. "I'll get them."

"And Ben," the QA rep added, softer, "this isn't me being slow. This is me being alive."

Ben held his gaze. For one second, he saw the rep not as an obstacle but as a person with a family photo on a desk somewhere, a mortgage, a fear he didn't name.

"I know," Ben said, and meant it more than he wanted to.

He walked away with his shoulders set hard, as if posture could keep the schedule from slipping.

The logistics bay sat at the edge of the integration floor, half office, half confession booth. Pallet jacks rattled over seams in the concrete. Cardboard dust hung in the air and stuck to sweaty skin. A shipping clerk sat behind a desk with stacks of stapled manifests and a coffee that had gone cold and bitter.

The clerk looked up when Ben approached, and something in his expression tightened.

That told Ben everything before any words did.

"Tell me you've got batch certs for last night," Ben said.

The clerk's eyes flicked to the side—toward a doorway marked AUTHORIZED PERSONNEL ONLY—then back.

"Depends," the clerk said.

Ben leaned his forearms on the counter, just enough to own the space without making it a threat. "Depends on what."

"Depends on what you think you need," the clerk replied.

Ben's pulse kicked. He kept his face neutral. "I need what keeps my build legal."

The clerk swallowed. "We got certs for most of it."

"Most isn't a number," Ben said.

The clerk pushed a stapled packet across the counter. The pages were warm from the copier, faintly smelling of machine heat. Ben flipped through them with efficient anger, eyes scanning for the missing line item.

There.

A critical component flagged not for Starbase, not for Cape, not for any of the public routing codes Ben had memorized in his bones. Destination: HOLD FOR CONTINUITY TRANSFER.

Ben felt his body go still in a way that had nothing to do with calm. The noise of the bay dulled for a beat, like the building held its breath.

He looked up. "What's 'continuity transfer.'"

The clerk's gaze dropped to the counter. "It's... it's not ours."

Ben kept his voice steady. "Not ours meaning what."

The clerk's mouth tightened. "Meaning it's not on your build plan."

Ben tapped the paper with one finger. "It's on my manifest."

The clerk's hands twitched as if he wanted to snatch it back. He didn't. That told Ben there were eyes on this desk that weren't his.

"Where's it going," Ben asked.

The clerk shook his head. "I don't get told. I get a code. I get a driver. I get told to shut up."

Ben's stomach turned. He heard the sentence the way it was meant: not explanation, not complaint—warning.

Ben lowered his voice. "Who authorized the reroute."

The clerk's laugh came out thin. "You think authorizations look like a person? It's a contract code. It's a stamp. It's a name you don't say in here."

Ben stared at the packet again. The words sat there in black ink as if they belonged. As if they were normal.

Three-check rule, Ben told himself, not as comfort, as weapon.

Check the numbers.

He traced the part number with his finger. It matched the build.

Check the people.

He watched the clerk's eyes. Fear. Not performance.

Check the consequence.

If a critical component walked out under a private code, this wasn't a clerical error. This was a decision.

"What's the driver name," Ben asked.

The clerk hesitated.

Ben didn't push closer. He kept his hands flat on the paper, palms down, controlling his own body.

"I'm not gonna blow you up," Ben said. "I'm gonna protect the mission."

The clerk's shoulders dropped a fraction. "You can't protect what you can't name."

Ben held his gaze. "Then give me the name."

The clerk exhaled like the air hurt. He pointed at a line on the manifest. His finger shook.

KLINE CONTINUITY GROUP.

The words looked too clean for what they meant.

Ben didn't react. He didn't let his face change. He folded the page back once, slow, like he was done with it.

His heart hammered anyway.

"Kline," Ben repeated, not as a question. A test.

The clerk's eyes darted to the doorway again. "That's all I'm saying."

Ben nodded once. "Where is it right now."

The clerk's lips pressed tight. Then he lifted his chin toward the loading entrance.

Ben turned and saw it immediately: a forklift easing a pallet—wrapped, tagged, sealed—toward the bay doors where a box truck waited with its back open like a mouth.

Two men stood beside the truck in clean boots and matching polos, no sweat stains, no hard hats. Contractors. The kind who never lifted anything heavier than a clipboard but somehow controlled where the heavy things went.

One of them held a folder. The other held a hand radio and didn't use it, just let it sit in his palm like a promise.

Ben's mouth went dry.

He straightened and walked toward the doors.

The closer he got, the louder every sound became: the beep of the forklift, the snap of shrink wrap, the scrape of pallet wood against metal. The air at the doors carried outdoor heat and a distant chemical tang from the flats beyond the facility.

The forklift operator slowed when Ben approached, eyes flicking to Ben's badge. "Hey, boss—"

Ben lifted his hand. Not to stop the machine. To pause the man.

"What's that pallet," Ben asked.

The operator glanced at the contractors. His throat bobbed. "Pick-up order."

"For who," Ben asked.

The operator swallowed. "Continuity."

Ben stepped around the forklift and faced the contractors.

"Hey," Ben said, voice level. "That hardware's on my build."

One contractor—taller, with a shaved jaw and a smile that never reached his eyes—looked Ben over. "You're integration lead."

Ben didn't like the way the man said it. Like he was reading from a profile.

"Where are you taking it," Ben asked.

The contractor's smile held. "Different site."

"That's not an answer," Ben said.

The second contractor—shorter, older, a watch too expensive for this bay—opened the folder and flipped it with quiet confidence. "It's authorized."

"Authorized by who," Ben asked.

The older one lifted the folder slightly. "By contract."

Ben stared at the folder. He imagined a stamp. A signature. A code that could erase him.

"The mission doesn't run on private side deals," Ben said.

The taller one's smile thinned. "The mission runs on what gets funded."

Ben felt heat rise under his collar. He wiped his brow with the back of his wrist and left a faint streak of grease across his skin. He hated himself for it. He didn't fix it. Not now.

"You're diverting critical components," Ben said.

The older contractor kept his tone mild. "We're reallocating assets in accordance with continuity planning."

There it was. The phrase that sounded like virtue until you watched it steal.

Ben stepped closer to the pallet and read the tag. The label adhesive tugged at his thumb when he touched it, tacky with heat. The part number matched.

He looked back at the contractors. "This part doesn't go to 'continuity.' It goes into a system that might keep people alive."

The taller one's gaze sharpened, something hard behind the polite mask. "You don't get to decide who 'people' are."

Ben felt the sentence hit his ribs. Scandal didn't always look like a mistress and a camera flash. Sometimes it looked like a pallet leaving a bay with paperwork so clean it could kill.

Ben forced his voice to stay steady. "Stop the load."

The forklift operator's hands tightened on the controls. He looked between Ben and the contractors like he was choosing who would ruin him.

The older contractor closed the folder with a soft clap. "If you interfere, you delay the program. You become the bottleneck. And the program remembers bottlenecks."

Ben didn't blink. "I'm not interfering. I'm verifying."

The taller contractor leaned slightly closer. Not enough to touch. Enough to press.

"You've got a reputation," he said. "Fast. Aggressive. Likes to be the hero."

Ben felt the insult wrapped in compliment. He didn't correct it.

"Three-check rule," Ben said quietly, more to himself than them.

The taller contractor's eyebrows lifted. "What's that."

Ben didn't answer.

He turned to the forklift operator. "Who signed your pick-up," Ben asked.

The operator's mouth opened, closed. He glanced at the contractors again.

Ben softened his tone. "I'm not trying to get you fired."

The operator swallowed. "It's... it's in the system."

Ben's jaw tightened. System. Invisible. Convenient.

He nodded once. "Then I need the physical manifest."

The older contractor's eyes cooled. "You already saw it."

Ben held his gaze. "I saw a page. I want the full chain."

"You're not cleared," the older contractor said.

Ben let the words hang for a second, then looked back at the pallet like it might answer him.

He didn't grab it. He didn't block it with his body. He didn't do anything that would turn him into the story they could tell about why a schedule slipped.

Instead, he stepped aside and watched.

The forklift eased forward. The pallet slid toward the truck's open mouth. Shrink wrap snapped tighter as it shifted. The operator avoided Ben's eyes.

Ben memorized every detail: the contractor's watch, the truck's license plate partially obscured by dust, the way the folder's corner had a crease like it had been opened and shut too many times.

When the pallet crossed the threshold into the truck, Ben felt something inside him rupture—a small, controlled breaking.

The taller contractor gave him a polite nod. "Good man."

Ben didn't respond.

The bay doors rolled down behind the truck as it pulled away, leaving a strip of bright daylight that narrowed until it disappeared. The noise of the integration floor rushed back in, uncaring.

Ben stood still for one beat, listening.

For a moment, the facility went quiet between alarms, like a held breath.

He felt it as warning.

He walked back to the shipping desk without running. Running looked guilty. Running looked afraid. He was both. He didn't show it.

The clerk's eyes widened when Ben returned. "You saw it."

Ben leaned in, close enough that his voice didn't need volume. "I need a copy of that manifest."

The clerk shook his head fast. "I can't."

"You can," Ben replied. "You just don't want to."

The clerk's lips trembled. "You don't know what they do to people who—"

"I know," Ben cut in, and surprised himself with how certain it sounded. "That's why I'm asking for paper."

The clerk stared at him for a long beat. Then he opened a drawer and pulled out a carbon-copy sheet, the old-fashioned kind that left smudges on your fingers.

He slid it across like contraband.

Ben's hand covered it, hiding it from any eyes that might be watching. The paper felt warm, as if it had absorbed heat from the lies printed on it.

"Don't put my name on your mess," the clerk whispered.

Ben met his gaze. "I won't."

He folded the manifest page small enough to hide in his pocket, then unfolded it again and smoothed it flat on the counter, as if he was choosing honesty over fear one crease at a time.

Then he folded it again, tighter.

He tucked it into his pocket and felt the weight settle against his thigh like a secret that could bruise.

Back on the integration floor, Ro caught him near the whiteboard station.

"Where the hell were you," Ro snapped. "QA's holding traceability, range just emailed about a potential protest block tomorrow, and you're out sightseeing?"

Ben forced his face into something that could pass as irritation instead of dread. "I was fixing a supply problem."

Ro shoved a tablet toward him and then, at the last second, seemed to remember Ben hated tablets right now. Ro pulled it back, annoyed. "We're losing time."

Ben's eyes flicked to the QA rep across the bay. The rep watched him, expression unreadable.

Ben thought of the pallet sliding into the truck.

Time wasn't the only thing they were losing.

"Give me ten minutes," Ben said.

Ro's laugh came out sharp. "Ten minutes? You gonna rewrite federal law in ten minutes?"

Ben didn't answer. He walked to the QA rep instead.

The rep looked up as Ben approached. "You get the certs."

"I got some," Ben said.

"Some," the rep echoed, not amused.

Ben held his gaze. "Enough to keep your gate from becoming a weapon."

The rep's eyes narrowed. "What does that mean."

Ben lowered his voice. "There are parts moving through this bay under private codes."

The rep's mouth tightened. "If you're accusing—"

"I'm not accusing," Ben said. "I'm telling you to watch your chain. Three-check rule. Don't sign what you can't physically verify."

The rep studied him. Ben didn't give more. More turned into a statement. A statement turned into a file. A file turned into a target.

The rep nodded once, slow. "You're rattled."

Ben tightened the glove strap again. "I'm awake."

The rep's gaze flicked to Ben's pocket, to the slight bulge the folded paper made. "You carrying something."

Ben didn't flinch. "I carry a lot."

The rep watched him for a long beat, then said, "Be careful who you think will protect you."

Ben's mouth went dry. "Yeah."

He walked away before the rep could say more that sounded like prophecy.

By the time Ben made it to his workspace—a metal desk wedged into a corner with a rolling chair and a stack of binders that smelled like dust—his muscles ached like he'd been lifting the pallet himself.

He sat, just for a second, and felt the chair complain under his weight.

He pulled the manifest out and stared at it.

KLINE CONTINUITY GROUP.

A name printed like it belonged in normal daylight.

He grabbed a pen and wrote the words in his own notebook, not the official one. He wrote the part number. He wrote the time. He wrote the shipping clerk's warning in shorthand.

Scratch of pen on paper. A sound so small it felt obscene against the scale of what it meant.

He exhaled slowly until his hand stopped shaking.

Then he closed the notebook and slid it under a stack of binders labeled innocuous things—FASTENER LOGS, TORQUE SPEC SHEETS, RANGE COMMS.

Camouflage wasn't only for war.

A coworker stepped into the corner without knocking, a man Ben recognized from test stand operations. Miguel. Friendly when the day allowed. Tight when it didn't.

Miguel took one look at Ben's face and stopped.

"Yo," Miguel said, voice low. "You look like you saw a ghost."

Ben kept his eyes on the desk. "What do you need."

Miguel didn't take the dismissal. He leaned against the partition and watched Ben like a friend who knew when to push.

"They're saying you're trying to stir things up," Miguel said.

Ben's pulse kicked. He lifted his gaze. "Who's 'they.'"

Miguel's mouth twisted. "People who don't like it when you ask why a pallet goes somewhere it shouldn't."

Ben didn't move. He let silence do the work.

Miguel blew out a breath. "Listen. I'm not telling you to shut up because I like being told what to do. I'm telling you because this place eats people when it needs a clean story."

Ben stared at him. "You think I'm wrong."

Miguel shook his head once, sharp. "I think you're right in a way that'll get you buried."

Ben's throat tightened. "So what. We let it happen."

Miguel's gaze softened for a split second. "We survive it. We keep our heads down long enough to do something that matters."

Ben wanted to laugh. He wanted to punch the wall. He did neither.

"Speed matters," Ben said.

Miguel nodded. "Yeah. And so does not getting your badge deactivated in the parking lot."

Ben held his gaze. Miguel wasn't a coward. Miguel was scared. There was a difference.

"I'm not sabotaging," Ben said.

Miguel's eyes flicked to Ben's pocket again. "You're collecting."

Ben didn't answer.

Miguel pushed off the partition. "Just... be smart. Don't be loud."

Ben watched him go, feeling the word *loud* settle in his chest.

Loud got you killed in a quiet war.

The afternoon bled toward evening without the mercy of a real sunset. Outside, the sky darkened in slow bruises, thunder building somewhere beyond the facility like a distant engine.

Ben finished the mandatory steps. He signed what he could sign without lying. He refused what he couldn't. He swallowed the looks people gave him when he said *no*.

By the time he reached his locker, the integration floor had thinned to skeleton crew and night shift. The clang of metal sounded lonelier now. The air cooled just enough to remind him heat had a choice.

His locker sat in a row of identical doors, each one hiding a person's private life behind a padlock.

Ben opened his. The metal squealed.

He pulled out his notebook and slid the folded manifest inside, behind a pair of work gloves and a spare safety vest. He pressed it flat against the locker wall, like he could force it to stay put through will.

He stared at it for one beat longer than necessary.

Then he shut the locker.

The door slammed harder than he meant.

The sound echoed.

A few heads turned.

Ben didn't apologize. He didn't smile. He just grabbed his keys and walked.

In the parking lot, the wind tugged at his vest. The air smelled like hot concrete cooling and distant rain. Test stand roar rumbled from somewhere far, a low animal sound that shook the ground under the cars.

Ben paused by his vehicle and looked back toward the facility.

He thought of the pallet leaving the bay, the contractors' clean boots, the way the word *continuity* had tasted in the clerk's mouth like poison.

A schedule was a story someone wanted believed.

Ben slid into his car and sat with his hands on the steering wheel, not turning the key yet.

Three-check rule, he told himself again.

Check the numbers. He had them.

Check the people. He had one scared clerk, two contractors, a forklift operator trying not to die for someone else's decision.

Check the consequence.

If he took this to leadership, he became the problem. If he stayed silent, he became complicit.

He started the car.

Thunder rolled somewhere beyond the facility, deep and slow, like the sky clearing its throat.

Ben drove out of the lot with the manifest's folded weight locked behind metal, and the sense that the real launch window wasn't just about rockets anymore—it was about who got to keep a door closed when the rest of the world started knocking.

Chapter 5 - No Glass After Dark

Lila's editor didn't wave her over.

He pointed at the conference nook and kept talking to the lawyer on speaker as if Lila was another piece of equipment that had arrived late.

Plastic cups sat where the glass carafe used to live. Someone had taped a handwritten sign to the kitchenette cabinet: **NO GLASS AFTER DARK.** Building policy, not theirs. A nervous little rule that told you what kind of week the city expected.

Lila slid into the chair without taking her backpack off. Her camera dug into her shoulder blade. The footage inside it had weight. Not sentimental weight—legal weight. The kind that could crack a career if you swung it wrong.

The lawyer's voice came through tinny and calm.

"Your reporter needs to stop calling this an imminent threat."

Lila watched her editor's fingers. They drummed once, then stilled.

"I haven't called it anything," Lila said. "I wrote 'uncataloged object.' I wrote 'unconfirmed.' I wrote—"

Her editor held up one finger without looking at her. Not *wait. Don't make this harder.*

"We aren't debating adjectives," the lawyer said. "We're debating liability."

Lila leaned forward, elbows close, keeping her body small. She'd learned that trick young: don't give anyone a big target.

"What's the actual problem," she asked.

Her editor finally looked at her. His eyes were tired in a way that had nothing to do with sleep.

"The actual problem is you're making powerful people nervous," he said, low.

He pushed a single sheet of paper across the table.

Not email. Not a forwarded PDF. Paper. Heavy stock. Clean corners. Official seal pressed in the top left like a raised bruise you could feel with a thumb.

Lila didn't touch it yet.

"Where'd that come from," she asked.

"Hand-delivered," her editor said. "To reception. Addressed to me. About you."

The lawyer kept talking, but Lila stopped listening. The world narrowed to the sheet between them, the kind that turned private work into public risk.

Her editor tapped the page with his knuckle.

"Read it."

Lila pulled it closer and read the first line.

ADVISORY NOTICE — REQUEST TO CEASE AND DESIST CERTAIN INQUIRIES

Her throat tightened. Not fear, not yet. Anger, contained.

She scanned down.

...national security...

...potential violations of contractual nondisclosure...

...defamatory implications...

The language didn't claim she'd done anything illegal. It didn't need to. It painted a fence around her and waited for her to step into it.

At the bottom, in smaller text, a reference string:

PHM-COMMS / EXTERNAL CONTACT PROTOCOL

Lila stared at the letters until they stopped being letters and became a code.

"What's PHM," she asked, not looking up.

Her editor shrugged once, tight. "No idea. I'm guessing you will."

The lawyer's voice sharpened. "Ms. Reyes, if you continue to contact individuals under nondisclosure agreements—"

"I don't know who has an NDA," Lila cut in. She kept her tone even. "That's the point. Everything's paywalled, redacted, locked. You want me to verify without talking to anyone who might know."

A pause.

"Ms. Reyes," the lawyer said, "your employer can be enjoined. Your sources can be compelled. Your devices can be subpoenaed."

Her editor didn't flinch at *devices*. His eyes flicked to Lila's backpack like it had teeth.

Lila sat back. The cheap chair squeaked. She hated the sound. It made her feel smaller than she was.

"So what," she said. "You want me to drop it."

Her editor exhaled through his nose. "I want you to keep your job."

"I want to keep my job," she said, and heard how flat it came out.

The lawyer pushed again. "If you publish insinuations without on-record confirmation from an authorized agency representative—"

"Authorized by who," Lila asked.

No answer. The silence was answer enough.

Her editor leaned toward her, one forearm on the table.

"Here's what I can do," he said. "I can give you a lane. You stay in it. You bring me something I can defend in court. Not vibes. Not 'my friend saw something.' Not grainy sky footage that the internet will shred."

"My footage isn't grainy," Lila said.

He held her gaze. "It's not enough."

The words hit harder because she'd been afraid they were true.

Lila pressed her fingertips to the paper. The seal's raised edge caught the pad of her finger.

"Who told you to send this," she asked the lawyer.

"I represent parties who have an interest in preventing harm," the lawyer said.

"Harm to who," Lila asked.

"Harm to the public."

Lila almost laughed. It wanted out. She swallowed it instead.

"No glass after dark," she said, glancing at the sign behind her editor. "That's harm prevention too, right? Because people throw bottles when they're scared."

Her editor's mouth tightened. He understood what she was doing. He didn't stop her.

The lawyer ignored the comment. "Your editor is offering you an off-ramp. Take it."

Lila looked at her editor.

He didn't give her softness. He gave her reality.

"Bring me a second confirmation," he said. "Independent. Credible. On-record or admissible. Until then, you don't publish another line. You don't tweet. You don't go on air. You don't turn yourself into a headline."

Lila nodded once. A small motion that kept her from saying something that would burn her.

She slid the notice back across the table.

"Fine," she said. "I'll get you what you need."

Her editor's gaze held, steady and worried.

"And Lila," he added, "don't be alone when you do it."

She stood, backpack strap cutting into her shoulder again, and walked out before her face could betray her.

The newsroom was quieter than it should've been for a city this size. A couple of late-shift reporters hunched over desks, shoulders tight, chasing safer stories. The monitors on the wall played muted footage of a press conference somewhere else, someone else's crisis. The captions crawled. The sound stayed off. Everyone acted like volume could draw trouble.

Lila stopped at her desk and pulled her camera out.

She didn't plug it into anything. She didn't send the clip. She didn't trust the wires in the walls tonight.

She hit playback and watched the smear in the sky again on the tiny screen: the pale tail hanging over Houston's orange glare like a mistake that refused to correct itself.

Then she watched the second thing, the thing that didn't belong in a normal sky-watching night: men in matching uniforms moving in coordination on the next building's roof, hard cases snapped open, radio chatter she couldn't hear but could read in body language.

Watching it, her pulse didn't spike anymore.

It steadied.

Someone had cared that she looked up.

That was the only honest confirmation she had, and it was the kind she couldn't print.

She slipped the camera back into her bag and dug out her notebook. Her pen hovered over the page, then stopped.

Not the names. Not the codes. Not the things that could turn into a neat trail for somebody else.

She wrote what she could without gifting anyone a shortcut: times, locations, descriptions of movements, the shape of cases, the way one man's hand stayed near his belt when he turned.

She wrote **PHM** in the margin and circled it once.

Then she closed the notebook and shoved it into the bottom drawer of her desk.

Her phone buzzed.

A number she didn't recognize.

She answered anyway.

"Ms. Reyes," a man said. No greeting. No courtesy. "This is Office of Public Affairs."

"For who," Lila asked.

A breath. Controlled. Like he'd practiced calm the way you practiced a smile for photos.

"A federal agency," he said. "You have been making inquiries."

"So have you," Lila replied.

A pause, sharp.

"You are advised," he continued, "to refrain from contacting individuals employed by or contracted with agencies under federal mandate. Your current line of inquiry intersects with matters of national security."

Lila kept her voice low. "You read that off a card."

"I'm informing you," the man said.

"Inform me of something useful," Lila said. "Is the object real."

Silence.

Then, "You are not authorized to receive that information."

Lila felt her teeth grind. She forced her jaw loose.

"My editor got a notice," she said. "Did you send it."

"I can't speak to communications from counsel," the man said. "But I can tell you this: continuing down this path will have consequences."

There it was. Not a threat with teeth. A suggestion with paperwork behind it.

"You're calling a local reporter at night," Lila said. "That's your job now."

"My job is to prevent harm," he said.

"By making sure nobody knows enough to prepare," Lila said.

His voice chilled. "Your words could cause panic."

Lila looked around the newsroom. The fluorescent lights hummed. The air-conditioning fought the humidity and lost in small ways. People kept their shoulders drawn in.

"Panic's already here," she said. "You're just trying to control who gets to name it."

The line went quiet.

Then he said, "Do you have anyone dependent on you, Ms. Reyes."

Lila went still.

Not because she didn't understand. Because she did.

Manuel's inhaler sat on her kitchen counter at home. Three doses left, if she spaced them with care and luck.

She didn't answer.

The man didn't need an answer.

"Be careful," he said, and ended the call.

Lila stared at her phone until the screen dimmed.

Her editor's words came back: don't be alone.

She grabbed her bag, her notebook, and a single manila folder from the supply cabinet—blank, innocent—and walked out of the building like she wasn't carrying anything worth taking.

Outside, Houston heat clung even after dark. A thin film of sweat gathered at the base of her neck. Streetlights made the sidewalks look wet. A bus sighed at the curb, half-empty, and the driver's eyes tracked her as she passed as if he was counting passengers the way you counted remaining stock.

At her apartment building, the lobby smelled faintly of bleach and tired flowers. The manager had taped another sign to the glass door:

NO GLASS AFTER DARK. PLEASE USE PLASTIC ON BALCONIES.

Under it, someone had written in marker: **LIKE THAT'LL HELP**

Lila didn't smile.

She climbed the stairs instead of using the elevator. She didn't trust the elevator's slow, boxed pause between floors tonight. She wanted the option to turn around fast if she heard footsteps behind her.

On the third-floor landing, she heard Manuel before she saw him—breath, uneven, a soft rasp that made her body move without thought.

She opened the apartment door and found him sitting on the couch with his elbows on his knees, shoulders hunched, trying to make himself small enough to breathe.

He looked up when she came in.

"Hey," he said, and tried to make it casual. He failed. His voice carried strain.

Lila dropped her bag and crossed to him.

"You use the inhaler," she said.

He shook his head, stubborn. "Was saving it."

"For what," she snapped, then softened because anger was useless here. "For a better night."

He swallowed, eyes glossy. "Pharmacy still open?"

"Not for long," Lila said.

She took the inhaler from the counter and pressed it into his hand.

"Now," she said.

He took it, breathed in, held, released. Again. His shoulders lowered a fraction.

Lila watched his chest rise and fall until it steadied enough that her own ribs stopped squeezing.

"Sit back," she said.

He leaned into the couch, head tipped against the cushion, eyes half-closed.

"You eat," she said, because she needed him to do something normal.

"I'm not hungry."

"Then you pretend," she said.

He cracked a small smile that looked like effort. "Bossy."

"Alive," she said.

She went into the kitchen and opened the cabinet where she kept the medicines. Two bottles left of the steroid inhaler refill, both dated, both precious. She checked the labels like the act could change what they said.

She picked up her phone and called the pharmacy again.

A recording answered.

Due to supply constraints, certain medications may be limited...

Lila hung up before it finished. She didn't need the rest.

She poured Manuel a glass of water—plastic cup, no glass after dark—and watched him drink with small, controlled swallows like he was measuring how much breath each swallow cost.

"You went back there," he said, not looking at her.

"Work," Lila replied.

He turned his head and looked at her then, eyes sharper.

"You're still on that sky thing."

Lila didn't deny it. Denial wasted time.

"I'm on truth," she said.

Manuel let out a breath that turned into a cough he tried to hide.

"Truth doesn't clear your lungs," he said, and the line carried more than it should've. Not cruelty. Fear.

Lila sat on the edge of the coffee table so he could see her hands, her face, her intention.

"I know," she said. "That's why I'm being careful."

He studied her like he was trying to find the lie.

"You're not careful," he said. "You're stubborn."

Lila's mouth tightened. "Same thing sometimes."

He shook his head once. "If somebody's calling you at night—"

She held up a hand. "Don't."

"Lila—"

"Don't make me choose between you and my job," she said, voice low. "Because I already chose you. Every day. I just don't want to live in a world where choosing you means shutting up when it matters."

Manuel stared at the ceiling.

"World's gonna do what it does," he muttered.

"People decide what the world becomes," Lila said.

He closed his eyes. "Then decide we sleep."

She stood. She could do that much for him.

But sleep didn't come with empty hands. It came with plans.

When Manuel's breathing settled into a rhythm she could trust, Lila moved back to the kitchen table and pulled her phone close.

She didn't call from the couch. She didn't want Manuel hearing the tone of her voice change.

She dialed the number she'd been given two days ago by a colleague who owed her a favor and hated owing anyone anything.

A man answered on the third ring.

"Yeah."

Lila didn't use his name. Names were handles.

"You told me you could confirm something without putting yourself in the ground," she said.

Silence.

Then, "You're the reporter."

"I'm the reporter," Lila agreed.

"You got the footage?"

"I got footage," she said. "I'm not calling you to admire it. I'm calling because you said you could see what I can't."

"I can," he said.

Lila heard the fear he tried to hide behind a flat voice.

"You're under contract," she said.

A rough laugh. "Everybody's under something."

"What do you need," she asked.

"Time," he said. "And discretion."

"I'm giving you both," Lila replied. "I need one thing: confirmation that there is an object that isn't being acknowledged."

Silence stretched long enough that Lila felt her pulse in her fingertips.

"I can't say it like that," he said finally.

"Say it how you can," she replied.

A breath. "There's a discrepancy."

"That's not enough," Lila said. "My editor will bury me with 'discrepancy.'"

"You want me to break my NDA on a recorded line," he said, and now his voice carried edge. "You want me to ruin my life so you can run a story?"

Lila swallowed. Manuel's breathing drifted from the living room, soft and uneven at the edges. It kept her honest.

"I'm not asking you to ruin yourself," she said. "I'm asking you to help me build something that doesn't rely on you being a martyr."

Another pause.

"You sound like you've done this before," he said.

"I sound like I want you alive," she replied. "Tell me what you can, and we meet in person. No devices. No recordings. You show me what you're allowed to show me. You tell me what you're allowed to tell me. I take notes. I don't take your identity."

He breathed out, a small exhale that sounded like relief and disgust in equal measure.

"You think that protects me," he said.

"It protects you more than a phone call does," she replied.

Silence.

Then, "Where."

Lila didn't pick a cute place. She picked a place where people went to disappear into ordinary life.

"Twenty-four-hour diner on Westheimer," she said. "Back booth. I'll be there in an hour."

"You bring anyone," he said, "I walk."

"I bring nobody," she said.

"You follow me," he said, "I disappear."

"I don't want your address," she replied. "I want the truth."

Another long pause.

"You keep saying that like truth is a thing," he said. "Truth is a weapon."

Lila's grip tightened on the phone.

"Then hand me the part that can cut through the right target," she said, and hated herself for how it sounded like a plea.

He exhaled again, rough. "Fine."

The call ended.

Lila sat there with the phone pressed to her ear, listening to nothing, as if the dial tone could tell her whether she'd just saved herself or doomed both of them.

She stood, moved quietly to her room, and dressed without turning on the overhead light. Dark jeans, hoodie, sneakers tied in double knots.

She checked the lock twice, then forced herself to stop checking. She didn't have the luxury of spiraling.

In the hallway, she paused by Manuel's door and watched his chest rise. It rose. It fell. It rose again. Enough.

"I'll be right back," she whispered into the dark, not sure if she meant it as promise or spell.

Outside, the night pressed warm against her skin. Cars passed in slow streams, headlights sliding over her like hands she didn't want. She kept to the brighter parts of the sidewalk, not because light meant safety, but because darkness made it easier for someone to stand too close.

At the diner, the neon sign buzzed and blinked on one corner where a letter had gone half-dead. The air inside smelled like burnt coffee and frying oil that had been used too long.

Lila chose a booth with her back to a wall and a view of the door. She didn't order food. She ordered coffee in a plastic cup and watched the waiter's eyebrow lift at the request.

"No glass," she said.

The waiter gave a small, understanding nod like he'd heard it all week.

She waited.

Ten minutes.

Twenty.

A man in a baseball cap walked in and scanned the room too slowly. Another man, older, with a work badge clipped to his belt, slid into a booth two rows away and stared at his hands like he couldn't bring himself to look up.

Lila's phone buzzed once.

A number. Unknown. Again.

She answered.

A whisper came through, harsh and rushed. "Don't come."

Her spine went cold.

"What," she said.

"They came to my office," the voice said. "Two of them. Not police. Not... not anybody with a badge you can name. They asked about you like they already knew. They told me to stop making myself useful."

Lila pressed her free hand to the table to keep it from shaking.

"Where are you," she asked.

"Doesn't matter," he said. "You don't know me. You never called me. You never—"

"I need one line," Lila cut in. "Off the record. For me. Not for print. Is it real."

Silence. Then a sound—breath catching, like he'd swallowed something sharp.

"It's real," he said.

Lila's throat tightened.

"And the reason they're scared," he added, "is because it's not supposed to be yours to name."

The line went dead.

Lila sat there with her phone to her ear as the diner's noise rushed back in: forks, plates, a laugh from the counter that sounded too loud.

She didn't move for a beat because movement felt like admission. Then she stood.

She walked out without finishing the coffee.

In the parking lot, the security light above the dumpster flickered, buzzing in a way that made her skin itch. Her car sat under it, hood reflecting the pale glare.

She unlocked the door, got inside, and locked it again fast.

Her breath came shallow.

She forced it deeper.

In the rearview mirror, her own eyes looked too bright.

She drove home with both hands on the wheel, checking mirrors without making it obvious, taking the longer streets instead of the straight ones because straight lines made you easy.

At her building, she didn't park in her usual spot. She parked one row over, under a different light, and watched the lobby door for a full minute before she got out.

Nothing moved.

That didn't mean nothing watched.

Inside her apartment, Manuel's breathing met her like a fragile gift. Still there. Still holding.

Lila went to the kitchen and pulled her folder out. She opened it and stared at the empty space as if the paper could fill itself with what she now knew.

She didn't have a second confirmation she could cite. She had a frightened voice and a silence that had been managed.

So she did the only thing she could do that didn't rely on anyone else's courage.

She built her own protection.

She pulled out her notebook and tore out three pages, careful to rip along the perforation so it didn't look frantic. She wrote down what mattered in clean block letters: times, locations, the call's content without the number, the exact words **IT'S REAL** with a line under it, then she crossed it out and rewrote it as **CONFIRMED BY PRIVATE SOURCE — ID PROTECTED** because words were evidence and also bait.

She went through her bag and took out the advisory notice copy she'd stolen from her editor's table when he'd turned his head for one second. She hadn't asked permission. She didn't trust permission anymore.

She made two photocopies at the small printer in her room. The machine whirred, dragged the page through, spit it out warm. She stacked the copies, squared the corners.

She didn't put the originals back in her bag.

She didn't trust her bag.

She opened a drawer and found a screwdriver she'd used once to tighten a loose cabinet hinge. She carried it to the kitchen vent near the floor, the one that always rattled when the AC kicked on.

She knelt.

The vent grille was held by four screws, each one filmed with dust and kitchen grease that clung no matter how often she cleaned. She turned the first screw slow, keeping pressure so it didn't drop and clatter. She set it on the tile. Then the next. Then the next.

The cover came free with a faint tug, metal cold under her fingertips.

Inside, the air smelled stale and warm, like trapped years.

She slid the hard copies in, wrapped in the manila folder to keep them from sticking to the duct walls. She pushed them far enough back that a quick glance wouldn't find them, but not so far she couldn't reach.

Her hands moved steady.

Not because she wasn't scared.

Because she didn't have room to be anything else.

She set the grille back in place and tightened the screws until the metal held firm. The screwdriver bit into her palm on the last turn, a small sting that anchored her to her body.

She sat back on her heels and listened.

Manuel coughed once in the other room, then settled.

Lila rested her fingertips on the vent cover for a moment, feeling the vibration of the building's air moving behind it—thin, constant, necessary.

She stood and washed her hands at the sink, scrubbing longer than needed, not to clean but to reset. The water ran warm. The plastic cup by the faucet reminded her of the sign at work, the rule in the lobby, the way the city had started rearranging itself around fear without admitting fear was the architect.

She turned off the faucet and breathed until her chest loosened.

Then she picked up her notebook, flipped to a fresh page, and wrote four words at the top:

WHO BENEFITS FROM SILENCE.

No flourish. No metaphor.

Just a question that could pull the right thread.

Chapter 6 - Pelican Case Silence

Naomi's badge beeped the same way it always did, a small chirp that pretended to be neutral. The sound still tightened her shoulders because she knew what it meant tonight: every door recorded her, every hallway kept a quiet score, every choice left a timestamp she couldn't argue with later.

The lab floor sat half-lit, harsh white over workbenches and shadows pooled under chairs. Cooling fans pushed dry air that made her eyes sting. Somewhere deeper in the building a compressor kicked on, then settled into a low hum like a throat clearing behind a wall.

She stood at the printer tray and watched a page slide out, warm at the edges. A trajectory plot, black lines on white, the curve clean enough to look confident. Confidence was the one thing she couldn't manufacture.

She lifted the page with both hands. The corner brushed her thumb. It left nothing behind, but her skin still crawled as if the room could read what she touched.

"Still here?"

The voice came from the aisle between racks. Jun Park—not related, and he always joked about it until someone laughed too hard and then stopped—rolled a chair with one foot and held a stale granola bar like it was a cigarette.

Naomi didn't turn right away. She let her gaze travel across the plot, because her body needed the ritual: look, check, breathe, decide.

"Still here," she said.

Jun's chair wheels squeaked soft. He stopped beside her without stepping into her space. He'd learned that early, too. In a building full of people who wore authority like armor, distance mattered.

"You're going to go home eventually," he said.

Naomi set the plot on the counter and squared it with the edge as if alignment could steady her pulse.

"I went home," she said. "Two hours. Shower. Tried to sleep."

Jun lifted his eyebrows.

"Failed," Naomi added.

He nodded once, understanding without commentary. His eyes slid to the plot, then away. He didn't ask what it showed. Asking was how you gave someone else a reason to keep you out.

Naomi reached into the folder under her arm and pulled a second sheet free: a single printed line-item from a compilation of observational reports. The amateur entry sat there like a splinter.

A date. A time. A location label that didn't match anything she'd been told in briefings.

She'd circled it back at T–428, during the first meeting when the room had decided to name the program and thereby decide the rules of speech. Sixty-eight days ago, she'd told herself it was noise—some hobbyist's misread streak, a glitch, a misfiled notation. Anything that let her keep working inside the lane they'd drawn.

The number still didn't move.

Jun's gaze flicked toward the sheet in her hand and stayed there a beat too long. He caught himself and looked at the floor.

"You keep staring at that like it owes you money," he said.

"It does," Naomi replied. "It stole time."

Jun's mouth twitched at the edge. "Time isn't on your payroll."

Naomi didn't smile. She lifted the sheet and tapped the amateur entry once with her fingernail, a tiny percussive act that felt louder than it should have.

"This predates what we're allowed to say was the first detection," she said.

Jun didn't answer. His granola bar stayed suspended halfway to his mouth.

Naomi waited. She wasn't asking him to confirm it. She was asking him not to pretend he didn't hear her.

When he spoke, he kept his voice flat. "You already flagged it."

"I flagged it," Naomi said. "And the response was a memo that told me not to use the word 'predates.'"

Jun's eyes sharpened, then softened again like a shutter closing.

"I got told not to use the word 'spike,'" he said. "Everyone's getting trained out of verbs."

Naomi folded the sheet back into her folder. Her fingers moved careful, controlled, like she was packing something breakable.

"Who else saw this entry," she asked.

Jun took a bite of the granola bar. He chewed longer than necessary.

"People who don't want to remember it," he said at last.

Naomi looked down the lab aisle toward the secure corridor. The hallway lights stayed on even at night, as if darkness itself was a liability. The doors at the end sat closed, a pair of blank expressions.

She felt the familiar fork: push and risk being labeled difficult, or swallow it and risk becoming part of the silence she despised.

Jun watched her shift her weight.

"Naomi," he said, quieter now, "it's late."

"It's always late," she replied.

His gaze slid toward the ceiling cameras and back. "Just... don't make yourself the problem."

Naomi took that in without flinching. A warning from someone who didn't like giving warnings because warnings implied belief.

She tucked the folder under her arm and started toward the corridor.

Jun called after her, low. "If you get shut down again, you come back here first."

Naomi glanced over her shoulder.

"Why," she asked.

Jun's jaw worked once. "Because if you walk straight out of an office after a conversation like that, people see your face."

Naomi nodded and kept moving.

At the badge reader, she slowed, not because she needed time, but because rushing looked guilty in places like this. Her badge hit the sensor. The reader chirped. The lock released with a heavy thunk that sounded like a decision being made for her.

Inside the secure corridor, the air ran cooler, too conditioned. The carpet swallowed her footsteps and made her feel like she was moving through someone else's house.

A door opened ahead and closed again. Laughter—short, strained—slipped out and then got cut off as if someone had grabbed it by the throat.

Naomi adjusted her grip on the folder. Her fingers pressed so hard into the cardboard she could feel the ridge under the pad of her thumb.

At the next badge reader, she paused and listened.

No footsteps.

No voices.

Just the building's constant breath.

She swiped in.

A figure sat behind the administrative desk inside, hair pulled tight, glasses set low on her nose. Tasha from access control. Gatekeeper by job description and by instinct.

Tasha looked up and smiled without warmth.

"Dr. Park," she said. "You're back."

Naomi kept her tone polite, which meant clipped. "I need a request filed."

Tasha's eyes dropped to the folder under Naomi's arm. She didn't reach for it.

"What kind of request," Tasha asked.

Naomi chose her words the way you chose a path in tall grass: step wrong and you made a trail someone else could follow.

"Analyst support," Naomi said. "A broader review of observational discrepancies."

Tasha's pen stopped moving over whatever she'd been doing. She looked up again, eyes steady.

"Discrepancies," she repeated.

Naomi held the gaze. "Consistency matters."

Tasha's mouth tightened. "In what way."

Naomi didn't answer that. She didn't have permission to say "timeline." She didn't have permission to imply "manipulated." She didn't have permission to admit she was afraid.

She slid a single page from her folder and placed it on the desk, angled so Tasha could read the header without Naomi shoving it at her.

"Triage request," Naomi said. "I'm asking for a limited circle expansion. Two more orbit analysts. One independent verification team from outside the current pool."

Tasha didn't touch the page. She read it as if touching could implicate her.

"You know what the directive is," Tasha said.

Naomi kept her face still. "Designated channels."

"And designated channels have designated hours," Tasha added. "It's late."

Naomi leaned in a fraction. "It's not late for the object."

Tasha's eyes flicked—just once—toward the hallway beyond the desk, where another locked door waited.

"You're not the only one who's asked," Tasha said.

Naomi's stomach tightened. "Who else."

Tasha's gaze held. "No one you want to drag into your argument."

Naomi exhaled slowly. "I'm not dragging anyone. I'm trying to keep us from making decisions with missing information."

Tasha's voice softened by a hair. "Missing information isn't a bug here. Sometimes it's a feature."

Naomi straightened. Anger rose, hot and fast, and she tamped it down the way she tamped down nausea: breathe through it, don't feed it.

"File it," Naomi said.

Tasha picked up the page between two fingers like it had a residue. "I can submit it," she said. "It will be reviewed."

"By who," Naomi asked.

Tasha's mouth pressed into a line.

Naomi already knew the answer. By people who had learned how to say "no" without writing it down.

Naomi slid her folder back under her arm. "I need to speak to Dr. Kwan."

Tasha's eyebrows lifted. "At this hour."

Naomi didn't blink. "Yes."

Tasha nodded toward the phone on her desk. "Call first."

Naomi didn't take the phone. She didn't like leaving a recorded request she couldn't control. She walked past the desk toward the door that led into the offices and paused at the reader.

Tasha's voice followed her, not loud, just enough to reach.

"Dr. Park," she said.

Naomi stopped.

Tasha's gaze held hers. "If you open certain doors, you can't pretend you didn't."

Naomi's mouth went dry. "I'm not pretending anything."

Tasha's expression didn't change. "That's what I'm saying."

Naomi swiped her badge and stepped through.

Dr. Kwan's office light still burned. That alone told Naomi her request had already been anticipated. Kwan lived inside meetings the way some people lived inside cars—always moving, always tense, always one wrong turn away from a crash.

Naomi knocked once, not timid, not aggressive. A middle note.

"Come in," Kwan called, voice already tired.

Naomi entered and shut the door behind her. She didn't let it click. She guided it closed with her hand so it stayed quiet. Silence was currency here.

Kwan sat behind his desk, jacket off, tie loosened, a stack of printed briefs fanned out like the aftermath of a storm. He looked at Naomi without surprise.

"Dr. Park," he said. "You're working late."

"So are you," Naomi replied.

Kwan glanced down at the folder in her hands and then back to her face.

"What do you need," he asked.

Naomi moved to the chair opposite his desk and stayed standing. Sitting made it feel like a plea. Standing made it feel like business.

"I need to widen the analyst circle," she said.

Kwan didn't answer right away. He picked up a pen, rolled it between his fingers, set it down again in the exact same spot.

"We already addressed this," he said.

"We addressed the optics of it," Naomi said. "We did not address the risk of being wrong because we shrank the pool."

Kwan's eyes narrowed. "You're implying the current pool is incompetent."

"I'm implying the current pool is pressured," Naomi said, and her voice stayed level because she'd rehearsed the tone in her head before she walked in. "Pressure distorts. We need independent verification."

Kwan leaned back in his chair. The leather creaked.

"And what exactly are we verifying," he asked.

Naomi knew that line. The trap where he forced her to say something that would make her look like she was reaching beyond her clearance.

She opened her folder and pulled out the amateur entry page. She didn't shove it across the desk. She placed it down between them with care.

"The observational report we flagged at T–428," she said. "The one that predates the official discovery record."

Kwan's gaze fell to the page. He didn't touch it. His eyes tracked the line-item, paused at the date, then lifted back to Naomi.

"That's noise," he said.

Naomi didn't move. "It's either noise or it's evidence that the discovery timeline is being massaged."

Kwan's jaw tightened. "Careful."

Naomi kept going, because stopping now would be the same as surrender.

"If it's noise, we can prove it's noise," she said. "Let two more orbit analysts review it. Let one outside team do a blind check. We lose nothing by verifying."

Kwan gave her a look that held both warning and fatigue.

"We don't lose nothing," he said. "We lose control of language."

Naomi's nails dug into the folder edge. "Language isn't the goal."

Kwan's eyes sharpened. "Language is the only thing keeping the public from running into the street with canned goods and rifles."

Naomi heard the fear inside the statement and didn't dismiss it. She'd seen people in grocery lines already fighting over bottled water when the weather forecast mentioned a tropical depression.

But she also heard something else: the assumption that truth was a luxury you rationed.

"We are not holding back truth to protect people," Naomi said. "We are holding back truth to protect a timeline. Those are different."

Kwan's gaze stayed steady. "You're not in the rooms where that decision gets made."

Naomi nodded once. "Then let me be in one."

A knock came at the door. Kwan's face didn't change, but his shoulders went tight.

"Come," he called.

The door opened. A man in a dark suit stepped in, badge clipped, hair too neat for this hour. Interagency liaison. Naomi had seen him once at the T–428 briefing, a quiet presence who spoke only when the room needed something to harden.

He looked at Naomi like she was a line item.

"Dr. Park," he said. "Still keeping unusual hours."

Naomi didn't offer a smile. "It's a busy program."

The liaison's mouth twitched as if he almost smiled and then decided against it.

"We're all busy," he said. He turned to Kwan. "I need the latest probability range for the morning call."

Kwan pointed to a stack of briefs without looking at Naomi. "Top packet."

The liaison picked it up, flipped through, stopped on a page, and frowned.

"This is the tightened solution," he said.

"Yes," Kwan replied.

The liaison's gaze flicked to Naomi's amateur entry page. He didn't ask about it. That was the first thing that made Naomi's skin go cold: he knew what it was without asking.

Kwan cleared his throat. "Dr. Park was just leaving."

Naomi didn't move.

The liaison looked at her again, and this time his eyes carried something like pity.

"Dr. Park," he said, "you have done excellent work. Everyone recognizes that."

Naomi hated compliments in rooms like this. They were never free.

He continued, "Part of excellent work is understanding what is yours to solve."

Naomi kept her voice calm. "I'm trying to solve an inconsistency."

The liaison nodded as if she'd said something cute.

"Inconsistencies exist," he said. "We manage them."

Naomi stared at him. "By burying them."

Kwan's breath caught. The liaison's expression stayed smooth, but his eyes sharpened.

"Be careful with your assumptions," he said.

"I'm careful with my numbers," Naomi replied. "I want the same care applied to our timeline."

The liaison placed the stack of briefs back on Kwan's desk and didn't pick it up again. The movement felt deliberate, like he was setting down a weapon he didn't need yet.

"You're asking for a broader circle," he said.

"Yes."

"Denied," he said, softly. "For now."

Naomi felt her pulse in her throat. She forced her shoulders down.

"For what reason," she asked.

The liaison's voice stayed polite. "For the reason you already know."

Naomi held his gaze. "Say it."

Kwan looked pained. "Naomi—"

"Say it," Naomi repeated, because she needed it spoken. If it stayed unspoken, it stayed flexible.

The liaison's mouth tightened the slightest fraction.

"National coordination requires containment," he said. "Containment requires designated channels."

Naomi stared at him. "Designated channels are slow."

"Designated channels prevent leaks," he replied.

"Leaks aren't the only threat," Naomi said. "Delay is a threat."

The liaison's gaze didn't move. "You're thinking like a scientist."

Naomi's hands tightened on the folder. "I am a scientist."

He nodded once. "Tonight, you need to think like a person with a clearance."

Naomi understood then: he wasn't telling her to stop. He was telling her she'd already been noticed.

Kwan's voice came out low, careful. "Naomi, go home."

Naomi looked between them. Two men, both tired, both scared, both complicit in a structure that made fear look like protocol.

"I can't sleep," Naomi said. "Not with this."

The liaison's expression softened in a way that didn't reach his eyes.

"You'll learn," he said, and the sentence landed as a threat dressed as mentorship.

Naomi picked up the amateur entry page and slid it back into her folder. She didn't let her hands shake.

"One more question," she said.

Kwan's eyes pleaded with her to stop. The liaison's gaze waited.

"If the entry is noise," Naomi said, "why is it dangerous to verify."

No one answered.

That silence was the answer.

Naomi opened the door and stepped out. The corridor light made her eyes water. She walked back toward the access desk with measured steps, not fast, not slow. She kept her face neutral, because Jun had been right—faces got read like documents in buildings like this.

Tasha looked up as Naomi approached.

Naomi didn't speak. She slid her triage request page back across the desk.

Tasha's mouth tightened. "You didn't submit it."

Naomi leaned in. "If it goes in, it gets flagged as me pushing. I'm already flagged. Keep it."

Tasha didn't reach for it. "You want me to hide it."

Naomi held her gaze. "I want you to wait until a moment when submitting it doesn't make you collateral."

Tasha watched Naomi's face a long beat, as if weighing whether Naomi had crossed into reckless territory.

Then, without touching the page with her bare fingers, Tasha lifted it with the corner of a file folder and slid it into a drawer.

"I didn't see this," Tasha said.

Naomi nodded once. "Thank you."

Tasha's gaze flicked to the hallway behind Naomi, where Kwan's office sat.

"They told you no," Tasha said.

Naomi's throat tightened. She kept her voice low. "They told me to stop asking."

Tasha exhaled slowly. "And will you."

Naomi looked at the desk phone, then at the locked doors behind it, then at the metal cabinet that held archived routing binders.

"I'm going to do what I can without making you a witness," Naomi said.

Tasha's eyes narrowed. "That sounds like you're about to make yourself one."

Naomi didn't answer. She turned toward the records room door.

Tasha's voice followed her, sharper now. "Dr. Park."

Naomi stopped.

Tasha leaned forward. "Those cabinets are logged."

Naomi met her gaze. "So are my thoughts."

Tasha didn't smile. "Then keep your thoughts in your head."

Naomi swiped her badge and stepped through.

The records room smelled like old cardboard and air that hadn't moved enough. Metal cabinets lined the walls, each drawer labeled with neat block letters and dates that stretched back further than Naomi's career.

A motion sensor clicked somewhere overhead, and the lights snapped brighter. Naomi blinked against the glare.

She moved to the cabinet where the routing binders lived. She had a legitimate pretext: reconcile discrepancies in reported discovery dates. Pretexts mattered. They kept your actions inside a frame others could tolerate.

She pulled open the top drawer. It resisted at first, then slid out with a heavy rasp. Inside, binders sat upright, spines labeled with month and year.

Naomi ran her fingertip along the spines until she found the range she needed. The binder rings inside the spine pressed against the cover when she lifted it free, stiff and resistant, like it didn't want to open.

She set it on the table and flipped it open.

Routing slips. Stamped approvals. Administrative cover sheets with codes and sign-off blocks. Most of it dull enough to numb a mind.

Naomi turned pages anyway.

She watched for patterns: stamps in the wrong order, signatures missing where they should be, addressee lines rerouted to offices that didn't exist on the org chart she was allowed to see.

She turned another page and stopped.

A cover memo sat clipped to a packet thicker than the others. The routing stamps looked clean at first glance, too clean. Then she noticed the dates.

The top stamp read RECEIVED. The next read REVIEWED. The next read CLOSED.

The spacing between them was wrong. Too tight. A process that should've taken days compressed into a single afternoon as if someone had shoved it through a chute.

Naomi's breath caught.

She read the header.

EARLY WARNING — OBSERVATIONAL ANOMALY REPORT

SUBJECT: UNCATALOGED OBJECT / TRAJECTORY REVIEW REQUEST

Her throat went tight. Not fear. Recognition.

She flipped the cover memo and saw the first page of the packet.

Printed plots, calculations, a plain-language summary written for people who needed a narrative, not equations. A recommended action list. Names in the routing list that were not in her current briefing circle.

And a stamped line near the bottom that made her stomach drop:

CONTINUITY PLANNING — ROUTE TO EXTERNAL COORDINATION DESK

Her fingers went numb at the edges, like her body wanted to detach from what her eyes were reading.

She scanned the signature line.

A name she recognized from the T–428 room. Not the liaison—someone higher, someone whose face appeared in televised science segments when the public needed reassurance. A senior official with a voice built for certainty.

Next to the signature block: a second stamp.

HOLD — NO ACTION / REASSESS AFTER DESIGNATION

After designation. After the program got a name. After speech got a fence.

Naomi stared until the letters blurred. She forced her eyes to refocus.

This wasn't noise.

This wasn't a delay because someone was busy.

This was a choice made on paper, with a hand that didn't shake.

A soft sound came from the doorway behind her.

Naomi's head snapped up.

A woman stood there with a janitorial cart, keys clipped to her belt, mop handle angled like a staff. She looked at Naomi, then at the binder, then away as if she hadn't seen anything she could later be asked to describe.

"I'm supposed to clean in here," the woman said, voice flat.

Naomi swallowed. "Give me five minutes."

The woman's eyes stayed on Naomi's face, not the binder.

"Five," she said, and rolled the cart back into the hallway.

Naomi's pulse hammered in her throat. Her hands moved before her mind caught up.

She flipped through the packet again, faster now, looking for the amateur entry reference. A line buried in the appendix caught her eye: a cited observation source labeled AMATEUR NETWORK / LOCAL REPORT.

Next to it: a timestamp.

The same date she'd circled weeks ago.

Naomi pressed her fingertips to the page as if touch could make it more real.

A knock on the wall outside—two taps. Not the janitor. A different rhythm.

Naomi froze.

Footsteps approached, then stopped. The handle didn't turn.

A voice came through the door, muffled. Tasha's.

"Dr. Park," she called, too calm.

Naomi's stomach tightened.

"Yeah," Naomi replied.

Tasha's voice stayed even. "You good."

Naomi stared at the packet. She could hear her own breath, too loud in her ears.

"I'm good," she said.

Silence.

Then Tasha, quieter. "Don't take anything out."

Naomi's throat went tight. "I'm not."

Tasha's voice softened by a hair. "Then you need to decide what you are."

Footsteps retreated.

Naomi stood over the open binder and felt the room tilt inside her. Not dizziness—orientation shifting. A before and after line drawn clean.

She couldn't remove classified material. She couldn't photograph it. She couldn't even stand here too long without creating a trail.

But she also couldn't unknow this.

She reached into her folder and pulled out a blank request form—plain administrative stationery she used for interdepartmental documentation. She set it beside the binder and wrote the only things she could safely carry: the routing stamps' dates, the exact language of the HOLD stamp, the continuity desk label, the senior official's name.

She wrote slow, careful, making the letters legible, because legibility mattered when you were building something meant to survive scrutiny.

She stopped before writing the amateur timestamp. Her hand hovered.

If she wrote it down and someone found it, they could claim she mishandled sensitive information.

If she didn't, she risked losing the connective proof that this packet had been buried around the same discrepancy she'd flagged.

She wrote the timestamp without the source label. Just the numbers. Just the fact that it existed.

Then she wrote a note to herself, small in the margin: VERIFY WHAT IS UNCLASSIFIED.

Naomi closed the binder and pushed it back into the drawer. The metal rasp sounded loud now, accusatory in its own way, like the building knew what she'd found.

She slid the drawer shut and rested her palm on the cabinet face until her heartbeat slowed enough to think.

The janitor rolled back in, cart squeaking soft. She stopped at the threshold and waited without impatience, like she'd seen people in labs have private moments before and knew how to give space.

Naomi tucked her handwritten sheet into her folder and turned.

"Sorry," Naomi said.

The woman nodded once. "People get stuck in the lights."

Naomi didn't know what to say to that. She walked out.

Back on the lab floor, the harsh lights seemed louder. The hum of fans felt like pressure against her skin. Jun's chair sat empty now, his granola bar wrapper on the counter like a small surrender.

Naomi went to her workspace and shut the door behind her. Not locked—she didn't have that authority—but closed enough to create a sliver of privacy.

On her desk sat a rugged equipment case, black, scuffed at the corners. Someone had dropped it off earlier in the week with a sticky note: FIELD KIT — RETURN AFTER USE.

Pelican brand. Overkill for most things. Waterproof, crushproof, built to survive the kind of chaos Naomi had spent her career pretending science could outrun.

She flipped the latches open. The case smelled like foam and plastic, the sterile scent of manufactured protection.

Inside, empty slots waited.

Naomi set her folder down and pulled out what she could legally duplicate: the cover memo header, the routing stamp page that held no sensitive equations, the administrative HOLD line. She went to the copier down the hall—the approved one inside the secure suite—and fed the pages through, one at a time, hands steady.

The machine whirred and pushed out warm sheets.

She didn't make a thick stack. Thick stacks drew attention. She made enough to prove the process existed: one copy for her secure office file, one copy for a contingency if hers got "lost."

Back at her desk, she wrote brief summaries on separate sheets. Not emotional. Not rhetorical. Dates. Names. Actions. Routing.

She didn't write what she thought it meant. She wrote what it was.

When her hand cramped, she flexed her fingers and kept going. The ache in her shoulders deepened. She took a sip from the coffee she'd poured earlier and tasted nothing but bitterness and heat.

On the edge of her desk, the amateur entry printout waited, a single line that had dragged her into this. She stared at it and felt the shame of how long she'd tried to talk herself out of being bothered.

A knock came at her door.

Naomi's muscles tightened.

Jun's voice came through, low. "You alive."

Naomi didn't open the door. "Yes."

Another pause. "You find anything."

Naomi's throat tightened. She wanted to say everything. She wanted to pour it out and make it real by sharing it.

She also remembered Kwan's office, the liaison's smooth face, the way denial had slid into the air without leaving fingerprints.

"Not something I can talk about," Naomi said.

Jun didn't push. He exhaled once, audible. "Okay."

His footsteps moved away.

Naomi looked at the equipment case again.

She placed the copies and her summaries inside, arranged flat, edges aligned. She set the amateur entry printout in last, not because it belonged in the same category, but because it was the origin of her doubt.

The latch clicked when she closed it. The sound echoed in her office, sharp in the quiet.

She stood with her hand on the case lid and realized her breathing had changed. Slower. More controlled. Less like a person hoping the system would do the right thing.

More like a person preparing for the system to do the predictable thing.

She pulled a blank request packet from her drawer: probe-data request forms. The kind you used for small missions, for incremental clarity. The kind that needed approvals and patience and language that didn't frighten administrators.

Naomi laid the forms out and aligned them, corners square. She filled in the fields in her careful block handwriting: objective, justification, parameters, expected yield. She chose words that sounded safe.

CHARACTERIZATION REQUEST. STRUCTURE AND COMPOSITION. RISK REDUCTION SUPPORT.

She didn't write "catastrophe." She didn't write "impact." She didn't write anything that would trigger a reflex.

Her hand hovered over the final section: requested priority.

If she marked it routine, it would sit behind everything else until time ran out.

If she marked it urgent, it would attract attention.

She thought of the buried packet's HOLD stamp. The clean compression of dates. The decision to wait until designation made containment easier.

Naomi checked the urgent box.

Her pulse jumped. She kept her face still, as if someone could see her through the walls.

She placed the packet in an interoffice envelope and wrote the destination: the approval desk inside the program's designated channel. The same channel that had told her no. The same channel she still had to use, because she wasn't ready to burn the building down with a leak that would cause harm without preparation.

She set the envelope on the corner of her desk and stared at it.

The shame came back, hot in her throat. Shame that she had to behave like a defendant to do her job. Shame that she had to hide administrative pages like contraband just to protect the truth from polite erasure.

She pushed the shame aside and focused on process.

Naomi wrote a second note for herself—short, precise—and slid it into the equipment case: PROBE REQUEST SUBMITTED — DATE/TIME.

Then she snapped the latches shut again.

Click.

Click.

The sound felt different now. Not protection. Commitment.

Naomi turned off her desk lamp and stepped into the corridor. The lights overhead buzzed faint, the building's constant insistence on being awake. She walked past Tasha's desk. Tasha didn't look up, but her voice came, quiet.

"You leave."

Naomi stopped. "I'm leaving."

Tasha's pen moved over a form. "You shouldn't have gone in there."

Naomi's throat tightened. "I shouldn't have had to."

Tasha's pen paused. "People get disappeared in softer ways than you think."

Naomi's fingers clenched around her badge. "I'm not trying to be brave."

Tasha looked up then, eyes tired and sharp. "Then what are you."

Naomi answered without drama, because drama was a luxury.

"I'm trying to make sure there's a record," she said.

Tasha held her gaze a moment longer, then looked down again. "Go."

Naomi walked to the exit corridor. The air changed near the doors, a faint hint of outside—cooler, damp with night. She swiped out, the reader chirped, and the door released.

Outside, the night air hit her face and made her inhale deeper. Distant freeway noise rolled like constant surf. The parking lot lights cast harsh circles on asphalt, leaving darkness in between like gaps you could fall into.

Naomi walked toward her car and felt her badge hang heavy against her chest, a physical reminder that the building still owned what she could say.

She didn't look over her shoulder too often. Too often looked like fear.

She looked once.

Nothing moved.

That didn't soothe her.

She got in her car and sat without starting the engine, hands on the steering wheel, staring at the lit windows of the facility as if she could see the buried packet through concrete.

Inside, in her office, a rugged case sat shut with a small stack of documents that could ruin her if someone decided she was the problem.

Naomi started the engine and drove out slow, headlights sweeping the curb, her jaw locked as if she could hold the entire system in place by force.

Chapter 7 - Badge Stays Visible

The cold hit Malik's lungs hard enough to make him cough once, the sound sharp in the open parking lot. He kept walking anyway, shoulder bag tight against his side, eyes scanning the spill of fluorescent light from the lobby onto the asphalt. Dawn sat low and gray beyond the freeway. A helicopter pushed across the sky, rotors beating the air in steady thumps that made every car alarm in his head start blinking.

He'd arrived early on purpose. Early meant he could watch who showed up and how. Early meant he could catch panic before it picked a direction.

Two staffers crossed from the far row, huddled inside jackets, heads down like they'd learned to hide their faces. One of them—Marta from admin—had her badge turned inward against her chest, the photo pressed flat to her sweater like she was ashamed of it. Malik recognized the move because he'd done it himself at a gas station two nights ago when a man at the pump had stared too long at the lanyard around Malik's neck and said, half a joke, half a threat, "Y'all got a list, don't you."

Malik had smiled back with his mouth only and driven away with the tank half full.

Now he stood beside his car and watched Marta's steps shorten as she neared the building. The second staffer—tall, broad-shouldered, a logistics specialist Malik had brought over from the port months ago—kept glancing behind them, as if someone might rise from between vehicles.

Malik raised his hand in a small wave that didn't ask for warmth. Just acknowledgment. Marta's eyes caught his. For a beat, she looked like she wanted to run back to her car and lock herself inside it.

She kept moving.

"Morning," Malik called, voice neutral.

Marta's answer came out thin. "Morning."

The tall man—Trevor—nodded, jaw tight. His badge also faced inward.

Malik didn't correct them yet. Not out here. Out here, correction sounded like command, and command sounded like certainty, and certainty was the one thing he couldn't sell without hating himself.

A siren rose somewhere near the freeway, slid past, faded. The sound left a residue in the air, like smoke you couldn't see.

Malik checked his phone without unlocking it, just the screen waking under his thumb. Three missed calls. Two from an unknown number. One from a contact saved as "D." He stared at the single letter until the screen dimmed again.

He could call back. He could ask what was wrong. He could also put a voice to his fear and let it sit in his ear while he tried to keep a building full of people from breaking apart.

He shoved the phone into his pocket and started toward the entrance.

Inside, the lobby smelled like carpet cleaner and hand sanitizer. The security desk sat to the right, glass panels scratched from years of keys and bracelets and people leaning in too hard. A guard Malik hadn't met before stood behind the desk, posture straight, eyes tired. His uniform looked new. His hands didn't.

"Mr. Carter?" the guard asked.

Malik stopped at the desk, kept his shoulders relaxed. "Malik is fine."

The guard nodded like he'd been told not to do that. "They said you'd be coming in early."

"They say a lot," Malik replied.

The guard didn't smile. He slid a laminated sheet across the desk. "We're supposed to ask everyone to sign this."

Malik leaned in. The sheet was simple. Visitor log language. A line about conduct. A line about not bringing weapons into the building.

"What happened," Malik asked, eyes still on the paper.

The guard's throat moved. "Yesterday afternoon. A guy tried to come in and film the front desk. Wanted names. Wanted badge numbers. Said he was going to post them."

"Did he?" Malik asked.

The guard's gaze flicked toward the glass doors, then back. "He got bored when we didn't bite. He left. Said he'd be back with friends."

Malik stared at the laminated sheet. It wasn't protection. It was theater. It was a way for leadership to say they'd done something if someone got hurt.

He signed anyway. His signature looked too calm on the line.

Behind him, the badge scanners chirped as more staff came through. Malik turned and watched them enter in small groups, each person's body telling the truth their mouths wouldn't.

A woman with a purse clutched tight to her chest, knuckles pale. A man who usually joked loud enough to fill a hallway now talking with his head angled down, voice contained. Another admin staffer with her badge tucked away, lanyard looped around her wrist like a leash.

Malik stepped out from the desk and caught Marta's attention.

"Hold up," he said, gentle.

Her gaze sharpened. "What now."

He lifted his own lanyard, let it hang where anyone could see it. The photo showed his face under fluorescent light, the expression neutral by training.

"Badge stays visible," Malik said.

Marta's lips pressed together. "So they can find us faster."

"So we can find each other," Malik replied.

She stared at him like he'd offered a prayer in a place that didn't deserve one. Then, slowly, she turned her badge outward.

Trevor didn't.

Malik didn't push. Not yet.

A door hissed open and a supervisor stepped into the lobby, eyes darting.

"Malik," she said. "Huddle in five. Conference room B."

He nodded and followed her toward the elevators. The carpet swallowed their steps. In the reflection of the elevator doors, Malik saw his own face, the corners of his mouth held in place like he was wearing something that didn't fit.

Conference room B sat off a hallway that used to feel ordinary. Now it felt like a corridor in a hospital: too clean, too bright, filled with people trying not to touch the walls.

The room was already crowded. Paper cups of bad coffee steamed on the table. Someone's phone buzzed again and again against a chair, the vibration like an insect trapped under plastic.

Malik stepped to the front without calling for attention. He waited until the room's scattered conversations collapsed into quiet.

"Look," he said, voice steady, "I know everyone's hearing things."

A few people laughed, brittle.

"Understatement," someone muttered.

Malik nodded like he'd earned it. "I'm not going to insult you by pretending I can answer every rumor. I'm also not going to stand here and tell you 'everything's fine.'"

Silence settled, heavy, not calm.

A woman near the back—hair pulled into a tight bun, eyes red as if she'd cried in her car—lifted her chin. "Are we on a list," she asked.

The question hit the room like a thrown object. A couple heads snapped toward Malik. Others looked away, as if not looking could keep the question from becoming real.

Malik held the pause. He didn't rush to fill it. He let the gap show. Let them see he heard her.

"What I can tell you," he said, "is this: if you feel unsafe coming in, I'm not going to call you weak. I'm going to call you honest."

A man near the table scoffed. "Honest doesn't pay my mortgage." A few people murmured agreement.

Malik kept his gaze on the scoffer. "No," he said. "It doesn't. But if you get hurt trying to prove you're brave, that doesn't pay it either."

That got a sharp exhale from someone. Not laughter. Something closer to relief that he wasn't going to shame them.

The woman with red eyes spoke again. "My neighbor called me a traitor last night. Said I'm helping 'the chosen' get out while everybody else dies. He knows where I park."

A man beside her put a hand on her shoulder, then pulled it back like touch might make things worse.

Malik let his hand rest on the edge of the table, fingers spread. "We're going to start coming in pairs," he said. "No one walks from the far lot alone. If you're here early, you wait by the doors until someone else arrives."

Trevor's voice cut in, sharp. "So we're supposed to huddle up like kids."

Malik looked at him. Trevor's jaw flexed. His badge still faced inward.

"You'd rather pretend you're not scared," Malik said.

Trevor's cheeks flushed. "Don't do that."

"Don't do what," Malik asked.

"Make it sound like I'm the problem," Trevor snapped.

Malik didn't raise his voice. "You're not the problem. The problem is the world outside this room is getting mean, and our job title is turning into a target."

A woman at the table let out a short laugh. "Target. Like we're important."

Marta's voice, quiet but cutting, slipped out. "Like we're visible."

A phone buzzed again. Someone finally shut it off with a hard swipe of their thumb.

Malik nodded once. "Visible," he repeated. "That's why the badge stays visible. Not because it keeps you safe. Because it keeps you accountable to each other. Because if someone gets grabbed or followed or shoved, I want people to be able to say a name without guessing."

The red-eyed woman swallowed. "What if they use the badge to find us at home."

The room tightened.

Malik's mouth went dry. He chose his next words like he was stepping onto a brittle surface.

"If you're worried about home," he said, "talk to me after. We can adjust parking. We can do ride shares. We can do quiet entry routes."

"Quiet routes," Trevor echoed, with a faint edge. "Like we're sneaking."

Malik met his gaze. "Like we're staying alive."

That shut Trevor up, but it didn't soften him. Malik saw it in the set of his shoulders: resentment turned inward, looking for somewhere to land.

A supervisor near the back cleared her throat. "We also need to talk about the wristbands."

The room's attention snapped to her.

Malik's pulse ticked once in his neck. He hadn't heard that word in this building yet. He'd heard it in port chatter. He'd heard it in a half-joke from a procurement contact who'd said, "You'll see, it'll be wristbands like a club."

"What wristbands," someone asked.

The supervisor's gaze flicked to Malik and then away. "They're... discussing it at higher levels," she said. "Color-coded lines for intake. To manage crowds."

A man near the door barked a laugh that turned into a cough. "Color-coded lines. Like an amusement park."

The supervisor's voice dropped. "It's being called the red wristband line."

A shiver ran through the room that had nothing to do with the air conditioning. The phrase sounded like a joke until you pictured it on skin, until you pictured someone deciding who got red.

Marta whispered, "That's sick."

Trevor muttered, "That's real."

Malik didn't comment. He watched faces. He watched who leaned forward and who leaned back. Who looked angry and who looked hungry.

He ended the huddle without a speech. "Pairs," he said again. "Badges out. No one stays late alone. If anyone sees something outside, you call security and you call me. Not after. In the moment."

A few nods. A few blank stares. A few people already halfway gone inside their own heads.

The meeting broke into small clusters. Malik stepped into the hallway, shoulders tight, and felt the building's hum press against his eardrums.

He didn't make it ten steps before shouting cut through the lobby.

A sharp male voice. A woman's cry. The sound of bodies moving fast.

Malik ran.

His shoes skidded on the lobby tile. The glass doors ahead vibrated with the impact of something—someone—hitting them. Through the glass, the parking lot flashed bright, shapes jerking in the pale morning.

He pushed through the doors.

Cold air slapped his face. Gravel shifted under his feet.

A man had someone backed against a car, forearm pinning them at the throat. The pinned person's hands clawed at the arm, fingers shaking. Malik recognized the coat—Dana from logistics, the one who always carried cough drops and offered them like currency.

The attacker shouted, voice raw. "Say it! Say you got the list!"

Dana's face was mottled red, eyes wide, mouth open but no sound coming out.

Malik sprinted, heart hammering. "Hey!" he shouted, voice big enough to cut. "Get off her!"

The man's head snapped toward Malik. His eyes were bloodshot, wild. He was close enough now that Malik could smell him: stale sweat, cheap liquor clinging under a layer of cold.

"You one of them," the man snarled. "You're the one."

Malik kept moving, hands open, palms out. "Step back," he said. "Nobody's got to get hurt."

Dana's badge had slipped free. It lay on the pavement near the car's rear tire, lanyard stretched out like a fallen vein.

The attacker's gaze flicked to Malik's own badge. His mouth twisted. "Look at you," he said. "Wearing it like a crown."

"It's a badge," Malik said, and his voice stayed calm because calm kept other people alive. "Back up."

The man tightened his forearm against Dana's throat. Dana gagged, a sound that snapped something in Malik's chest.

Malik moved faster.

Security spilled out of the lobby—two guards, one older with a baton, one younger with empty hands. Trevor appeared from the side, eyes wide, then darted in like his body had decided before his pride could.

Malik lunged for the attacker's wrist, caught skin slick with sweat, and yanked down hard. The man's grip loosened just enough for Dana to suck air.

The attacker swung his free hand, nails raking Malik's cheek. Pain flared hot. Malik didn't back off.

"Now," Malik barked, and the older guard grabbed the attacker's shoulder and wrenched him away from Dana. The younger guard caught the attacker's other arm. Trevor moved in front of Dana like a wall.

The attacker fought, feet scraping on gravel, voice breaking into a shout that carried across the lot. "They're killing us! They got seats! They got seats!"

A car horn blared. Someone shouted from inside a vehicle, "Leave her alone!"

Someone else yelled, "Ask him about the list!"

Malik's breath came hard. His cheek burned where the nails had hit.

The attacker jerked his head toward Malik. "Tell them!" he screamed. "Tell them who gets red!"

Malik didn't answer. He couldn't. His silence wasn't moral. It was enforced.

Security dragged the man toward the lobby doors. The older guard hissed under his breath, "Don't spit," like that was the kind of warning you gave every day now.

Dana sagged against Trevor. Her hands shook so hard she couldn't pick up her badge.

Malik crouched, grabbed the lanyard, and held it out to her.

Dana stared at it like it was poison. Tears had pooled at her lower lashes and didn't fall, trapped by shock.

"I can't," she whispered.

Malik's throat tightened. He didn't tell her she could. He didn't tell her she had to.

He slid the badge into his own pocket instead.

"Inside," Malik said.

Trevor's voice cracked. "She can't breathe right."

Malik nodded. "Lobby. Now."

They half-walked, half-carried Dana through the doors. The lobby's warm air hit Malik's face and made the cold outside feel unreal, like a dream you woke from but couldn't shake.

Dana collapsed into a plastic chair near the security desk. Her knees bounced. Her hands kept trying to grab at her throat, then stopping.

Marta rushed over with a bottle of water and knocked it against Dana's lip. "Sip," she said, voice thick. "Small."

Dana tried. Water spilled down her chin.

The guard at the desk picked up the phone with shaking fingers. "EMS," he said into it. "We need—"

A supervisor hurried out of the hallway, eyes sharp with panic and calculation. "Not in the lobby," she snapped.

Malik's head turned. "What."

The supervisor gestured toward the glass doors, toward the parking lot where staff and a few bystanders had begun to gather, hungry for a story. "Not here," she said again. "Move her to the back."

Dana's eyes widened. "No," she whispered.

Malik stood, the movement fast enough to make his vision flare for a second. "She got attacked on our property," he said, voice low. "We're not hiding her."

"We're not hiding her," the supervisor hissed back. "We're controlling escalation."

The phrase hit Malik like a slap. He'd heard it before from people with clean hands who never stood in gravel.

Marta's face twisted. "She's bleeding," she said.

Dana wasn't bleeding. Not visibly. But her throat looked raw, skin already bruising.

The supervisor's gaze flicked to Malik's cheek. "So are you," she said, as if that made it manageable.

A man in a suit appeared from the hallway—HR, Malik thought, or legal. His face held the careful blankness of someone who spoke only in ways that could be defended later.

"Mr. Carter," he said, tone soft. "We need to document the incident."

Malik stared at him. "We need a medic."

"We've called," the guard said, voice small.

The man in the suit didn't look at the guard. He looked at Malik. "Back corridor," he suggested. "Less visibility."

Dana made a sound that wasn't a word. She tried to stand and nearly fell.

Trevor's hand shot out to steady her. He didn't speak. His eyes were fixed on the doors like he expected the attacker to come back with friends.

Malik took a breath and forced his voice into something Dana could hold. "Dana," he said, "we're going to move you to the conference room by the back offices. It's quieter. You'll have space. You won't be alone."

Dana's gaze flicked to the glass doors, to the gathering shapes outside. Her mouth trembled.

"Please," she whispered, and the word didn't land as weakness. It landed as a decision.

Malik nodded. "Okay."

He leaned in and spoke low enough only she could hear. "I've got your badge," he said. "You don't need it right now."

Dana's eyes closed for a beat. She nodded once, shallow.

They moved her through the side hallway, away from the lobby. The building's hum returned, steady, indifferent.

In the back conference room, Marta grabbed paper towels and pressed them gently to Dana's neck as if pressure could erase what had happened. Trevor stood near the door, body angled like he'd learned to guard without being told.

Malik hovered a step back, hands flexing, trying not to shake.

The man in the suit placed a form on the table. "We need your statement," he said.

Malik stared at the form. His eyes skated over blank lines meant to turn fear into neat text.

"Later," Malik said.

The man's expression didn't change, but his voice cooled. "Now is preferable."

Malik's cheek throbbed. He tasted blood when he swallowed. He wanted to spit, but spitting felt like losing control.

He leaned forward, palms on the table. "You want a statement," he said. "Fine. The statement is: our staff got assaulted because people think we're hiding seats. People think we have lists. People think we're choosing who lives. And we are not prepared for what happens when that belief turns into a crowd."

The man in the suit blinked once. "That's not a statement. That's commentary."

Malik's jaw clenched. "It's the truth."

The man's voice stayed calm. "Truth is not always helpful in the moment."

Marta made a sound like a laugh but didn't smile. "That's rich," she muttered.

Trevor's eyes flicked to Marta, then to Malik, as if deciding which side he was on.

Dana's breathing hitched. She pressed her fist to her mouth. Malik watched her knuckles whiten and felt something in him harden.

The supervisor stepped into the room, eyes sharper now. "We're implementing new entry protocols," she said. "Effective immediately."

Malik didn't look away from Dana. "Good."

The supervisor faced him. "Badge visible at all times," she said. "Escort pairs from parking lot. Quiet routes. No one uses the front entrance alone."

Malik nodded, already moving through the steps in his head.

"And," the supervisor added, hesitating just long enough to show she didn't want to say it, "we're restricting movement on certain supplies. Access only."

"Certain supplies," Malik repeated, voice flat.

The supervisor glanced at the man in the suit, then back to Malik. "You know what I mean."

Malik did. He'd seen the way pallets at Pier 22 had been marked. He'd seen how a strip of blue tape could turn a crate into something people stopped asking about.

He had told himself that was port culture—temporary labels, rushed sorting, someone's lazy shorthand.

It hadn't been.

"Show me," Malik said.

The supervisor's mouth tightened, but she nodded and led him into the hallway.

They walked past offices with doors shut, blinds angled down. People glanced up as Malik passed, eyes lingering on the scratch on his cheek. A story traveled faster than policy.

The supervisor stopped at a side door Malik hadn't paid attention to before. The door had a new sign taped to it. No printed letterhead. No official stamp. Just handwriting in block letters:

AUTHORIZED ACCESS ONLY.

A strip of blue painter's tape ran across the doorframe. On the tape, someone had written three letters: PHM.

Malik's stomach turned.

He stared at the tape until the supervisor shifted, uncomfortable.

"You've seen this," she said, more question than statement.

Malik didn't answer right away. He moved closer, eyes narrowing. The tape looked fresh. The handwriting looked careful, as if someone had practiced it before committing it to the strip.

"Where else," Malik asked.

The supervisor pointed down the hall toward a storage area. "There," she said. "And on the loading dock doors. And on the route boards."

"Route boards," Malik repeated.

The supervisor nodded once. "Blue only. No photos."

Malik's gaze snapped to her. "No what."

Her jaw flexed. "No photos," she repeated, voice lower. "People keep taking pictures of everything and sending it to... wherever."

Malik thought of the buzzing phones in the huddle. Thought of rumors outrunning trucks.

He held his voice steady. "This is how you think you stop it."

The supervisor's eyes hardened. "This is how we stop theft."

Malik stared at the blue tape. The letters PHM sat there, small and confident, like the building itself had chosen a side.

He turned and walked toward the storage area without waiting for permission.

Inside, the air was cooler, heavy with cardboard and plastic wrap. Shelves rose in neat rows. On the end of one shelf, another strip of blue tape marked a bin. On the floor, two pallets sat wrapped tight, corners dented, each with the same tape on the top edge.

Malik stepped closer and read what was written beneath PHM in smaller letters:

CONTINUITY — HOLD.

His chest tightened.

"You're telling me continuity is in our building," Malik said, voice low.

The supervisor's gaze stayed on the shelves. "Continuity is everywhere," she said.

"That's not an answer," Malik replied.

"It's the only one you're going to get," she said.

Malik looked at the taped pallets and felt the ground shift. Not the comet. Not the calculations. The human part. The part where someone had already decided who got held back from the chaos and who got pushed into it.

He thought of Dana's bruising throat. Thought of the attacker screaming about red.

He turned back to the supervisor. "Who has access," he asked.

The supervisor's eyes flicked away. "Authorized staff."

"Names," Malik said.

She exhaled hard. "Malik."

He leaned in. "If we're putting tape on doors and calling it safety, I need to know who's walking through those doors. Because the next person who gets grabbed in the parking lot might be the person someone thinks is carrying keys to that room."

The supervisor's mouth tightened. "You're making it worse."

Malik stared at her. "It's already worse," he said. "You're just trying to keep it quiet."

The supervisor's eyes flashed. "And you're trying to make it clean. Neither of us is getting what we want."

They stood there, the hum of the building filling the space between them. Malik could hear his own heartbeat, a steady thump that matched the helicopter noise from earlier, as if the day had its own soundtrack.

He stepped back from the pallets and forced his voice into a workable shape. "Badge visible," he said. "Escort pairs. Quiet routes. I'll walk the lot and set the pattern. I'll get volunteers."

The supervisor's shoulders loosened a fraction. "Good."

"And," Malik added, "I want one more guard posted outside at dawn."

The supervisor's eyes tightened. "We don't have the staffing."

"Then pull someone from inside," Malik said. "Because right now, the threat isn't someone stealing a printer. It's someone grabbing a person."

The supervisor didn't answer. She didn't have to. Malik could see the calculation: budget, optics, politics. How many bodies could they afford to lose before the numbers mattered enough to justify the cost.

Malik walked back into the lobby with the weight of the blue tape stuck behind his eyes.

By midday, the parking lot felt like a different planet. Sunlight hit windshields and turned them into hard mirrors. Every reflection looked like someone watching.

Malik stood at the entrance with two volunteers—Marta and Trevor, surprisingly—and the older guard from the morning.

Marta's badge hung outward now. Trevor's did too, though his fingers kept rubbing the lanyard cord like it itched.

"All right," Malik said, voice low, "front entrance is for groups. Back entrance is for pairs. No one crosses the lot alone. If you arrive and you don't see anyone, you wait in your car and you text—"

He stopped himself. He didn't want to say "text" like it was a solution. Phones were rumor engines right now.

"If you arrive and you don't see anyone," he corrected, "you call the desk. You do not walk."

Trevor scoffed, then caught Malik's gaze and swallowed the scoff back down.

A staffer approached from the far row, steps fast, head swinging side to side. Malik recognized her—Nina from procurement. She'd always been efficient, sharp, the kind of person who could find a missing shipment with one phone call and a raised eyebrow.

Today her face looked thin. Her eyes were glassy.

"I'm not doing this," Nina said, voice tight.

Malik stepped forward. "You're already here."

"I'm not wearing the badge," she snapped, hand clenched around the lanyard in her pocket. "Not after what happened to Dana."

Malik kept his voice even. "Dana is inside. She's breathing. She's going to be out for a while. You not wearing your badge doesn't change that."

Nina's eyes flashed. "It changes who can find me."

Marta spoke, soft. "We can find you too."

Nina's gaze snapped to Marta, anger sharp and displaced. "You think I trust any of this," she hissed.

Malik didn't argue. He stepped closer until Nina could see his cheek scratch, the faint swelling.

"I don't trust it either," he said. "I'm still standing here."

Nina's throat moved. Her eyes flicked to the parking lot, to the cars, to the bright glass. She pulled the lanyard out, hands shaking, and clipped it on.

She didn't look at Malik when she walked past.

Behind her, another staffer approached, then another. Malik watched each face. He watched who flinched at the sight of security. He watched who looked relieved and who looked furious.

A man in a polo shirt stopped short when he saw the escort arrangement. "What is this," he demanded.

"Safety," Malik said.

The man's laugh came out harsh. "Safety. You mean control."

Malik held his gaze. "Call it what you want. It's the difference between you walking in and you getting grabbed."

The man's nostrils flared. "This isn't what I signed up for."

Malik nodded. "I know."

The man stared at him, waiting for an apology. Malik didn't give one. Apologies didn't stop bruises.

The man walked in anyway, badge out, jaw tight.

Marta let out a breath she'd been holding. "This is going to get ugly," she whispered.

Malik didn't answer. He watched the lot. He watched the sky.

A helicopter crossed again, low and loud, as if reminding him that nothing about this stayed inside one building.

His phone buzzed in his pocket.

He didn't pull it out right away. He didn't want Marta and Trevor watching his face change.

When he finally stepped aside and checked, the screen showed another missed call from D. No message left.

He stared at the letter until it blurred. Then he opened his car door and sat behind the wheel for a moment, hands resting on the steering wheel as if he could steady the day by holding something solid.

In the glove compartment, beneath registration papers, a small notebook sat tucked flat. His private record of conversations that were always verbal and never backed by an email he could print. He hadn't told anyone about it. He hadn't shown it to anyone. It felt like a shameful thing to need.

He didn't open it. He didn't write. He just touched the corner with his fingertips, a reminder that if the system ever turned on him, he would have something that proved he hadn't been freelancing with people's lives.

Outside his car, the morning light hit every window and turned the lot into a field of eyes.

Malik stepped back out, straightened his badge until it lay flat against his chest, and walked toward the doors with his shoulders squared—because if he looked hunted, the people he was trying to protect would feel it in their bones.

Chapter 8 - Cinder Coffee Newsroom

The generator's vibration came up through the floor tiles and into Lila's knees, a steady tremor that made every desk feel slightly alive. The building's lights held, then blinked once as if deciding whether to keep cooperating. Someone had dragged a hot plate onto the copy table. The coffee on it smelled scorched, like the last inch in a pot left too long—bitter enough to coat the back of her throat before she even lifted the cup.

She sat with her shoulders pitched forward, wrists hovering above the keyboard like she might spook the words if she touched them too hard. The newsroom around her had gone thin. Fewer bodies, fewer jokes, the same tired hum of printers and a phone that refused to stop ringing.

She didn't answer that phone. Not yet. She kept her eyes on the draft on her screen and on the paper copy beside her—two versions of the same truth, neither one safe.

Across the aisle, a night producer had pulled his chair close to the call station, writing down tips in block letters on a legal pad. Each time the phone rang, his hand tightened around the pen before he picked up, like he needed to anchor himself to something solid.

Lila's editor, Graham, stood at the end of her row with his sleeves rolled up and his tie loosened, hair flattened on one side like he'd rested his head against a wall at some point and decided sleep wasn't worth it. He looked at her screen, then at the paper, then at her face as if he might find a loophole there.

"You took out the part about the agency name," he said.

She didn't glance up. "You asked me to."

He rubbed the bridge of his nose until his fingers went pale. "I asked you to stop handing them a handle."

"Then stop asking for honesty," she said, and her voice came out flat, not sharp. She didn't have extra heat to waste.

Graham exhaled and leaned closer, reading the lede again. His lips moved on the words he didn't like.

"'A federal response program operating under emergency secrecy...'" he read, then stopped. "That sentence is going to get us an injunction."

"It's not a target. It's a description."

"It's an invitation," he corrected, and his eyes flicked toward the windows as if the street outside could hear.

Lila's fingers flexed. Her hands wanted to do something—tie a knot, scrub a surface, pick up a stack and make it neat. Instead, she slid the paper copy toward him and pointed to the margin notes in her own handwriting.

"I don't name locations," she said. "I don't name intake sites. I don't publish anything that tells people where to go, who to follow, who to hunt. I'm not putting blood on my keyboard."

Graham's jaw worked. He stared at the page as if it could start smoking.

"I know," he said, softer. "I know you're trying to be careful."

"Careful doesn't matter," Lila replied. "Truth does."

That made him flinch—not because he disagreed, but because it sounded like a line someone would quote back in court.

He straightened and glanced toward the corner office where the managing editor sat behind a half-closed door. The door had been open earlier. The door being half-closed felt like a decision.

"Legal's on speaker in five," Graham said. "They're already drafting a response. There's a—" He hesitated. "There was another advisory."

Lila's pulse ticked once in her throat. "Another letter."

Graham's eyes flicked down to his hand. He held an envelope. He hadn't been holding it a minute ago. Lila didn't remember seeing him pick it up.

He set it on her desk like it was ordinary mail.

The envelope wasn't sealed with wax or stamped with drama. It was plain, heavy paper, addressed in black type, return address a federal office she'd already memorized without wanting to. Someone had written a code in the top right corner, three letters, neat and small: PHM.

Lila stared at it until the edges of her vision went grainy.

Graham's voice lowered. "They keep saying it's for your protection."

"They keep saying a lot," she said, and her hand went to the envelope without opening it. The paper felt cool. Too clean.

"Don't—" Graham started.

"I'm not going to tear it up," she said. "Relax."

He looked like he might laugh, but his mouth didn't cooperate. "It's a warning," he said. "That's all it is."

Lila slid the envelope under the paper copy, covering the code. Not because she thought the code mattered, but because she hated the feeling of it watching her.

"Get legal," she said.

Graham hesitated. "Lila."

She finally looked up. His eyes weren't just tired. They were scared in a way he couldn't hide behind newsroom sarcasm.

"If you do this with your byline," he said, "your name becomes the story."

"My name's already on every story I've written for ten years," she said.

"Not like this," he replied.

The generator's vibration pushed up again through the floor, a reminder that even the building was running on borrowed patience.

Lila didn't tell him about Manuel's inhaler canister sitting on her kitchen counter at home, light in her hand when she'd shaken it earlier. She didn't tell him about the pharmacy tech who'd shrugged at her three days ago and said, "We can fill half."

She didn't tell him that she'd already been doing math in her head that had nothing to do with sentences.

"Bring legal," she repeated, and turned back to the draft.

The conference corner smelled like overheating plastic and stale carpet. Graham perched on the edge of a chair, one knee bouncing. Lila sat across from him with her paper copy spread out. The legal advisor's voice came through the speakerphone as if it had traveled through too many layers of permission before it reached them.

"We are exposed," the lawyer said. "If you publish without an on-record confirmation, you are inviting immediate relief."

Lila kept her face neutral. She watched Graham's hands. He kept turning his wedding band around and around, like friction could make a different outcome.

"I have a federal spokesperson's statements on background," Lila said.

"Background is not on record," the lawyer replied.

"And the advisory?" Graham asked.

The lawyer's pause was small but present. "It's framed as an advisory," she said. "Not a formal demand. That's intentional."

"It's intimidation," Lila said.

"No one is going to admit that," the lawyer answered.

Lila leaned forward and tapped the paper copy. "I'm not publishing rumors," she said. "I'm publishing what I can defend: a program exists, secrecy is being used, public resources are being repositioned under the cover of other threats, and we have documentation of pressure applied to me and this newsroom."

"You don't have documentation of the program's name," the lawyer said.

"I'm not publishing the name," Lila replied, and her eyes cut toward Graham. "I'm not even publishing the initials."

Graham's shoulders dropped a fraction. He knew what she meant. He'd seen the code on the envelope. So had legal. They were all pretending they hadn't.

"That helps," the lawyer said. "But it doesn't fix the underlying."

Lila stared at the speakerphone like she could force it to become human. "What do you want," she asked. "A dead quiet newsroom in a dead quiet city while people with money move early and everyone else gets fed slogans?"

Graham's knee stopped bouncing. His gaze sharpened on her, warning. Don't say too much.

Lila didn't look away.

The lawyer's voice stayed careful. "I want you to survive the next seventy-two hours," she said. "I want the outlet to survive. You can publish, but you must strip anything that reads as operational. No suggestions. No lists. No 'here's what to do.'"

"I'm not a siren," Lila said. "I'm a reporter."

"And you're in a moment where the difference is thin," the lawyer replied.

Graham leaned in. "What about the byline," he asked. "Can we run it as staff?"

The question wasn't legal. It was personal, dressed up as policy.

Lila watched Graham's face. He didn't meet her eyes.

She kept her voice even. "If you strip my name," she said, "you're telling them it worked."

Graham's jaw tightened. "I'm telling you I don't want you dead."

Lila held his gaze now. "Then don't publish," she said.

Silence thickened. The generator's tremor filled the gap.

Graham swallowed. "Don't do that," he muttered, barely audible. "Don't make it binary."

"It is binary," Lila replied. "Either we publish and deal with the fallout, or we keep a clean hallway and let other people decide what the public deserves."

The lawyer cleared her throat through the speakerphone. "If you publish," she said, "do it with one more safety step."

"What," Lila asked.

"Print the final copy," the lawyer said. "Keep the notes in physical form. Keep your chain clear. If someone claims you invented pressure, you show the paper."

Lila's mouth went dry. She didn't like being advised to live like a defendant.

"Fine," she said.

Graham's eyes flicked toward the newsroom. "And after," he said quietly, "you don't go home."

That hit harder than any legal phrasing. Lila thought of Manuel's bedroom doorway, the soft light she left on for him, the sound of his breathing when the medication finally kicked in.

"I'll decide that," she said, and hated herself for how stiff it sounded.

Graham nodded once like he'd expected the resistance. "Okay," he said. "Decide fast."

When they stepped back onto the newsroom floor, it felt louder. Not because it had changed, but because Lila's body had.

The night producer at the call station raised two fingers at Lila, signaling he had something. She crossed to him, weaving past desks where screens glowed with half-finished headlines and weather alerts that had become background noise.

He covered the phone's mouthpiece with his palm. "We're getting weird calls," he said.

"Define weird," Lila replied.

He looked at his notes, then back at her. "People talking about private departures," he said. "Not flights you can buy. Security convoys. A family loaded up at a hangar like it was Tuesday."

"A tip," Lila said.

"Not one," he answered. "Three. Different parts of town. Different voices. Same shape."

Lila's stomach tightened. "Write it down," she said. "No names unless they give consent. No addresses."

He nodded and flipped the page on his pad. The paper was smudged from his palm sweat.

A photographer came in through the side door, hair damp, shirt sticking to his back, camera strap cutting a red line across his shoulder. His face had the pale, tight look of someone who'd seen something that didn't fit inside a normal night.

Graham spotted him and lifted his chin. "Eli," he called.

Eli walked toward them, eyes scanning, then landing on Lila. "You're publishing," he said, not a question.

Lila didn't answer. She watched his hands. One held the camera. The other held nothing, but his fingers kept curling like he wanted to grab air.

"I went out there," Eli said to Graham, "because I thought it was going to be a rumor. It wasn't."

Graham's voice stayed low. "What did you see."

Eli's gaze flicked to the windows. "A hangar door rolled open," he said. "A man in a polo shirt with an earpiece walked out first. Then two more. Then a woman in a blazer holding a kid's hand like the kid was a suitcase."

He swallowed. His throat moved hard.

"And then," Eli continued, "the family. Not famous. Not politicians. Just... expensive. The kind of expensive that doesn't look at lines."

Lila's nails pressed into her palm. "How do you know it was connected," she asked.

Eli's laugh came out short and humorless. "Because they didn't look surprised," he said. "They looked scheduled."

Graham's face tightened. "You got anything we can use."

Eli hesitated, then lifted his camera slightly. The screen faced him, not them. "I got images," he said. "But I'm telling you: the images aren't the story. The story is what it does to people when they believe it."

Lila nodded once. "That's why I'm being careful," she said.

Eli's eyes held hers. "Careful won't stop it," he said. "But it might keep it from turning into a hunt tonight."

A phone rang again. Someone answered. Another voice rose, sharp, then cut off.

Graham stepped closer to Lila. "We run it," he said. "Now."

Lila walked back to her desk with the sound of Eli's words stuck behind her teeth. She sat, hands hovering again, and reread the lede out loud under her breath once—just to hear whether it sounded like a match being struck.

It didn't. It sounded like a door being opened.

Her cursor blinked at the end of the first paragraph. The newsroom lights flickered again, and the generator caught itself with a shudder.

She reached for the paper copy and slid it into the printer tray, hitting print. The machine whirred and spat out the pages warm, the heat blooming against her fingertips as she stacked them.

Graham leaned over her shoulder. He didn't touch her. His presence felt heavy anyway.

"Last chance," he said.

Lila stared at the screen. She thought of Manuel. She thought of the advisory envelope with those three letters. She thought of people in a hangar moving like the future belonged to them.

She clicked once.

The key made a sound too loud in her skull.

For a beat, nothing changed. The generator kept vibrating. The coffee kept smelling burnt. The newsroom kept being a room.

Then the phones started to ring like they'd been waiting for permission.

The call station lit up. The night producer's pen flew. Someone at the far desk swore softly, then louder. A siren outside rose and didn't fade.

Lila's own phone buzzed on the desk. She turned it facedown without looking. The vibration kept pushing against the wood, insistent.

Eli stepped toward the windows and peered down at the street. "Look," he said.

Lila stood and walked to the glass. The window reflected the newsroom behind her—faces lit by screens, mouths moving, shoulders hunched. Beyond that reflection, the street below had shifted. Cars slowed. People clustered near the corner, staring at their phones, pointing at the building like it had become a monument.

A man on the sidewalk lifted his phone toward the windows, arm extended, recording. Another person shoved close beside him to see.

Graham came up beside Lila. "We're going to have to lock the doors," he said.

Lila watched the cluster grow. "It's fast," she murmured.

"That's how it works," Eli replied from behind them. "They copy behavior. They don't wait for confirmation."

A scream of tires echoed from somewhere down the block. Someone shouted. The sound bounced off the buildings and came back sharper.

The night producer called out, "We got one repeating the same thing—over and over."

Lila turned from the window and crossed to the call station. The producer covered the mouthpiece and leaned close.

"He keeps saying, 'Kline has seats,'" the producer whispered. "Like it's a phone number."

Lila felt her stomach drop a notch. "Say it again," she said.

The producer's eyes narrowed. "He said 'Kline has seats.' That if you have money you call Kline and you get a seat. He said it like—" His throat moved. "Like instructions."

Lila stared at him. The name meant nothing to her yet. The certainty in the caller's voice meant everything.

"Don't air that as fact," she said. "Write it down. Keep it. If he calls again, ask where he heard it. Don't push."

The producer nodded, already scribbling.

Graham stepped in. "We're getting a call from the mayor's office," he said.

Lila's mouth went dry. "Already."

Graham's face tightened. "And a federal spokesperson wants to 'clarify.'"

"Clarify," Lila repeated.

Eli's laugh came out sharp. "That's cute."

Graham shot him a look. "Not helping."

Eli raised his hands and backed off. His eyes stayed on Lila, though, as if he could see what she was doing inside herself: measuring risk against the weight of everyone else's ignorance.

Lila went back to her desk and pulled the advisory envelope out from under her draft. She didn't open it. She didn't need the words. The presence of it was enough. She slid it into her bag anyway, next to her paper copy, like keeping it close could turn it into leverage instead of a threat.

Her phone buzzed again. She flipped it over this time and saw her name on the screen—not a contact, just text, her name floating in a message preview from a number she didn't recognize.

WHO DO YOU THINK YOU ARE.

Her hand tightened around the phone until the plastic creaked.

Graham was at her desk in two strides. "What," he asked.

She tilted the screen toward him without speaking.

Graham's face drained. "We need security," he said.

"We have a lobby guard," Lila replied. "He's a person, not a wall."

Graham's jaw worked. He looked toward the windows again. The cluster outside had grown. Someone had lifted a sign—made fast, marker on cardboard. Lila couldn't read the words from here, but she didn't need to. The gesture was enough.

She checked her phone again. Another message from a different number.

LIAR.

Another.

TELL US WHO GETS OUT.

The last one made her swallow hard. The phrasing was too close to the question Malik had faced months earlier without her knowing. The same hunger wearing a different shirt.

She turned her phone facedown again.

"Graham," she said, voice low, "we need to move me out of here."

His eyes flicked to hers. "Now."

"Now," she agreed.

Graham's mouth tightened. "You can't go home," he said again.

Lila's chest tightened like a fist. "Manuel is at home," she snapped, and the heat in her voice surprised her.

Graham held up both hands, palms out. "I know," he said. "That's why you can't lead anyone there."

Lila stared at him, the urge to argue sharp and immediate. She wanted to say her street wasn't on the internet. She wanted to say she'd been careful. She wanted to say she was allowed to go home.

Her phone buzzed again. This time it wasn't a message. It was a call from the unknown number.

She let it ring once, twice, then silenced it.

The generator hiccupped. The lights dimmed, then steadied.

Eli appeared near her desk again, eyes alert. "Street's getting louder," he said. "Somebody's yelling your outlet name."

Lila felt her throat tighten. "My name," she corrected, and hated how small her voice sounded.

Eli didn't contradict her. He didn't need to.

Graham leaned in, voice low. "Back stairwell," he said. "We can get you out to the alley. Marta's in the lobby—she'll distract if she can."

"Marta," Lila echoed, and the irony stung. Malik had Marta. Lila had a different Marta, a receptionist who wore sneakers and carried a stun gun in her purse, not because she wanted to fight but because she'd stopped believing doors were enough.

Lila grabbed her bag and stuffed the paper copy deeper inside, under a sweater. She glanced around her desk. The rooftop footage lived in her mind, not on the screen. Her notes lived in paper and in the hard place behind her ribs where fear sat.

She didn't pack her entire world. She packed what could keep her story alive if the building went dark.

Graham guided her through the back corridor. The hallway felt too bright. The ceiling lights buzzed. Each door they passed looked like a mouth that could open.

At the stairwell door, Graham paused. "Listen," he said.

Lila held her breath.

She heard muffled shouting through the walls. Not words she could parse, but tone—sharp, rising, hungry. She heard the distant wail of sirens threading the streets, moving closer, then sliding away, like the city was trying to decide which fires to chase first.

Graham pushed the stairwell door open. The metal creaked. The sound shot up the stairwell like a warning.

They moved down fast, steps thudding. Lila kept one hand on the rail, knuckles tight, and thought of Manuel's breathing—slow, then faster when he got anxious, then slow again when she coached him through it.

At the bottom, the alley door stuck for a beat before Graham shoved it open with his shoulder. Cold air rushed in, carrying exhaust, damp trash, and something metallic from the street.

The alley was darker than the newsroom, lit by one flickering security light. A dumpster sat near the far wall. The back of a delivery truck blocked part of the view to the street.

Eli was there, too—he'd beaten them down somehow, moving like he'd practiced getting out of buildings fast.

"Car's around the corner," Eli said. "If we cut left and hug the wall, we can avoid the crowd."

Graham looked at Lila. "Where are you going," he asked.

The question wasn't just logistics. It was the whole cost.

Lila's mouth went dry. She thought of home. She thought of Manuel alone if someone followed her. She thought of the street below the newsroom window, people copying the rich's movement like it was gospel.

"I'm not going to my apartment," she said.

Graham's shoulders dropped a fraction, relief and grief tangled. "Okay," he whispered.

Lila pulled her phone out again, thumb hovering. She had one call she had to make. Not to argue. Not to explain. To check breath and keep it steady.

She dialed Darius out of habit before she remembered Darius wasn't hers. The contact was D. It could be anyone. It could be Malik. It could be someone else. She canceled the call and scrolled until she found Manuel's number.

Her thumb hesitated over the screen.

Eli's head snapped toward the street. "They're moving," he said.

Lila shoved the phone back into her bag without calling. The shame of it burned, but the fear burned hotter. A call could be traced. A call could be listened to. A call could be a thread.

"Move," Graham said, and they did.

They hugged the wall, footsteps quick on the rough concrete. At the corner, the street noise hit them full—voices layered over each other, engines revving, the sharp clack of a metal gate coming down somewhere nearby.

A group stood half a block away near the front entrance of the building, faces lit by their phones. One person pointed toward the windows and shouted something Lila couldn't make out. Another voice responded, louder, and the crowd shifted like a single animal turning its head.

Lila kept her own head down, bag tight against her side, shoulders angled to make herself smaller without looking like she was running.

Eli's car sat at the curb, engine already on. He yanked the passenger door open for Lila. "Get in," he said.

She slid inside, breath shallow. The seatbelt dug into her collarbone when she snapped it into place. Graham leaned into the open window.

"Call me when you're settled," he said.

Lila met his eyes. In the streetlight, his fear looked older than him.

"You're staying," she said.

Graham's mouth twisted. "Someone has to keep the lights on," he replied.

The phrase landed wrong. The lights were already unstable. The truth was the only light they had left.

Eli pulled away from the curb, tires rolling slow until they cleared the corner. Then he accelerated, the car surging forward like it wanted to escape the city itself.

Lila looked back once through the rear window. The newsroom building rose behind them, windows bright against the dark. In the glass, she saw the reflection of the street—people clustered, faces washed in phone glow, arms lifted. Sirens laced through the streets below like thin red threads.

Her name wasn't painted on the building, but she could feel it there anyway, hovering, attached to the light.

She swallowed hard, throat tight enough to hurt, and faced forward as the car carried her into the night she'd just helped make louder.

Chapter 9 - Binary Nucleus Printout

The vents pushed hot air hard enough to make the room feel impatient.

Naomi sat at the conference table with her forearms on the laminate, palms flat, pretending her skin didn't stick when she lifted them. The HVAC's low rumble never stopped. It crawled under every sentence and made the silence between people sound staged.

A stack of printer paper waited near the center of the table, already curling at the corners from the warmth in the room. Someone had set out bottled water and forgotten the caps. The sharp, clean smell of plastic sat on top of stale coffee and whatever cleaner the night crew used to wipe fingerprints off glass.

Across from her, an interagency representative in a blazer that still held its crease checked a wristwatch like the mission answered to the same clock as his meetings. Beside him, her supervisor stood with a tablet she didn't look at, a hand on the back of a chair as if she might need it to keep from walking out.

Two analysts flanked Naomi—one with a ruler tucked under his notebook, the other with a pen gripped too tightly. They watched Naomi more than they watched the empty paper stack. That told her everything: this wasn't about data. It was about who would be blamed for it.

Naomi cleared her throat and tasted dryness. She forced herself to take a sip of water. It went down like a task.

"All right," her supervisor said. Her voice stayed neutral. Neutral was the only tone that didn't get you tagged as unstable. "We're here because your request finally produced returns. We need a briefing package by end of day."

The interagency rep leaned forward. "We need a clean answer," he said. "Binary. Yes or no."

Naomi didn't react to the word binary. She let her fingers press into the table instead until the urge to laugh turned into something that could pass as patience.

"We need an honest answer," she said.

"That's what I said," he replied, smiling without warmth. "Yes or no. Can we stop impact."

The analyst on Naomi's left swallowed audibly. Naomi heard it and didn't look. She kept her gaze on the paper stack, on the empty space where the evidence would land, because her eyes wanted something to hold.

"Your timeline for 'stop' assumes a single body," Naomi said. "Assumes a clean deflection. Assumes we have authority and time to do what your talking points promise."

Her supervisor's hand tightened on the chair. A tiny warning. Don't antagonize him. Not yet.

The interagency rep's smile thinned. "Doctor—"

"Dr. Park," Naomi corrected, softly. The room heard the correction anyway.

He nodded once, like conceding a small point cost him nothing. "Dr. Park. Public confidence is already brittle. The last thing we need is a scientist hedging on camera."

"I'm not on camera," Naomi said.

"You will be," he replied, and his eyes flicked to her supervisor. "Or someone will. That's how this goes."

Naomi felt the pull of it—the familiar squeeze that came when people treated truth like a prop they could swap out for something more useful. She had watched it happen for months, watched it happen in paper and meetings and half-closed doors. She had built a private record because she no longer trusted the official one to remain intact.

Her supervisor leaned forward. "Naomi," she said, using first name like a friendly hand. "Walk us through what you have, and what you don't. Keep it tight."

Naomi nodded. Tight. Like a tourniquet.

She tapped the empty stack. "The probe returns are coming in segments," she said. "There were delays. Dropouts. Missing packets. Some of what we asked for didn't make it."

The analyst on her right—Miguel, she reminded herself. Miguel who slept under his desk last week and still showed up—pushed his notepad toward the center. On it he'd written timestamps in block digits. Not digital proof. Human proof. The kind that could survive when systems failed.

"How incomplete," the interagency rep asked.

"Enough that anyone who wants to pretend can claim uncertainty," Naomi said. "Enough that anyone who wants to weaponize uncertainty can use it against us."

Her supervisor's eyes flicked toward her. A second warning. You're saying the quiet part out loud.

Naomi smoothed her hand across the table's edge and kept going anyway, because she'd already learned what silence cost.

A door opened at the back of the room. A technician rolled in a cart stacked with fresh printouts. The pages sat in uneven piles, still warm. The technician didn't meet anyone's eyes. He set the cart near the table and left immediately, like even delivering paper could get you burned.

The first analyst reached for the top sheet as if it might jump away. "Here," he said, voice too loud.

Naomi took it carefully. The paper bowed slightly from heat. She scanned the header, the codes, the abbreviated labels. She'd seen the request forms a hundred times. Seeing the returns felt different. This was the universe answering—late, partial, indifferent.

She read the first line. Then she read it again.

Her eyes did the thing they did when she didn't want to accept what she saw: they slid away, tried to find a friendlier number, a different phrasing. She forced them back. She read it a third time.

The room waited. The vents pushed hot air. Someone's chair squeaked.

"Give me the cross section," Naomi said.

Miguel slid another sheet toward her. His fingertips left a faint smear, the oil of his skin, the proof that a human had touched it. Naomi aligned the pages, edges tapping against the table until they matched. She lined them up like order could hold.

She took the ruler from the other analyst without asking and laid it across the printout, tracing the pattern that rose and fell like a lie detector. A predicted signature should have been smooth. It wasn't. It had shoulders. Repeated structure. Echoes.

Her chest tightened, then loosened in a way that didn't feel like relief.

Miguel leaned in. "It's not a single peak," he said.

Naomi didn't answer. She slid the ruler lower, compared to the earlier model output they'd printed days ago—predictions taped together with hope. The earlier curves were clean. They looked like a story that had a hero.

This did not.

The interagency rep cleared his throat. "What does it say," he asked.

Naomi's supervisor murmured, "Let them work."

The rep's gaze sharpened. He didn't like being told to wait.

Naomi kept the ruler steady. She held her breath, then released it slowly through her nose, controlled. She could feel her pulse in her neck, a small stubborn beat that didn't care about politics.

Miguel pointed with his pen. "You see that repeat," he said. "Two dominant lobes. Not noise. Not artifacts."

Naomi nodded once. A small motion. She didn't trust anything bigger.

"Say it out loud," Naomi said to Miguel.

He blinked. "What."

"Say the interpretation," Naomi replied. "Out loud. I need to hear it in a human voice. I need to know we're not inventing patterns because we're desperate."

The other analyst's eyes widened a fraction. Naomi could feel how it looked: the scientist who needed reassurance like a child. She didn't care. She'd learned humility was cheaper than being wrong in public.

Miguel swallowed. "It reads like a clustered nucleus," he said. "At least two substantial components. Possibly more."

Naomi didn't move. The words hung in the air and changed the shape of the room.

Her supervisor exhaled slowly. "Clustered," she repeated.

Miguel nodded. "Binary at minimum," he said. "If we treat it like one body and push, we risk... we risk turning one strike into a scattershot."

Naomi stared at the printout until the lines blurred. A decision could be hidden, but it couldn't be undone. She felt that line in her bones—not a quote, not a slogan. A rule.

The interagency rep leaned forward, voice sharpening. "Are you telling me the plan fails."

Naomi lifted her head.

"I'm telling you the plan changes," she said. "And if we pretend it doesn't, we make it worse."

He held her gaze. "Binary," he said again. "Yes or no."

Naomi felt something harden behind her ribs. Not anger. Not fear. A narrowed kind of clarity.

"No," she said.

The word landed heavy and plain.

Her supervisor's hand tightened on the chair until the knuckles showed. The other analyst stared at Naomi like she'd just volunteered to be pushed off a bridge.

The interagency rep sat back, lips pressing into a line. The smile was gone now. "That's not acceptable," he said.

Naomi kept her voice low. "It doesn't care what you accept," she replied. "The object is what it is."

He leaned forward again. "Then what do we tell them," he asked, and the them wasn't just the public. It was leadership. It was the people who could end careers with a sentence.

Naomi slid the printout across the table toward him. "You tell them we can reduce harm," she said. "You tell them we can shift the worst corridor toward open ocean. You tell them we can increase breakup in a controlled way so energy is spread—"

"Spread," he repeated, like it was obscene.

"Spread," Naomi echoed. "Because 'stop' is a story we wanted to believe."

Her supervisor finally moved. She sat, carefully, like any sudden motion might crack the thin calm. "Explain limits," she said to Naomi. "Now. Numbers, Naomi. Authority and physics."

Naomi nodded. This was where she could make it real, where she could keep it from turning into fantasy.

"We don't steer like a car," she said. "We nudge. We influence probability. We shift where the worst mass goes by degrees, not miles. And every intervention has risk—if we hit the wrong lobe, if we push asymmetrically, we could fragment in ways we don't predict."

Miguel added, voice tight, "The danger is making multiple city-killers instead of one."

Naomi looked at the interagency rep. "That's the scandal you don't want to brief," she said quietly. "But it's the one you'll own if you force us into a false yes."

The rep's jaw worked. "You're asking me to go upstairs and tell them we're moving from saving the world to... what. Choosing who dies."

Naomi didn't blink. "We were always choosing," she said. "We just pretended the choice didn't exist."

The room went still. The vents pushed hot air. A bottle cap rolled slightly on the table and stopped.

Her supervisor broke the silence. "We need a pivot packet," she said. "Today. A framework that leadership can brief without—" She stopped herself from saying panic. Panic had become a forbidden word and a daily reality.

The interagency rep's voice went cold. "And we need it to account for continuity assets," he said.

Naomi's gaze sharpened. "Meaning," she prompted.

He didn't flinch. "Meaning critical infrastructure," he said smoothly. "Sites. Command continuity. Facilities that cannot be compromised."

Miguel's eyes flicked to Naomi, then away. The other analyst's pen froze above his notebook.

Naomi felt her stomach tighten, not from the physics but from the implication sliding under it.

"You want the worst mass shifted away from your protected locations," Naomi said.

The rep's smile returned, smaller, controlled. "I want the worst mass shifted away from the highest-value assets," he corrected.

Her supervisor inhaled. "We are not doing this here," she warned, but her voice sounded less like a command and more like a hope.

Naomi leaned forward, palms flat. "You don't get to talk about 'value' like it's neutral," she said. "The moment you define it, you're deciding who counts."

The rep's eyes held hers. "People count," he said. "That's why we maintain governance. That's why we preserve command capability."

"And the people outside your facilities," Naomi replied, voice steady, "what are they. Noise?"

Her supervisor cut in, sharp now. "Naomi."

Naomi turned her head a fraction. "You asked for honesty," she said. "This is it."

The rep's jaw tightened. "We will not brief language like that," he said.

Naomi didn't look away. "Then you will brief something that hides the choice," she said. "And you will call it responsible."

The other analyst shifted in his chair, the squeak loud. He looked like he wanted to disappear.

Her supervisor's gaze flicked toward the door, toward the hallway beyond, toward the unseen weight of executive floors. She made a decision in her face before she made it in words.

"We're not debating ethics in this room," she said, and Naomi heard the compromise. Not now. Not in front of him. Not with your record already heavy.

Naomi sat back slowly. She tasted metal at the back of her mouth like stress had a flavor.

"All right," Naomi said. "We do the physics. We write probabilities. We write ranges. We write what we can do and what we cannot."

Her supervisor nodded once, relieved she'd stepped back from the edge.

The rep leaned forward. "And we draft messaging that keeps confidence stable," he said.

Naomi's eyes went to the printouts again. The curled corners looked like the paper itself wanted to lift off the table and escape.

"Confidence is not our problem," she said.

"It becomes your problem when you lose funding," he replied.

Miguel's fingers tightened around his pen until his knuckle went pale. He didn't speak.

Naomi looked at her supervisor. "We need to widen the analyst circle," she said. "We need fresh eyes. We need more than our team in a hot room with a deadline."

Her supervisor's expression tightened. "We can't widen without clearance," she said.

Naomi watched her carefully. There it was: the chain of permission. The same chain that had buried an early warning packet months ago. The same chain that had turned her into someone who carried paper in a rugged case because she didn't trust the system to remember honestly.

The rep rose from his chair. "I'll need a one-page summary in two hours," he said. "No ambiguity. No moralizing. Just deliverables."

He left without waiting for agreement. The door shut behind him with a soft click that felt final.

When he was gone, the room's air changed. Not cooler. Just less performed.

Miguel exhaled like he'd been holding it for an hour. The other analyst rubbed his forehead with the heel of his hand.

Her supervisor stayed seated, eyes on Naomi. "That," she said quietly, "was not strategic."

Naomi didn't answer immediately. She forced herself to drink water again. Her throat still felt dry.

"It was accurate," Naomi said.

Her supervisor's mouth tightened. "Accuracy isn't the only constraint."

Naomi watched the woman's hands. Her supervisor's fingers were clean. She'd never met a paper cut she couldn't avoid. Naomi wondered what that said about her, then stopped. Judging wouldn't help.

"You want me to package it," Naomi said. "Fine. But you don't get to make me promise a clean win."

Her supervisor nodded. "No one is asking you to promise," she said. "They're asking you to help them survive the briefing."

Naomi's laugh almost escaped. She trapped it behind her teeth. "And what about us," she asked, "surviving the physics."

Her supervisor's gaze dropped to the printouts. "We survive by doing the best possible work," she said. "And by staying inside the rules."

Naomi didn't argue. She gathered the papers in front of her, aligning edges. Her hands moved on their own into order. It was what she did when she needed to keep from shaking.

Miguel leaned close. "If it's clustered," he said softly, "and we push—if we screw up—we make it worse."

Naomi nodded once. "I know."

"And if we don't push," he continued, voice thinner, "we... we watch it happen."

Naomi looked at him. His eyes were red around the edges, not from tears but from exhaustion. She saw herself in him, months ago, before she'd found the buried packet and stopped believing the official story would stay clean.

"We push," she said. "We just push differently."

Her supervisor stood. "I need you in the hallway," she said. "Five minutes. Then back here. We have to brief our own, because this will leak inside before it leaks outside."

Naomi followed her out of the room.

The hallway lights were too bright. The floor wax reflected them in long white streaks. The sound of a printer somewhere down the corridor created a mechanical rhythm, steady, indifferent.

Two team members waited by the wall, not standing close enough to look like a conspiracy, not far enough to look like strangers. One was older, shoulders tight, eyes sharp with anger. The other was younger, jaw clenched, hands shoved into pockets like he could hold himself together by force.

The older one spoke first. "We should go public," she said, and didn't bother with pretense. "We're sitting on something that changes everything, and they're going to turn it into a one-page confidence plan."

The younger one cut in. "Public will riot," he said. "It's already bad. Have you seen what's happening out there. You want to pour gasoline on it."

Naomi kept her voice low. "We are not debating this in the hallway."

The older one's eyes flashed. "Of course not," she snapped. "We're not allowed to talk like humans."

Her supervisor stepped between them slightly. "We are allowed," she said, "to do our jobs."

The older one's laugh was bitter. "Our job is truth," she said.

"Our job is truth with consequences," Naomi replied.

The younger one's jaw worked. "If it's clustered," he said, "and we admit 'reduce harm,' we're telling the world we can't save them."

Naomi watched him. He wasn't wrong. He was just saying it like it was the first time anyone had forced him to look at that sentence.

"We were always going to lose people," Naomi said. "Now we're being honest about scale."

The older one leaned in. "And the continuity rep," she said, voice dropping. "Did you hear what he said. Value assets. Facilities. They're already carving the world into 'protected' and 'acceptable loss.'"

Naomi felt her hands curl into fists at her sides. She didn't let them rise. "I heard," she said.

"Then what are you going to do," the older one demanded. "Because they're going to use your work to justify it."

Naomi met her eyes. "I'm going to put the truth on paper," she said. "I'm going to make sure the pivot is documented. And I'm going to make sure when they brief, they can't claim later they didn't know."

The older one stared at her like that wasn't enough. Maybe it wasn't. Naomi didn't offer more than she could deliver.

The younger one shook his head once. "This is insane," he muttered. "We're writing the shape of extinction."

Naomi's supervisor stepped closer. "Keep your voice down," she said.

The younger one's mouth twisted. "Why," he asked. "Because the walls might hear."

Naomi looked toward the nearby door with a badge reader. The badge reader blinked, waiting, a little red eye. She remembered after-hours pulls logged and left in a queue until someone felt like reviewing them. She remembered how easy it was for a decision to sit unseen because everyone assumed someone else was watching.

"Yes," Naomi said. "Because the walls hear, eventually."

The older one's gaze softened a fraction, then hardened again. "I didn't sign up to be complicit," she said.

Naomi's throat tightened. She thought of the record she'd built, the papers in her case, the fact that she had started living like someone preparing for trial.

"Neither did I," Naomi said.

Her supervisor glanced at her watch. "Back in," she said. "Now."

Naomi returned to the mission support room with the printouts pressed against her torso, like holding them close could keep anyone from rewriting them. The table was still warm. The bottles still uncapped. The paper stack still curling at the corners as if the room itself refused to let truth lie flat.

She sat at her workstation afterward, away from the conference table, in a corner where she could hear the vents but not the conversations through the door. She spread the printouts out again. She wrote in the margins with a steady hand: clustered nucleus, two dominant lobes, risk of uncontrolled fragmentation. Probabilities. Ranges. Limitations.

She stapled the sheets into a packet—one clean stack, dated, labeled for internal record. The staple made a sharp click that echoed in the small space, too loud for something so ordinary.

Naomi slid the packet into a folder. She added a cover page with the plainest language she could manage: PROBE RETURNS SUMMARY — STRUCTURE UPDATE — OPERATIONAL IMPLICATIONS.

She didn't dress it up. She didn't make it dramatic. She made it undeniable.

Her wrist ached. She flexed it, then pressed her fingertips to the bridge of her nose until the pressure pushed back the headache threatening to bloom. She forced herself to drink water again. Another task. Another small refusal to fall apart.

The office door was open. People moved in the hallway. Voices rose and fell. A burst of laughter floated past—someone telling a story, someone enjoying a moment that belonged to an old world.

Naomi froze with her hand on the folder.

The laughter didn't stop when it passed her door. It receded, but it stayed in the air. It made her skin prickle.

She looked down at the packet again. The top page wouldn't stay perfectly flat. The heat in the building kept coaxing it into a curl, a stubborn lift at the corner. She pressed her palm over it, flattening it with steady pressure, as if that could make the truth behave.

Outside, the laughter faded into other sounds—footsteps, a distant door closing, the soft chirp of a badge reader. Ordinary noises, the kinds that used to mean nothing.

Naomi kept her palm on the page until the paper held still under her hand.

Then she lifted it, slid the packet into her rugged equipment case, and snapped the latches shut with a sharp click that cut through the room like a line drawn in stone.

In the hallway, someone laughed again—lighter this time, like they'd forgotten what time it was.

Naomi didn't move. She stood with her hand still resting on the closed case, feeling the hard plastic under her fingertips, and listened until the sound died away.

Chapter 10 - Red Wristband Line

The civic center smelled like disinfectant that never got a chance to dry.

Malik pushed through the side entrance with his badge out in front of him, lanyard straight, the plastic edge tapping his knuckles as he walked. Fluorescent light flattened everyone's faces into the same exhausted color. The concrete floors threw every footstep back at the ceiling, turning a handful of people into a crowd.

He could hear the real crowd anyway—muffled, distant, but present. A low animalless sound, all throat and impatience, pulsing behind the thick doors on the far end like a generator under load.

"Afternoon," the security supervisor said. His name patch read HERNANDEZ. The man had the squared-off look of someone who slept in short bursts and woke ready to be wronged. He held a radio in one hand and a paper cup of coffee in the other, like both were lifelines.

"Afternoon," Malik replied.

A woman stood beside Hernandez in a navy blazer with a visitor sticker stuck too neatly to her lapel. She carried a clipboard like it had weight beyond paper. Her hair was pulled tight enough to make her cheekbones look sharper.

"Malik Carter?" she asked.

He didn't correct her. If she was here, she already had his name in a folder somewhere.

"Yes."

"Janice Wu," she said. "City counsel. Risk and compliance. I'm observing, not interfering."

"People always say that," Hernandez muttered.

Wu ignored him, eyes on Malik. "We're rehearsing intake under the new capacity framework," she said. "Criteria, distribution rules, chain-of-custody for supplies. There will be press interest."

Malik didn't look toward the doors where the sound lived. "There's press interest in everything," he said.

Wu's smile didn't reach her eyes. "Not like this."

A staff trainer hustled past, juggling a bundle of plastic strips in one hand and a stack of printed forms in the other. A volunteer in a neon vest followed, wide-eyed, already sweating through the back. Malik watched the volunteer's hands. The hands flexed and opened and flexed again. Hands gave away what faces tried to hide.

He stepped into the staging area where stanchions formed corridors that looked clean and logical from above. From the ground, they looked like cages built for people who still believed in lines.

Hernandez gestured toward a cluster of tables. "We're set up in the back hall," he said. "We keep distribution away from the doors. Out of sight."

"Out of sight," Malik repeated, and felt the phrase stick.

On the far wall, blue tape marked the edges of a few crates and a doorway leading deeper into the facility. The tape sat flat, unremarkable, the kind of thing that could be mistaken for routine. Malik knew better now. He'd learned to see the small signals that decided who got access without ever saying the word.

He kept walking anyway.

A logistics aide met him near the tables. She wore her badge clipped to her pocket instead of hanging from her neck. Malik's eyes went to it automatically.

"Badge visible," he said.

She blinked like he'd spoken a foreign language, then moved the badge higher with a quick, embarrassed tug. "Sorry. Habit."

"No," Malik said. "Not habit. New rule."

Her throat bobbed as she swallowed. "Right."

The aide's name tag read RIVERA. She flipped open a box and the rubber smell rose up—sharp, chemical, almost sweet. Inside were spools of wristbands in bright colors, stacked like candy that didn't belong in a place like this.

"Inventory's here," Rivera said. "Green, yellow, red, blue. The red batch came in late."

Malik set his palm on the box edge and felt the cardboard give slightly. The table was sticky from tape residue and hurried hands. "Late from where," he asked.

Rivera's eyes flicked toward the blue tape-marked doorway. "Same truck as the bottled water," she said. "Same vendor list."

Hernandez snorted. "Same folks making a killing off all of us."

Wu's pen hovered above her clipboard. "Color coding must remain consistent with the documented criteria," she said. "Any deviation creates liability."

"People create liability," Hernandez said. "Bodies."

Wu looked up, unblinking. "Bodies create lawsuits."

Hernandez's mouth tightened. Malik held up a hand before the two of them could turn it into a contest.

"We're not here to win a debate," Malik said. His voice came out calm because he forced it. His thumb pressed into his palm under the table, hard enough to leave a dent.

Rivera slid a printed chart toward him. It listed categories in dry language: medical, essential personnel, minors, caregivers, special cases. Each category had a corresponding color and a set of conditions.

Malik scanned it, eyes catching on the phrase "Red wristband line" typed in small block letters near the bottom under a heading labeled PRIORITY ENTRY.

He could feel the wordline people used in the office, half-joking, half-afraid, turning into official policy in twelve-point font.

"Who decided red is priority," Malik asked.

Wu's pen made a small, impatient tick. "It aligns with emergency management practice," she said. "Red indicates immediate processing. It's intuitive."

"It's not intuitive to the people outside," Malik replied.

Hernandez's radio crackled. A voice said something about a gate, a van, a small group arriving early. Hernandez answered without looking at Malik, eyes already scanning toward the entrance corridor.

Rivera cleared her throat. "We've got volunteers ready for the mock line," she said. "Staff trainers are running them through behavior cues. Shouting, pushing, confusion."

"Acting," Malik said.

Rivera's eyes didn't meet his. "Some of them won't have to act," she said quietly.

Malik felt his jaw tighten. The crowd noise behind the doors rose and fell, a reminder that the rehearsal had an audience even if no one admitted it.

He reached into the box and lifted a red wristband spool. The plastic was warm from the room, the strips sticking slightly together. He turned it in his hand. No technology in it. No hidden chip. Just color and permission.

"Rules," he said, to no one in particular. "We're pretending the rules can replace trust."

Wu's gaze sharpened. "Rules are what we have," she said. "Trust isn't a policy tool."

Malik set the spool down. "Then we're in trouble," he said.

They moved toward the mock intake corridor where stanchions guided a line that didn't exist yet. Volunteers wore plain shirts and paper numbers taped to their chests. Staff trainers gave them quick instructions with tight smiles.

"Okay," a trainer called. "You're frustrated. You've been waiting. You don't believe what you're being told. You're tired. You're scared. You want your kids inside."

The word kids made Malik's throat tighten. He pictured Darius, not as a category on a chart but as a face he'd seen too many times in his mind in the quiet moments. A minor. A name. A promise he hadn't made yet but felt like it was already binding him.

A volunteer raised her hand. "Are we allowed to cry," she asked, half-laughing.

The trainer's smile faltered. "Sure," she said. "If you can."

Hernandez leaned close to Malik. "We're seeing phones," he murmured. "People on the sidewalk. Filming through the glass. They're already calling it a prison."

Malik didn't turn toward the doors. He kept his eyes on the volunteers' hands, on the way fingers curled around imaginary tickets.

"It's not a prison," he said.

Hernandez's mouth twisted. "Not yet."

Wu stepped up beside Malik. "Your people must be consistent," she said. "No improvisation. If you bend the criteria in rehearsal, they'll bend it under pressure. And then we can't defend it."

"Defend it," Malik repeated.

Wu's eyes stayed steady. "In court," she clarified.

Malik let the silence sit long enough to feel rude, then nodded. "We'll be consistent," he said. He didn't say the rest: until we can't.

The rehearsal started.

A staff member sat at the first table with a stack of printed forms and a pen. Another stood behind with boxes of wristbands. Volunteers shuffled forward in their assigned agitation. A third staffer played the role of "line monitor," trying to keep shoulders from pressing too close.

At first it worked. Bodies moved at a controlled pace. Voices rose and fell but stayed contained. Malik almost felt the pull of relief—almost let himself think, We can do this.

Then Rivera hissed his name. "Malik."

He stepped closer. Rivera held out a spool with red bands that looked slightly off, the shade more orange than the others. She had a strained expression that tried to be professional and failed.

"Mis-sorted," she said. "This batch got placed with red. It's not in the chart. It's... wrong."

Wu's pen stopped midair. Hernandez's shoulders lifted, a predator's readiness.

"How many," Malik asked.

Rivera's fingers trembled once, then still. "Two spools," she said. "Maybe three. Some got handed out already."

A volunteer in the line overheard the word wrong and leaned forward. "What's wrong," she demanded, loud enough for the people behind her to hear.

"It's fine," the staffer at the table said, too quickly.

The volunteer's eyes narrowed. "You said it's wrong," she snapped. "Is that because you're saving the real ones for your friends?"

Another voice rose behind her. "They're cutting the line!"

The words hit the corridor like a spark.

Bodies compressed. The stanchions rattled. A wave rolled forward, not from malice but from physics: everyone pressing because the person behind them pressed first.

Malik stepped toward the line monitor. "Hold!" he shouted, and the command landed on ears already full of fear.

A volunteer shoved against the barrier. A staffer grabbed her wrist to steady her and the volunteer yanked back like the touch burned.

"Don't touch me!"

"Back up," Hernandez barked, voice like a slap. Two security officers moved in, hands already on belts, eyes hard.

The corridor tightened. Malik smelled sweat and deodorant and the chemical tang of the wristbands. The air thickened with breath.

"Stop," Malik said, louder. "Stop moving."

The word stop didn't stop anything.

Someone screamed. Not dramatic. Not rehearsed. A short, sharp sound that made every head jerk.

A child's voice followed, crying, the pitch cutting through the roar. Malik didn't see the child. He saw hands rising, protective, desperate. He saw shoulders turning sideways to wedge through.

He pushed into the crush.

A hand clamped around his forearm—too tight, nails digging into skin. Malik turned, reflexive, ready to pull away, and saw a woman's face inches from his.

"You said red means inside," she spat. Her breath hit his cheek, hot and sour. "You said red means my boy doesn't die out there. So why are you taking it away?"

He didn't know her. That didn't matter. In her eyes, he was the person holding the door.

He tried to speak and his throat closed. Not fear of being hurt. Fear of what he was becoming in her story.

"It's a rehearsal," he forced out.

Her laugh was ugly. "You think this is pretend," she said.

The stanchion to Malik's left tipped under pressure. Metal scraped concrete. The sound jolted the line like a shot. People surged again.

Hernandez grabbed the fallen stanchion and shoved it upright, face hard. "Move back!" he shouted. "Move back or we clear you!"

Wu's voice cut in, sharp. "No threats," she snapped, and then her composure slipped for the first time. "Do not threaten."

Hernandez glared at her. "Do you want blood on this floor," he demanded.

Malik shoved his shoulder against the line just enough to create a pocket of space near the front table. He leaned close to the staffer distributing bands.

"Pull distribution," he said. "Now. Stop handing anything out."

The staffer's eyes went wide. "If we stop—"

"Stop," Malik repeated. "We reset."

The staffer hesitated long enough for Malik to feel rage at the delay, then slid the box of wristbands under the table like hiding it would make it safe.

The lack of movement at the front made the crowd behind press harder. People thought someone was being processed secretly. People thought someone was slipping through.

"Look," Malik shouted, forcing his voice into the sound. "Nobody is going in right now. Nobody. We're resetting."

A man in the middle of the corridor yelled, "Liar!"

Another voice: "They got a red line for the insiders!"

The phrase landed with a particular weight. Red wristband line. It didn't sound like slang anymore. It sounded like an open wound.

Hernandez stepped closer to Malik, jaw clenched. "We need to clear this corridor," he said through his teeth. "We can't lose control."

"We don't have control," Malik shot back. "We have consent. And we're burning it."

Hernandez's eyes flashed. "Consent," he echoed, like it was a luxury. "These people will crush each other."

Malik looked over the heads, saw the twitchy movement, the shifting weight. He saw what the trainers called behavior cues and what real fear looked like: not chaos for fun, chaos because the body wanted to live.

He raised both hands, palms out, and held them there until his shoulders ached.

"Everybody breathe," he called. "Hear me. Take one step back. One. That's it. One step."

A few people obeyed because they needed permission to do something other than push. A pocket of space formed. Not enough. But it changed the shape of the corridor.

"Again," Malik said. "One step."

The crying child's voice softened slightly, less trapped. Malik's lungs pulled in air that tasted like chlorine and sweat.

Hernandez muttered into his radio. "Hold the outer doors. Keep them closed," he said.

Outer doors. The real crowd. Malik felt it as a pressure even without looking.

The line monitor finally regained her footing and used her body as a wedge, arms out. "Back up," she said, not yelling, just firm. "Back up. We're not processing anyone right now."

The word processing made Malik flinch. He couldn't stop hearing it like a factory term.

Wu stepped forward, clipboard forgotten, voice trained into calm. "We had a sorting error," she announced. "We are correcting it. No one is being favored."

Her voice had the cadence of courtroom clarity. It didn't soothe. It sounded like a statement prepared for later, not a truth offered now.

The woman gripping Malik's arm loosened slightly. Her nails had left half-moon marks.

"You're going to get me killed," she whispered, and then she pulled away, swallowed by the bodies behind her.

Malik stood there as the corridor slowly loosened, stanchions still shaking, as if the building itself had nerves.

When the surge finally calmed enough to call it contained, Malik stepped back into the debrief corner near the service corridor. His shirt clung to his spine. His hands shook once, a small betrayal, and he clenched them until they stopped.

Hernandez paced in a tight square, radio crackling. "We need hard measures," he said. "We need barriers that don't move. We need officers in the corridor, not two yards back. We need to treat it like a hostile environment."

Wu lifted her clipboard again, regaining her armor. "We need documentation that the process remained consistent with policy," she said. "We need to note the deviation—distribution paused, criteria not applied—"

"We paused because you shipped us wrong bands," Malik said.

Wu's eyes narrowed. "We paused because your team did not perform inventory verification before distribution," she countered.

Rivera flinched as if struck. "We did," she said, voice small. "We—"

Hernandez cut her off. "You can write all the notes you want," he said to Wu. "You can't note your way out of panic."

Wu looked at him coolly. "And you can't intimidate your way into legitimacy," she replied. "If force escalates, the city will face consequences."

Malik watched them argue and felt the shape of his role: a hinge between two doors that both wanted to slam. Security wanted certainty. Legal wanted defensibility. The crowd wanted survival. None of them got what they wanted without taking from someone else.

Hernandez turned on Malik. "This is why I said keep the red line tight," he snapped. "You let them crowd the distribution point. You let them hear 'wrong.' You let them think they can negotiate. Next time, they don't negotiate. Next time, they rush and someone dies."

Malik's thumb pressed into his palm again, hard. "Don't talk about them like they're a storm," he said. His voice stayed low. "They're people."

Hernandez's eyes burned. "People who will trample you," he said. "I saw what happened last month outside our office. You want to be noble, be noble after we keep staff alive."

Wu's pen hovered. Malik could feel her recording the tension as if it were evidence in a case.

Malik looked at Rivera. "How many wrong bands went out," he asked.

Rivera swallowed. "Maybe twelve," she said. "We can track by counting."

"Count," Malik said.

Wu's eyebrows lifted. "You can't reclaim distributed wristbands," she said. "That creates confrontation. That creates claims."

Malik stared at her. "So we let wrong permission circulate," he said. "We let people believe we lied."

Wu's gaze didn't move. "We correct the system," she said. "We communicate. We maintain process integrity."

Hernandez scoffed. "Communicate," he repeated.

Malik felt something harden behind his ribs, not anger, not despair—something closer to refusal.

"We don't call them animals," Malik said, looking at Hernandez, then at Wu. "We don't call them hostile. We don't treat fear like it's a crime. We build steps that keep bodies from compressing. We keep distribution away from the corridor. We use teams. We speak plain."

Hernandez opened his mouth.

"And we do it without promising what we can't deliver," Malik added, before Hernandez could turn it into a lecture.

Wu's pen made a small scratch on her clipboard. Malik pretended he didn't notice.

A staff trainer approached, face pale. "There are people outside," she said. "Not volunteers. Real people. They heard the noise and they're at the doors."

Hernandez's hand went to his radio immediately. "Told you," he said.

Malik looked toward the doors now, finally. He could see the frosted glass vibrating faintly with impact—hands or fists, he couldn't tell. Shadows moved behind it, pressed close, restless.

He felt shame rise in him, hot and quick, because he could imagine what it looked like from the outside: men with badges rehearsing how to decide who got to live.

Wu followed his gaze. "We need to end rehearsal," she said. "We need to secure supplies. We need to avoid escalation."

"We're in escalation," Hernandez replied.

Malik turned away from the doors and walked into the service corridor, needing a pocket of quiet so he could think without the sound of the crowd crawling under his skin.

The corridor smelled different—dust, old paint, the faint stink of mop water that never fully left. The concrete here had scuffs that told a truer history than the polished public floor. A maintenance cart sat abandoned near a utility closet. The building held its breath.

Malik leaned his shoulder against the wall and listened. The crowd noise softened, muffled by distance, but it didn't disappear. It was a reminder: pressure didn't care whether you were ready.

He saw a side door marked STAFF ONLY. The kind of entrance that bypassed the main corridor. It opened into a loading area where ambulances could pull close without being seen from the front.

He stood there staring at it until the outline of a plan formed in his head, not elegant, not clean, but possible.

Hospital cases. Transfers. People too fragile to stand in a line that could turn into a crush. The ones who would die first if "order" failed.

And Darius—Malik didn't say it out loud. He didn't have to. The name sat behind his teeth like a vow he hadn't spoken yet.

If Darius ended up in a hospital corridor, if Darius ended up in a wheelchair or on a gurney, Malik could not imagine telling a kid to wait outside while paperwork moved through a system designed for calm.

He pulled his phone from his pocket out of instinct, then stopped himself and shoved it back. He didn't need a screen. He needed a door and a decision.

He found a folded sheet of paper in his clipboard pocket and a pen. He wrote in blunt, fast strokes:

SERVICE ENTRANCE — MEDICAL DROP
STAFF ESCORT REQUIRED
NO CROWD VISIBILITY

He stared at the words. They looked innocent. They weren't. They were a loophole. A way to bend.

He could already hear the arguments it would spark—corruption, favoritism, the fear that every loophole became a pipeline for the powerful. He could also see the other option: telling a frail person to stand in a line that could become a stampede and calling it fair.

Fairness didn't mean much when lungs failed.

A door down the corridor opened and Rivera stepped out, breath quick. "Malik," she said. "They're asking for you."

He folded the paper, tucked it back into his clipboard, and forced his face into something steady.

Back at the supply tables, the staff trainers packed up with fast, frantic movements. Volunteers peeled off their paper numbers and looked embarrassed, like they'd been caught playing a game that turned real.

Wu stood near the wristband boxes with her clipboard, speaking quietly to a man Malik didn't recognize. The man wore a laminated badge with a generic label—CONSULTANT—no agency name. His suit looked too good for a civic center.

Malik approached and caught the last line of their conversation.

"We can keep a dedicated red lane," the consultant said, voice smooth. "For continuity-critical personnel. It's standard. Minimal friction."

Wu nodded slightly. "It reduces liability," she said.

Malik stopped a foot away. "Red lane for who," he asked.

The consultant turned, smile easy. "Essential staff," he said. "Command continuity. People necessary to keep—"

"To keep what," Malik cut in. "Lights on. Governance intact. I've heard the pitch."

The consultant's smile held. "You know the stakes," he said. "Order matters."

"Order matters," Malik repeated. He looked at the red bands stacked in a box, the color bright under the harsh lights. "So does not building a fast lane that looks like a privilege pass."

Wu's eyes sharpened. "It is not privilege," she said. "It's operational necessity."

"It will not look like that to the people outside," Malik replied. "It will look like a separate door for people who already have one."

The consultant's gaze flicked toward the doors where the crowd waited. "Perception can be managed," he said.

Malik stared at him. "Bodies can't," he said.

For the first time, the consultant's smile faltered, just a crack. "You're emotional," he said, soft, like a diagnosis.

Malik felt heat rush up his neck. He pressed his thumb into his palm again until the sensation grounded him.

"I'm responsible," Malik said. "There's a difference."

Wu stepped between them slightly, shielding the consultant like he mattered more. "We will note your concerns," she said.

Malik almost laughed. He didn't. He watched Rivera lift a lid on one of the wristband boxes, fingers careful, as if the bands might bite.

Rivera whispered, "We found the misprints."

She held out a spool. The print on the bands was faintly wrong—letters smudged, alignment off. Nothing a desperate person would notice from ten feet away. Everything an auditor could use to claim fraud.

Malik took the spool. It stuck slightly to his skin.

"Discard," Wu said immediately. "Chain-of-custody requires destruction of misprints."

Hernandez's radio crackled again. "They're pushing the doors," a voice said. "We need direction."

Malik held the spool in his hand and felt its weight, small and shameful. A last-resort option that shouldn't exist. A thing that could save someone later and damn him if discovered.

He pictured a hospital corridor. A kid's face. A crowd moving like a wave. Thick doors muffling screams.

He closed his fingers around the spool.

"Discard," Wu repeated, sharper.

Malik met her eyes. "Later," he said.

Wu's eyes widened a fraction. "That's not—"

Malik slid the spool into his pocket. The plastic warmed against his thigh almost immediately, like it had always been meant to live there. His stomach turned.

Hernandez stared at him. "What did you just do," he asked.

Malik kept his face steady. "I secured a misprint," he said. "For documentation."

Wu's pen hovered, ready to make a mark that could become a weapon.

Malik didn't wait for her permission. He turned toward Hernandez. "We end rehearsal," he said. "We clear volunteers. We move supplies away from the front. We open a staff-only corridor to cycle people out without drawing attention."

"And the crowd," Hernandez asked.

Malik looked toward the doors. The glass shuddered again under impact. Shadows pressed close. Faces, maybe. Hands, definitely. The sound rose into a chant, indistinct, hungry.

"We don't open the main doors," Malik said. "Not yet. We bring in community liaisons if we can. We speak through the glass. We tell them the truth: this was a rehearsal, we're not processing. We give a timeline for information."

Hernandez's mouth tightened. "Timeline," he echoed.

Malik's throat tightened too. He understood what Hernandez meant: timelines became promises, promises became rage when broken.

"We give them something," Malik said. "Not a lie. Not a miracle. Something."

Wu's eyes stayed on Malik's pocket, as if she could see the spool through fabric. "You're making unilateral decisions," she said quietly.

Malik didn't look at her. "Someone has to," he replied.

He moved through the civic center with his shoulders squared, walking past staff who avoided his eyes and staff who watched him like he might become the villain they needed. He felt the misprinted spool warm in his pocket like a secret with a heartbeat.

Outside, the heat pressed against the building. The air smelled like exhaust and sun-baked asphalt. Helicopters thumped low over the freeway lanes, a steady reminder that someone else always had a better view.

Malik paused at a side door that opened onto a small service lot. He didn't step out. He let the crack of light and sound touch his face and then closed it again.

Inside, the crowd noise stayed muffled, held back by thick doors and policy and fear. The building kept its secrets. Malik kept his.

He walked toward his car with the weight of the spool against his leg and the echo of shouting behind him, swallowing hard as he accepted that "help" now came with consequences he could already taste.

Chapter 12 - Bunker Brunch Etiquette

The gatehouse looked like a small country club until the guard lifted his hand and the line of SUVs obeyed.

Lila sat in her car with the engine running, heat pressing through the windshield, and watched the guard's mirrored sunglasses tilt toward each vehicle as if he could read bank balances through glass. Behind him, manicured hedges formed a green wall that hid the house itself, and beyond that—somewhere deeper—laughter drifted, softened by air-conditioning and money.

Her hands stayed low on the steering wheel. She kept them there on purpose. The last time she'd walked into a controlled space with her shoulders tight and her eyes sharp, someone had noticed, and the consequences had followed her all the way home.

She reached down into the passenger seat, slid her fingers beneath a folded sweater, and checked the small recorder one more time.

Microcassette. Plastic. Nothing glamorous. The kind of thing her mother would've called "old-fashioned" and Manuel would've called "a toy" if he'd seen it, if he'd been the kind of kid who didn't live with a pill schedule that made the day feel like a series of alarms you couldn't afford to miss.

The recorder sat in her palm, warm from being hidden too long. She thumbed the switch. Off. Then on. Then off again. The tiny click sounded louder in the sealed car than it ever did in open air.

She put it back, but she didn't relax. Her notebook lay beside her—plain, cheap, already creased from being shoved into bags too fast. She didn't open it yet. She didn't want to look like she was preparing for anything.

The guard waved an SUV forward. It rolled through the open gate like it belonged on the other side of the world.

Lila's phone rested facedown in the cup holder. She didn't pick it up. Not because she'd sworn off it, not because she believed in purity. Because the last two weeks had taught her that attention had weight. It bent toward her, and it bent toward Manuel, and it didn't always care if she meant well.

She took her key ring out and rubbed her thumb along the notched edge of one key until the ridges stopped feeling sharp. The motion was small. It looked like nothing. It kept her breathing even.

A church office had let her use their landline that morning—no questions, just a sympathetic nod from an older woman with tired eyes. Lila had called a number written on a sticky note she'd kept in her wallet for months.

A neighbor. Trusted. The kind of person who didn't talk just to fill silence.

"Everything okay over there?" Lila had asked, keeping her voice casual while her stomach turned.

"Yes," the neighbor had said. "He's eating. He's mad because the cereal is the wrong kind. He's alive."

Behind that, a faint sound—Manuel's voice arguing about something unimportant. The relief had come so hard Lila had to press her fingers to her own throat to keep it from showing.

"You're sure you can stay?" Lila had asked.

"I'm not going anywhere," the neighbor had answered, and the certainty in the voice had steadied Lila more than the words.

Now, sitting outside a gate meant to keep the wrong people out, she held that certainty in her head like a talisman. She couldn't protect him by staying small. She also couldn't protect him by setting the world on fire and calling it justice.

A volunteer badge hung from her rearview mirror, the lanyard twisted so the name didn't show unless someone leaned in close. She'd gotten it through her editor's friend-of-a-friend—someone with a nonprofit title who liked Lila's work and also liked being invited to things. It had taken one donation she couldn't really afford and one phone call where Lila had kept her own name half hidden.

Not a trespass. Not a theft. A door held open because doors always held open for someone, and today she was willing to walk through it.

The line moved.

Lila eased forward. The gravel under her tires crunched softly, polite even in resistance.

When she reached the guard, he leaned down to her window with the ease of a man used to being obeyed. His uniform shirt was crisp, the kind of crisp that came from never having to sweat for real.

"Name?" he asked.

She offered a small smile that didn't touch her eyes. "Volunteer," she said, and handed him the printed confirmation page folded into quarters.

He didn't take it immediately. He stared at her face as if it were a familiar headline he couldn't place.

Lila let her expression stay smooth. She'd learned how to be harmless-looking. She hated that she'd learned.

The guard took the paper, scanned it, and then scanned her again. His radio murmured at his shoulder. Somewhere beyond the hedge wall, a sprinkler hissed, indifferent.

"You're late," he said.

"Traffic," she replied.

His mouth twitched like he almost smiled. "Everybody's got somewhere to be," he said, and handed the paper back. "Park where they tell you."

He lifted his hand. The gate swung wider.

Lila drove through.

The air changed instantly. The noise from the street fell away as if the hedge wall swallowed it. The road curved toward a large home that had been designed to look warm—stone façade, wide porch, flags that hung limp in the still air—but every feature also said controlled access. Cameras tucked beneath eaves. A small cluster of suited men near the front walk, pretending to look like staff.

She parked where a teenage valet pointed, his smile practiced and thin. When she stepped out, heat climbed up her back, and then a blast of cool air hit her face as the front doors opened.

Cold air in a polished foyer. Perfume. Catered food that smelled expensive without smelling like anything alive. Glassware clinking against quiet laughter.

Lila's skin tightened with goosebumps as she crossed the threshold.

A long check-in table sat just inside, staffed by women in pastel cardigans who looked like they'd once baked pies for school fundraisers and now managed donor lists like sacred texts. Pens were chained to the table. Name tags peeled at the corners. A bouquet of white flowers sat in the center like innocence on display.

"Hi, sweetheart," one volunteer said, bright enough to be sharp. "Name?"

Lila kept her shoulders loose. She softened her mouth into the half-smile that cost her jaw. "Lila," she said.

The woman's fingers paused over the printed roster. "Last name?"

"Reyes," Lila said, and watched the woman's eyes flicker—just once—like the name meant something she didn't want it to mean.

Another woman leaned in, whispering, "Isn't that—"

The first woman cut her off with a laugh that sounded like a cough. "No," she said too quickly. "Different."

Lila didn't react. She didn't let her throat tighten. She watched the woman's hands instead. Hands gave away what faces tried to hide.

A security man stood a few feet behind the table, arms crossed, suit too snug across his shoulders. He didn't look at the flowers or the guests. He looked at people's exits.

The volunteer slid a name tag across to Lila. It read LILA in neat block letters, no last name. Friendly. Anonymous.

"Volunteer team," the woman chirped. "Kitchen runner. You'll be bringing plates out and taking empties back. Stay out of the private rooms."

"Of course," Lila said, and the word came out clean.

She clipped the tag to her blouse. The metal pin bit into fabric. She felt it like a warning.

The foyer opened into a ballroom-sized living space dressed up with white tablecloth rows and low music that tried to convince everyone it was still just a luncheon. A stage stood at the far end with a lectern and a banner with a charity name printed in tasteful font—something about relief, resilience, community.

Lila scanned the room the way she'd started scanning every room: exits, blind spots, sightlines. She counted the doors without moving her lips.

A waiter passed carrying a tray of champagne flutes. Bubbles rose like small celebrations. Someone laughed too loudly and then glanced around, checking whether the laugh had been acceptable.

Etiquette as camouflage. Everyone knew it. No one said it out loud.

Lila moved toward the service area, past tables where donors sat with straight posture and bright smiles. Their hands rested on linen as if linen could make them decent. Silverware scraped softly. A tray wobbled in a waiter's grip and steadied again.

Two women at a table near the center leaned close together, their voices low but not as low as they thought.

"Kline said it's handled," one whispered.

"Kline says a lot," the other murmured. "But my husband—"

"Kline has seats," the first woman said, and the phrase landed between them like a password.

The second woman's eyes widened, hungry and embarrassed by the hunger. "Don't say it like that," she hissed, looking around. "Not here."

Lila's fingers tightened on the stack of plates she'd been handed near the kitchen. The porcelain edges dug into her palms. She kept walking.

She didn't look for Gideon Kline right away. Looking too hard made people notice. Instead, she let the room reveal him the way it would reveal any man who believed the world existed for his benefit.

He arrived with an assistant trailing him, a hand on his elbow like a handler. He didn't wear a suit that screamed wealth. He wore one that whispered it: perfect fit, soft fabric, no visible logo. His hair was touched with gray in a way that read deliberate. His smile looked practiced for cameras and intimate in person.

People shifted when he passed. Not because he was imposing physically. Because he carried the gravity of access.

Lila watched him take a seat at a table near the front, where the most expensive dresses gathered like petals. A man stood to greet him and bent a little too low, like he was offering himself for approval.

Kline touched the man's shoulder, smiling as if they were friends. "Always good to see you," Kline said, voice warm enough to melt steel.

The man laughed, too hard. "You're saving our lives," he replied.

Kline's smile stayed in place. "We're all doing our part," he said, and his eyes slid briefly toward the stage banner, toward the word community. He wore it like a joke only he understood.

Lila forced herself to keep moving. She carried plates to a side table. She took empties back. She listened with her whole body.

At a table near the back, a donor leaned toward another man and said, "I don't care what the official line is. My pilot filed a plan yesterday and got a call within ten minutes."

The other man's mouth tightened. "From who?"

"You know who," the first man said, eyes darting. "They asked questions they shouldn't have had access to."

The second man's voice turned brittle. "We're paying enough to be discreet."

Lila's stomach turned. Paying enough. Discreet. Like survival was a service tier.

She moved through the room, and a woman with a sharp bob haircut caught her eye.

The woman's gaze lingered on Lila's face a beat too long. Recognition tried to form and failed, but suspicion remained.

"You," the woman said, as Lila set down a plate near her table. "Have we met?"

Lila's heartbeat jumped. She kept her smile polite, light. "Not that I know of," she said.

The woman leaned back, examining her. "Your face is familiar," she said. Her tone stayed pleasant. Her eyes did not.

"I get that a lot," Lila replied, and hated herself for how easily it came out.

The woman's lips curved. "Right," she said. "Of course you do."

Lila didn't linger. She didn't give the woman another angle to study.

She slipped into the service corridor near the kitchen doors, where the air smelled of hot food and stressed bodies. The hallway was narrower, the walls plain. A corkboard held shift lists and handwritten reminders. Staff moved fast, their faces stripped of donor smiles.

The corridor offered a view into the ballroom through swinging doors. It also offered something else: proximity without spotlight.

Lila set her stack of empties on a counter and pretended to adjust her name tag. Her fingers slid beneath the edge of her blouse, finding the recorder nestled against her ribs beneath the fabric.

Warm plastic. A heartbeat away.

She held her breath and flicked the switch.

A tiny click, barely audible under the clatter of a tray and the hiss of a dishwasher. Her thumb shook once, then steadied.

She didn't press the recorder outward. She didn't hold it up like a microphone. She let it sit where it was, hidden by fabric and posture. She looked like a volunteer catching her breath.

The hallway door at the far end opened.

Kline's assistant stepped in first, scanning the corridor with quick, efficient eyes. Behind him came Gideon Kline and a man in a pale suit who looked like he'd never carried his own luggage.

The pale-suited man spoke fast, voice pitched low. "I need certainty," he said. "My wife—"

Kline lifted a hand as if calming a skittish animal. "Certainty is an expensive word," he murmured. "What I offer is capacity management."

The phrase hit Lila like a slap. Capacity management. Not hope. Not rescue. A term that belonged in supply chains and spreadsheets, used here for human bodies.

The pale-suited man swallowed. "You're saying you can move us," he said.

Kline's smile didn't reach his eyes. "I'm saying I can place you where the probability is acceptable," he replied. "If you can follow instructions."

The assistant opened a leather folder. He held a pen ready.

"Instructions?" the man asked, uneasy.

Kline glanced toward the ballroom doors. The music and laughter leaked through. He spoke softly, like a private tip. "Discretion," he said. "It's not complicated. You don't talk. You don't agitate. You don't become... a variable."

The pale-suited man's jaw tightened. "You want silence," he said.

Kline's smile sharpened. "I want stability," he replied. "And stability requires adults to behave like adults."

Lila's fingers curled around her own pen inside her pocket. She forced herself to relax them. She couldn't afford to look like she was listening.

The pale-suited man's voice dropped further. "And the seats," he said. "The—"

Kline cut him off with a quiet chuckle. "Don't say it like that," he said. "It sounds crude."

The man flushed. "People are saying it," he muttered.

Kline's eyes flicked toward the assistant. "People say a lot," he replied. "People say there are lists. People say the government is lying. People say panic is justified. People say it's every man for himself."

He leaned a fraction closer to the pale-suited man. "People are wrong," he said, still soft. "It's every man for himself only if you can't afford a better arrangement."

The man's face went still. "My check cleared," he said, and the entitlement in the words turned his mouth ugly.

Kline smiled warmly, like a father indulging a child. "Yes," he said. "It did. That's why you're here and not outside a warehouse screaming at a shuttered door."

The pale-suited man flinched as if he'd been slapped.

"Florida?" he asked, trying to regain footing. "Or—"

Kline shook his head slightly. "Florida is crowded," he said. "Crowds create problems. Problems create headlines. Headlines create... complications."

His gaze drifted, casual, toward the corridor corner where Lila stood with a tray in her hands. It was the kind of glance that could've been nothing.

It wasn't nothing.

His eyes didn't widen in recognition. They didn't need to. His focus sharpened for the length of a breath, then softened again into charm.

Lila's throat tightened. She kept her face neutral. She stared at the tray, not at him.

Kline continued, voice smooth. "If you want something exclusive, you pay for exclusive," he said. "Ground transport, air, whatever makes your wife sleep. And you sign what my assistant puts in front of you."

The pale-suited man's voice caught. "What is it," he asked.

Kline's assistant answered this time, tone professional. "Non-disclosure, non-disparagement," he said. "Compliance."

The pale-suited man swallowed hard. "And if someone talks," he said, trying to sound brave.

Kline's smile never moved. "Then they lose their arrangement," he replied. "And arrangements are fragile. They can vanish if you mishandle them."

He said it kindly. Like advice.

Then he added, almost as an afterthought, "Families are fragile, too."

The words landed in Lila's ribs.

Her skin prickled under her blouse. The recorder felt suddenly too warm against her.

Kline continued speaking as if he hadn't just reached into her life. "A rumor becomes a riot," he said. "A riot becomes a tragedy. I'm preventing tragedy."

The pale-suited man's eyes darted. "So you're doing this for the greater good," he said, sarcasm bleeding through.

Kline's smile hardened. "I'm doing this because the greater good needs sponsors," he replied. "And sponsors don't appreciate chaos."

The assistant slid a document forward. The pale-suited man reached for it with hands that didn't quite stop shaking.

Lila forced her breath out slowly through her nose. She counted silently—one, two, three—so she didn't move too fast.

A catering worker stepped into the corridor behind her, pushing a cart piled with linen. The worker paused, hearing Kline's voice, and their face shifted—confusion, then something like disgust. Their gaze snapped to Lila's name tag and then away, as if they didn't want to be implicated just by standing there.

Neutral. Witness. Lila didn't grab them. She didn't need to. She just needed them to stay within earshot long enough to hear the words that mattered.

Kline's voice carried, low and confident. "Your wife wants a guarantee," he said. "Tell her this: the only guarantee is being prepared."

Prepared. A word that sounded noble until it meant letting other people drown.

The pale-suited man nodded too quickly. "We'll be prepared," he said. "We'll do whatever you say."

Kline's eyes flicked again toward the corridor corner. Not directly at Lila this time, but close enough to make her stomach turn. "Good," he said. "Because the ones who think they can expose things—make noise—don't understand what noise costs."

Lila's grip tightened on her pen. Her notebook lay tucked under the tray, hidden beneath plates. She didn't open it. She didn't write in the moment. She didn't want to look like she was documenting. She just held the phrases in her head and let the recorder do its work.

Kline's assistant spoke again, efficient. "We'll need signatures," he said. "Today."

"Today," Kline echoed, and the word had weight. "Because capacity shrinks. And people who hesitate end up in the wrong line."

The pale-suited man swallowed. "The red line," he said, almost whispering.

Kline's smile turned faintly amused. "You've heard that," he said.

The man's face flushed. "Everyone's heard it," he admitted. "It's—"

Kline cut him off with a gentle touch to his elbow. "Then you know why we do this quietly," he said. "We manage capacity. We maintain order. We keep the public from tearing itself apart while the work gets done."

Work. He said it like he was building something holy.

Lila stood still until they moved away, until the assistant guided the pale-suited man toward a side door marked PRIVATE, until the corridor air shifted again to kitchen noise and staff footsteps.

Only then did she flick the recorder off.

The click sounded like a gunshot in her own head.

She didn't check the tape. She didn't rewind. She didn't do anything that looked like confirmation. She kept the recorder warm against her ribs and moved like a volunteer with plates.

She walked toward the catering worker with the linen cart, keeping her pace normal.

"Hey," Lila said softly, as if asking for a tray. "You okay?"

The worker's eyes flicked to her face. Close-up, their age was hard to place—young enough to have acne scars, old enough to have exhaustion baked into their posture.

They swallowed. "He always talks like that?" they asked.

Lila didn't answer the question directly. "You heard it," she said.

The worker's mouth tightened. "Capacity management," they repeated, voice bitter. "Like we're... like we're inventory."

Lila's throat tightened again. "What's your name," she asked, gentle.

The worker hesitated, then nodded toward the name stitched on their apron. "Marisol," they said. "Why?"

Lila didn't tell her why. She let it sit between them. "If someone asks you what you heard," Lila said, "tell the truth."

Marisol's eyes narrowed. "Who are you," she asked.

Lila gave her the smallest, saddest smile. "Someone who needs the truth to survive being called a lie," she said.

Marisol stared at her, then looked away down the corridor where Kline had disappeared. "He said families are fragile," she murmured.

Lila's jaw tightened. She nodded once.

Marisol's voice dropped. "That was a threat," she said.

Lila didn't deny it. Denial would've been a comfort she didn't have the right to offer.

Marisol shoved the cart forward hard enough that the wheels squealed. "I'm just here to work," she snapped, as if saying it louder could make it true. "I'm not— I don't want—"

"I know," Lila said quietly. "I'm not asking you to be brave. I'm asking you to be honest."

Marisol's shoulders rose and fell. She didn't nod. She didn't agree out loud. But she didn't walk away from the truth either.

Lila moved back toward the ballroom, her pulse in her fingertips.

On the luncheon floor, Kline had returned to his table, his smile back in place. He lifted a glass as someone toasted resilience. Applause spread, neat and contained.

Lila carried empties, her face set into polite neutrality. She passed near Kline's table and heard a woman laugh lightly.

"We're all so grateful for your leadership," she said.

Kline's smile widened. "It's a privilege," he replied. "I'm here for the community."

The word community came out clean. Lila tasted bile.

A man at the table leaned in, voice low, and said, "The press is getting ugly."

Kline's eyes flicked up briefly. "The press needs a story," he said. "Stories keep them paid."

"And if they publish the wrong one?" the man asked.

Kline's smile didn't move. "Then they learn," he said, soft and warm. "Everyone learns eventually."

Lila's skin tightened. She kept walking.

She slipped into the hallway near the bathrooms, where the air smelled of floral soap and polished tile. The noise of the ballroom dulled behind her.

Inside the bathroom, the lighting was harsh enough to strip color from skin. Lila gripped the sink edge and turned the faucet on. Cold water splashed over her wrists. She kept them under longer than necessary, scrubbing as if she could wash off the feeling of Kline's voice reaching into her life.

She lifted her head and stared at her reflection.

Her face looked too pale under the lights. Her eyes looked older than they had six months ago. Her mouth was set in a line she didn't recognize.

She took a paper towel, tore it too fast, and pressed it against her palms until her knuckles stopped trembling.

Publishing wasn't the same as saving.

She'd believed, once, that truth landed like light—that if you showed people what was real, they would correct course.

Now she could see the other physics: crowds didn't follow facts. They followed behavior. They followed the rich leaving early. They followed rumors like "Kline has seats" because the phrase offered something facts couldn't: a door, a gate, a promise that you wouldn't be the one left outside.

If she dropped this tape into the world raw, it would ignite. Not the way a journalist dreams about—reform, accountability, justice. It would ignite into fists and broken glass and armed men defending gates like this one.

And somewhere in that fire, Manuel's name might get said.

Her phone vibrated again in the cup holder memory of her mind. She'd left it in her pocket this time, facedown. She pulled it out just enough to see the missed calls: her editor. Twice.

She couldn't call him from inside the venue. She couldn't be seen in a bathroom stall whispering into a phone like a teenager. She couldn't leave a trail that could be used to call her reckless.

She slipped the phone back, breathed out slowly, and practiced her face again. Polite. Harmless. Volunteer.

When she stepped out, the hallway felt narrower.

A woman in a cocktail dress stood near the doorway, eyes locked on Lila's name tag.

"Lila," the woman said, smiling. It was the woman with the sharp bob haircut. "There you are."

Lila kept her voice light. "Hi," she said.

"I knew it," the woman purred, taking a step closer. "You're her."

Lila didn't ask who. She let the woman say it.

"The reporter," the woman continued, voice still pleasant. "The one who decided she could stir things up for clicks."

Lila held her posture steady. "I'm a volunteer," she said.

The woman laughed softly. "Oh, sure," she said. "And I'm a kindergarten teacher."

Lila didn't flinch. She kept her smile small. "Do you need help finding your table?" she asked, weaponizing politeness.

The woman's eyes narrowed. "You think you're clever," she said. "You think you can walk into rooms like this and listen."

"I'm carrying plates," Lila said.

"You're carrying stories," the woman replied, and the word stories came out like a dirty thing. "Do you know what stories do now?"

Lila didn't answer. She knew. She'd watched it happen after she hit publish.

The woman leaned closer, perfume sharp. "Gideon hates variables," she whispered. "And you, sweetheart, are a variable."

Lila felt the recorder against her ribs, warm, heavy. She kept her voice calm. "If you have concerns, you can speak to the organizers," she said.

The woman smiled wider. "Oh, I will," she said. "But I wanted you to know I saw you. Because you look like someone who thinks she's protecting someone."

Lila's throat tightened. The woman's gaze dropped briefly toward Lila's chest, toward where the recorder sat hidden. It didn't linger long enough to prove anything. It didn't need to.

"You should be careful," the woman murmured. "Families are fragile."

The same words. Same cadence. Like a script passed around.

Lila's pulse surged. She forced herself not to react. Reaction would be admission.

"Excuse me," Lila said smoothly, and stepped around the woman without brushing her, without giving security a reason to intervene.

She walked back toward the ballroom, then angled toward the exit path through the venue grounds, her pace measured. Not fast. Not slow. Normal.

Outside, heat slapped her face, thick with exhaust from idling cars. Lawn sprinklers hissed over the grass, casting mist that made the air feel falsely clean.

She kept moving toward the valet stand.

A suited security man stepped into her path, smiling politely. "Ma'am," he said. "Hold on a second."

The words were gentle. They were also a trap.

Lila stopped. She didn't stop too sharply. She didn't freeze. She turned her face toward him with the calm smile she'd practiced in mirrors since she was a kid trying not to be noticed in rooms where she didn't belong.

"Yes?" she said.

"Are you with catering?" he asked, eyes flicking to her name tag.

"Yes," Lila replied, and lifted the stack of plates in her hands slightly, as if to prove it. Her arms started to ache. She welcomed the ache. It made her body feel honest.

He smiled wider. "They told us there might be... media," he said, tone careful. "We have policies."

"Of course," Lila said. "I'm just returning these."

His gaze lingered on her face. "What's your last name?" he asked.

She didn't hesitate. Hesitation was guilt in his world. "Reyes," she said, and watched his eyes flicker again, that tiny shift that said he knew the name.

Behind him, the woman with the bob haircut stood near the doorway, watching. Her mouth curved as if she'd won something.

The guard's radio murmured at his shoulder. He lifted a hand slightly, palm open, still polite. "We'd like you to come back inside for a moment," he said. "Just to clarify—"

Lila's stomach dropped, but her face stayed calm. "I can't," she said, still polite. "The kitchen manager is waiting on these. If they're short staffed, it becomes a safety issue. Hot trays, knives, crowd—"

She watched his eyes. She watched the moment his brain grabbed the word safety and tried to use it.

He opened his mouth.

Lila added, softly, "If you need my information, you can get it from the volunteer coordinator. It's all in the roster at check-in."

She gave him a helpful smile. A cooperative smile. The smile of someone who wasn't hiding anything.

He hesitated. His gaze flicked toward the check-in table visible through the open doors. He didn't want to walk back through the ballroom. He didn't want to make a scene. He didn't want to be the reason donors felt uncomfortable.

The woman with the bob haircut stepped closer, her voice carrying just enough to reach them. "She's press," she said, bright and light. "She's the one who—"

The guard's jaw tightened. His eyes stayed on Lila. "Ma'am," he said, still polite, "we're going to need—"

A voice called from the valet stand. "Hey! We need these plates cleared!"

A young staffer waved toward them, panicked.

The guard's eyes flicked toward the staffer. He looked irritated. Not at the staffer. At the inconvenience.

Lila held her plates up slightly again, as if she wanted to help. "I should go," she said, and started moving before he could decide.

He reached out—then stopped short of touching her. Touching her would create a story. Even he knew that.

"Ma'am," he called, sharper now.

Lila didn't run. She didn't speed up dramatically. She walked with the quiet urgency of someone doing her job, slipping into the normal flow of staff movement.

At the valet stand, she handed the plates off quickly, smiled at the panicked staffer, and said, "Sorry," like she'd truly been delayed by nothing more than logistics.

The staffer didn't look at her face. He looked at the plates. He was too tired to care who she was.

Lila turned toward the parking area, sun beating down. Her car sat between two black SUVs with tinted windows. She kept her head down as she walked, not because she was ashamed but because she didn't want to offer her face to any watching phone.

She unlocked the door, slipped inside, and shut it.

Only then did her hands start to tremble.

She pressed her palms against the steering wheel until the shaking slowed. Sweat slicked the leather. Her throat tasted metallic.

She didn't pull the recorder out yet. She didn't rewind. She didn't let herself check. Checking would make it feel like it was over.

It wasn't over.

She started the car. The air-conditioning kicked on and then coughed weakly, blowing warm air that smelled faintly like old plastic. Her chest tightened anyway. Even bad air felt like relief compared to the foyer's cold politeness.

She backed out carefully.

In the side mirror, she saw the security guard step into the parking area, scanning. The woman with the bob haircut stood near the doorway, watching the cars leave like she was counting.

Lila kept her face forward. She didn't give them eye contact. She drove out of the gated suburb with the same measured pace she'd used to enter, passing the guardhouse again.

The guard with mirrored sunglasses looked into her car once more. His gaze slid over her face, then away.

The gate swung open.

She left.

Only when she hit the main road did she let herself breathe deeper. The city noise returned in layers—horns, distant construction, a siren threading through heat.

She drove for fifteen minutes before pulling into a strip mall parking lot that smelled like fried food and asphalt. She chose it because it was ordinary. Ordinary meant invisible.

She parked near a laundromat whose door stood propped open with a plastic chair. The air inside looked cool. People moved in and out, arms full of clothes, eyes on their own lives.

Lila stepped inside and walked to the counter where a woman sat behind bulletproof glass, reading a magazine.

"Can I use your phone?" Lila asked, voice steady.

The woman's eyes lifted, suspicious. "For what?"

"To check on my kid," Lila said, and the word kid came out clean even though she hadn't defined Manuel that way out loud before. It was close enough to be true.

The woman watched her for a beat, then slid a corded handset out through a small slot. "Two minutes," she said.

Lila dialed the neighbor's number from memory, fingers sure even as her pulse hammered.

The neighbor picked up on the second ring. "Hello?"

"It's me," Lila said.

A pause. Then the neighbor's voice softened. "He's fine," she said immediately, as if she'd been waiting.

Lila's throat tightened. "He took his meds?" she asked, keeping her voice casual in case anyone listened.

"Yes," the neighbor replied. "He rolled his eyes like a professional."

Lila almost laughed. The sound stuck in her throat.

"Can I—" she started, then stopped herself. Can I talk to him. Can I hear him. Can I steal a second of normal.

The neighbor didn't make her ask. "Hold on," she said.

A muffled shuffle. Then Manuel's voice, distant but unmistakable, complaining about something small. "No, I don't want that one—"

Relief hit Lila so hard her eyes stung. She blinked fast, staring at the laundromat floor.

"Tell him I'm—" she started.

The neighbor cut in softly, "I will," and the voice carried the same certainty from earlier. "Go do what you have to do."

Lila swallowed. "Thank you," she said, and meant it like prayer.

She hung up and slid the handset back through the slot.

The woman behind the glass watched her with a face that held no curiosity, only fatigue. "You good?" she asked.

Lila nodded. "Yeah," she said. She left before her voice could break.

Back in her car, she pulled the recorder out at last.

It sat in her palm, warm from her body heat. She held it against her ribs for a second, feeling her own heartbeat thud against plastic.

She forced her breathing even and rewound the tape a few seconds. She pressed play, just long enough to hear Kline's voice—soft, confident—say capacity management.

She stopped it immediately. She didn't need to hear the whole thing now. She needed to keep it safe.

She tucked the recorder back under her blouse, close to skin, where it wouldn't be forgotten. Then she opened her notebook and wrote, quick and blunt, the phrases she could not afford to lose: capacity management, discretion, "families are fragile," non-disclosure, "the red line."

Her pen pressed hard enough to dent the paper.

When she finished, she shut the notebook and held it on her lap until her hands stopped shaking.

Her phone buzzed again.

This time she flipped it over.

EDITOR. 3 MISSED CALLS.

She stared at the screen a beat too long, then hit call.

He answered immediately, voice tight. "Where the hell are you?"

"Alive," Lila said.

A pause. A breath. "Do you have it?" he asked, and the question sounded like both hope and dread.

"Yes," Lila said. "It's real. It's clean. It's—"

"Don't say it over the phone," he snapped, then softened, because he heard something in her voice. "Okay. Okay. Where are you?"

"A laundromat," she said. "Not far."

He exhaled hard. "Jesus," he muttered.

Lila stared through the windshield at a man loading clothes into his trunk. Ordinary. The world still doing laundry while the rich negotiated survival.

"They know me," she said, voice low.

Silence on the line.

"They said it," she continued. "They used the same words. Families are fragile."

Her editor's voice sharpened. "Did he say your name?"

"No," Lila replied. "He didn't need to."

Another pause, and she could hear her editor's mind working through consequences—injunctions, threats, the kind that arrived on letterhead and the kind that arrived without warning.

"We can't dump this," he said finally, voice grim. "Not raw."

"I know," Lila said.

He swallowed. "So what do we do?"

Lila looked down at her notebook. At the creased cover. At how her grip had warped it.

"We need someone who understands the lines," she said. "The intake. The logistics. The real-world physics. If I put this out without guidance, people will die trying to break gates."

Her editor's voice went wary. "Who?"

Lila hesitated. Not because she didn't know. Because saying the name made it another kind of risk.

"The FEMA guy," she said. "Malik Carter."

Silence. Then her editor exhaled sharply, like he'd been holding that name in his own head too. "How do you—"

"Don't ask me that," Lila said, voice tight. "Just tell me if you can get me to him without sending messages into the void."

Her editor's voice dropped. "I can," he said. "Not directly. But my cousin's church has a relief coordinator. He knows people. He's the kind who still uses paper lists and landlines."

"Good," Lila said.

"I'll call him," her editor continued. "He'll call someone. It'll take—"

"No time talk," Lila cut in. "Just do it."

Her editor swallowed. "And Lila," he said, voice turning softer. "Don't go home."

Lila stared at the steering wheel, slick with sweat. "I wasn't planning to," she replied.

A beat. Then she said, quieter, "Is Manuel safe?"

Her editor didn't answer immediately. He didn't ask who Manuel was. He already knew. He just didn't like saying it out loud.

"As safe as we can make him," he said. "Keep doing the landline thing. Don't light up your location."

Lila shut her eyes briefly. The smell of detergent from the laundromat drifted through the cracked window. A siren wailed somewhere in the distance and faded.

"I'm not trying to be brave," she said, voice low. "I'm trying to be responsible."

"I know," her editor said, and the certainty in his voice steadied her, just a fraction.

They hung up.

Lila sat with the phone in her hand for a moment, then flipped it facedown again like it could burn her.

She stared at the strip mall storefronts until her breathing normalized.

Then she typed a message to Manuel—ordinary on purpose.

Need anything from the store?

She sent it and immediately regretted the tenderness. It felt like a flare.

But she couldn't live entirely in fear. Not if she wanted him to have any kind of future.

Her phone stayed silent.

She pulled the notebook closer and tucked it into her bag. The recorder stayed against her ribs. She checked her rearview mirror, then the side mirrors, tracing the parking lot, the cars, the faces reflected in glass.

Nothing obvious.

And still, she knew: she had walked through a gate and heard the truth spoken like etiquette, and now the truth was a thing that could get people killed if handled wrong.

Outside, heat shimmered over the asphalt. Exhaust hung in the air. Somewhere a siren rose again, threading through traffic like a warning no one could afford to misunderstand.

Lila gripped her notebook until the cover creased deeper, and she kept her eyes on the road ahead, because every car window caught the sun and threw it back at her, bright and watchful.

Chapter 13 - Storm Net at Starbase

Rain hammered the trailer roof like it wanted inside.

Naomi's badge swung against her chest as she leaned over the central table, trying to ignore the way the sound drilled straight through the thin metal and into her teeth. The air smelled like damp fabric and coffee that had been kept hot long past the point of kindness. Every surface held a fine sheen of humidity—paper edges softening, jackets hanging heavy, the backs of chairs slick where exhausted bodies had sat and stood and sat again.

The trailer's monitors threw a pale wash over faces that had stopped pretending they were fine. A weather liaison in a rain-darkened polo kept tapping a marker against his knuckle. Two engineers hovered near the trajectory plots, shoulders bunched as if the fluorescent lights weighed something.

Naomi kept her hands on the table because she didn't trust them anywhere else. When she lifted her fingers, she felt the urge to rub her eyes until they burned. She didn't. She kept her gaze on the printouts, the time windows, the sequence steps she had written out in her own blocky handwriting because her brain started skipping when she stared too long at glowing screens.

"Say it again," she told the guidance specialist without looking up.

The specialist—a woman with hair pulled into a tight knot that made her cheekbones look sharper—blinked hard and pointed at a line Naomi had underlined twice. "Beacon alignment begins at minus twenty-three minutes. Mirror staging completes at minus eleven. The corridor shift effect—"

"Don't summarize," Naomi said, voice low. Not harsh. Just flat. "Numbers."

The specialist inhaled, steadying herself. "We're nudging the b-plane corridor by point-seven degrees, plus or minus point-two, assuming the fragment distribution stays within the last packet bounds."

"Point-seven," Naomi repeated, and wrote it down. Her pen dragged slightly against damp paper. "Not miles. Not a miracle. Degrees."

An engineer across the table snorted softly—too tired to hide the bitterness. "Point-seven degrees of what," he murmured. "A rock that's already coming apart."

Naomi's throat tightened. She didn't correct him. Correction would turn into a fight, and fights wasted energy they didn't have. She turned her gaze to the flight director type—a man everyone called Drew even though his name tag said Andrew in small letters.

Drew's eyes were red-rimmed. He looked like he'd slept in his car and argued with his own thoughts the whole time. "We still have Ben's window?" Naomi asked.

Drew lifted a paper schedule and ran a finger down it, leaving a faint wet streak from condensation. "We have a window," he said. "We have a storm. We have a public that thinks we're making this up to cover a budget grab."

"And we have a tropical system turning our margin into a joke," the weather liaison said, almost gently.

Naomi watched the liaison's mouth as he spoke. She watched what he didn't say. He didn't say if the storm would intensify. He didn't say if the winds would cross the safety thresholds. He didn't say if their "no-go" rules would hold when the wrong phone call came in.

She had learned, in the last months, that rules didn't break loudly. They softened. They were "interpreted." They were "temporarily adjusted."

She kept her voice even. "I need the next update at the top of the hour," she said to the weather liaison. "Not 'soon.' Not 'when you can.' Top of the hour."

The liaison nodded, marker tapping his knuckle once. "Yes, ma'am."

That word—ma'am—still sat wrong in her stomach. It sounded like deference. It sounded like blame waiting to happen.

A young engineer at the far end of the trailer shifted his weight and winced. Naomi noticed the bruise on her own forearm when she moved, a tender patch from bumping into a metal rack earlier. She pressed her thumb into it, hard, until the pain sharpened her focus.

Someone's radio hissed with static near the door. The sound came in and out like the world breathing through teeth.

A man in a suit stepped into the trailer, rainwater dripping from his jacket cuffs onto the floor. He didn't look like he belonged here. Not because he was clean; everyone was clean in theory. Because he carried the calm of someone whose sleep hadn't been rationed.

He had a badge clipped to his lapel that said LIAISON in large print. The smaller agency name beneath it meant nothing to Naomi. Everything meant something to someone, and she didn't have time to memorize the whole ecosystem of power.

Drew straightened as if a string had yanked him. "We're in a briefing," he said, polite.

The liaison in the suit smiled like he'd expected that. "I won't take long," he replied. "I'm here to ensure alignment."

Alignment. Naomi's jaw clenched. The word belonged to optics, not physics.

She didn't stand. She didn't offer her hand. She just looked at him until his smile thinned.

"Which alignment," she asked.

His eyes flicked to her name tag. "Dr. Park," he said, and he pronounced it correctly, like he'd rehearsed. "I'm being told we may need to revise the sequence to preserve the window."

The guidance specialist gave a small, involuntary laugh—pure exhaustion. "Revise," she echoed. "Sure. We'll just revise the weather."

The suit-liaison's smile held. "I'm referring to safety constraints," he said. "Launch commit criteria. There's flexibility, within reason."

Within reason. Naomi felt the room tilt. Not physically. Psychologically. A familiar pressure, the kind that came with carefully chosen words and implied consequences.

She kept her tone mild. "We don't have flexibility on lightning," she said. "We don't have flexibility on wind shear. We don't have flexibility on people getting killed by pretending rules are optional."

The suit-liaison's gaze didn't flinch. He didn't look offended. He looked amused, like she'd said something quaint. "No one is suggesting we endanger anyone," he said. "We're suggesting we weigh risk appropriately."

Naomi leaned forward, palms flat on the table. "Say what you mean," she said softly.

The room went still enough that the rain sounded louder.

The suit-liaison's smile didn't change, but his eyes cooled. "We cannot afford to miss this window," he said. "If we miss it, we lose more than a sequence."

"Lives," Naomi said.

He hesitated. A fraction of a second. Then, "Capability," he corrected, and the correction landed like a confession.

Capability meant contracts. It meant control. It meant who got to steer the story of what happened next.

Naomi stared at him until his smile finally slipped at the edges.

Drew cleared his throat, stepping into the gap. "We'll evaluate with weather," he said. "We'll follow criteria."

The suit-liaison nodded, satisfied with the phrase follow criteria as if it was a prayer that made consequences vanish. He turned toward the door as if the conversation was done.

Naomi watched him leave and felt her pulse climb.

The guidance specialist leaned closer to Naomi, voice low. "That was a warning," she murmured.

Naomi didn't answer. She picked up her pen and wrote the liaison's phrase in the margin of her paper: WEIGH RISK APPROPRIATELY.

She didn't write it for drama. She wrote it because paper didn't forget.

When the trailer door shut again, the static hiss resumed in the small silence left behind.

Drew exhaled hard. "Ignore him," he said, not convincing himself.

Naomi kept her eyes on the schedule. "I can't," she replied. "He wasn't here to be ignored."

The rain intensified, striking the roof so hard the metal vibrated. A drop slipped from the window frame and trailed down the inside glass.

Naomi's stomach rolled. She pressed two fingers to the bridge of her nose and held them there until the ache behind her eyes stopped spreading.

"Top of the hour," she repeated to the weather liaison, as if she could anchor time with her voice.

The liaison nodded again, marker finally still.

Naomi forced herself to eat a protein bar she had found in her bag. The taste was bland, cardboard with a hint of sweetness. She chewed without thinking. Swallowed. Kept working.

Outside, thunder rolled somewhere far enough away to feel like a warning and not an immediate threat.

She had learned to measure fear in distance.

When the weather update came, it arrived with wet paper and a voice that had lost its softness.

The liaison spread the printouts on the table. Damp edges curled upward under the trailer's stale warmth. "The system tightened," he said. "Wind profiles at altitude are changing faster than forecast. Lightning probability stays elevated through the next three hours."

Drew's jaw tightened. "We lose the window," he said, not a question.

The weather liaison shook his head. "We lose the wide window," he corrected. "We may have a narrow break. It's not clean."

Naomi's pulse thudded in her neck. She leaned over the printouts, scanning. She saw the numbers, the probabilities, the little footnotes that translated into real bodies.

The guidance specialist ran a finger down a line and muttered, "This is cruel."

No one argued. Cruel was accurate.

Naomi didn't say she felt anything. She didn't name it. She kept her voice steady because steady meant the room could keep breathing.

"Give me the break window," she said.

The liaison pointed. "Between twenty-three forty-five and zero-oh-fifteen," he said. "If the lightning pattern shifts south like the model suggests. If."

If. That word was a door that might not open.

Drew glanced at Naomi. His eyes were asking her to carry it.

"We can stage sequence to be ready," Naomi said. "We can't force the sky. We can be ready."

The engineer who had snorted earlier looked up. "Ready to do what," he asked. "Pretend this shift matters?"

Naomi turned toward him. She didn't glare. She didn't snap. She just held his gaze until he looked away first.

"It matters," she said quietly. "Not enough. Not the way you want. But it matters."

He swallowed. "And if it fails," he whispered.

Naomi didn't answer the way he wanted. Comfort would've been a lie. She pointed at the paper. "Then the corridor stays where it is," she said. "And the ocean isn't what it could be."

Someone laughed softly in the hallway outside the trailer—bright and careless—and the sound threaded through the door seam like an insult.

Naomi flinched anyway.

She pushed away from the table and stepped toward the trailer door. "I need thirty seconds," she said, not asking.

No one stopped her.

Outside, the rain hit her face immediately, cold and sharp. Floodlights threw halos in the mist, turning the world into a smeared watercolor of light and shadow. Mud sucked at her boots as she stepped off the small metal stairs.

She tilted her head back and let the rain strike her cheeks, her eyelids. It didn't cleanse anything. It just reminded her the world did whatever it wanted.

Her breath tasted metallic.

The wind slapped her hair against her jaw. She pushed it back with a wet hand and looked toward the distant outlines of larger buildings, toward the silhouettes of structures that were supposed to represent human ingenuity and now felt like thin shells beneath a sky that didn't care.

A security fence gleamed under floodlights, wet wire shining. Beyond it, she could make out a cluster of people in ponchos gathered near a barrier. Their voices carried faintly—chants, fragmented words, anger diluted by rain.

She couldn't hear what they said clearly. She didn't need to. She knew the rhythm of a crowd that had decided it was owed answers.

She had answers. She also had uncertainty, and uncertainty sounded like betrayal in a world starving for certainty.

Naomi pressed her palm to the side of the trailer, metal cold and slick. She counted her breaths again—one, two, three—until her pulse stopped climbing.

She thought of the rule change they'd already made. Stop had become reduce. Save had become shift. Every word had gotten uglier because it had to hold truth.

Inside, someone called her name. Not loud. Not urgent. Just a reminder: she couldn't stay outside and let the rain do the thinking for her.

She went back in.

The air hit her like a wall—warm, damp, smelling of clothes that had never dried. A chair creaked as someone shifted.

Drew pointed at the screen where trajectory arcs glowed. "We need confirmation," he said. "We need to know the sequence still moves the corridor off the densest land path."

Naomi moved to the guidance station. Fingerprints fogged the protective glass over the display. She didn't touch it. She wrote the key numbers on her own paper instead, forcing her brain to translate light into inkless pressure—just pen and paper, the way she trusted when she stopped trusting herself.

"Read it aloud," she told the guidance specialist.

The specialist blinked. "I just did."

"Again," Naomi said softly. "Not because I don't believe you. Because I don't believe fatigue."

The specialist's shoulders dropped, then lifted. She read the numbers, careful, slow. Naomi listened for any slip. A digit swapped. A decimal moved. A mistake that would look tiny on paper and become catastrophic in the sky.

When the specialist finished, Naomi exhaled once, controlled. "Okay," she said.

The engineer at the end of the table muttered, "This is like steering a truck with a sewing needle."

Naomi didn't correct the metaphor. She just said, "It's what we have."

A small argument started near the monitors—two engineers disagreeing over a tolerance assumption. Their voices stayed low, not because they were calm but because they knew what loud voices signaled in a trailer like this: fracture.

"You're using the optimistic distribution," one engineer said.

"I'm using the latest packet," the other snapped.

"The latest packet is incomplete," the first shot back. "You're filling gaps with hope."

Hope. Naomi stepped closer. "Stop," she said, and the word cut through them without volume.

They turned toward her.

"We fill gaps with ranges," Naomi said. "We state the ranges. We state the failure modes. We don't hide behind a clean number because clean numbers make people comfortable."

The second engineer's mouth tightened. "Leadership wants a clean number," he said.

Naomi's gaze flicked toward the trailer door as if she could see the suit-liaison through the metal. "Leadership can want whatever it wants," she said. "Physics doesn't care."

Silence settled again, tense and thin.

A radio crackled near the table. Drew leaned over it, listening. His face shifted—worry, then calculation.

"Ben's on," he said.

Naomi's pulse jumped.

Drew pressed the talk button. "Ben," he said. "We're looking at a narrow break. You have eyes on your side?"

A voice came through—distorted, rain and static layered over it. Ben's voice. Tired. Focused. The kind of focus that sounded like it had been carved out with a knife.

"We have weather holds," Ben said. "We have people outside the gate who think they're saving the world by blocking a truck. We have federal folks who want signatures."

Naomi's fingers tightened around her pen.

Drew's voice stayed professional. "We're coordinating sequence readiness. We need you to confirm you can hit the break window if it opens."

A pause. Static hissed. Then Ben's voice again, lower. "We can hit it," he said. "If the rules stay the rules."

Naomi felt the words land in her ribs. Ben knew. He knew rules weren't always rules anymore.

Drew glanced toward Naomi, a quick question in his eyes. Naomi stepped closer to the radio. She didn't take it from him. She didn't perform authority. She just spoke as herself.

"Ben," she said.

Another pause. "Dr. Park," Ben replied, and the way he said it carried respect and something else—fear that she would become another person telling him to do the impossible.

"We're being pressured," Naomi said, careful. She didn't name names. She didn't say Kline or continuity. She didn't offer a hook for anyone listening. "If the break opens, we may have to commit faster than we like."

Ben exhaled, audible even through static. "That's what they want," he said.

Naomi stared at the paper schedule. "I know," she replied. "I need you to tell me—if you hit it, can you do it without pretending the margin is larger than it is?"

Silence. Then Ben's voice came back, rougher. "I can do it," he said. "I can't promise it won't cost."

Naomi's throat tightened. "Say that again," she said.

A faint sound—almost a laugh—came through the radio, but it held no humor. "It'll cost," Ben repeated.

Naomi nodded once even though he couldn't see it. "Okay," she said.

Drew took over again, voice brisk. "Stand by," he told Ben. "We'll call the decision."

The radio clicked off. The static hiss remained, like a ghost of the conversation.

For a moment, no one spoke. The rain filled the silence, relentless.

Naomi felt the room waiting for her to carry the weight they couldn't say out loud: if she signed off, people might die because she had decided the window mattered more than the caution that made everyone feel moral.

She had a choice. It wasn't a good choice. It was still a choice.

Drew cleared his throat. "We need the call ready," he said.

The suit-liaison returned before Naomi could reply. He slipped inside with the ease of someone who didn't ask permission. He carried a folder in his hand, protected from the rain beneath his jacket.

"We're prepared to move," he said, setting the folder on the table. "Authorization is ready."

Naomi looked at the folder. The top sheet had her name printed in the signature block.

Printed.

Her skin prickled. "Who prepared this," she asked.

The suit-liaison smiled. "Counsel," he said. "We're streamlining."

Streamlining. Naomi's fingers curled into her palm. She pressed her thumb hard into the heel of her hand until the pressure steadied her.

She flipped the top page over with two fingers. The paper stuck slightly from humidity. The language on the sheet was clean, almost cheerful: APPROVED TO PROCEED UNDER CONTINGENCY WEATHER CONDITIONS.

No mention of reduced safety margin. No mention of lightning probability. No mention of the narrow break being a gamble.

This wasn't paperwork. It was a story they wanted her to sign.

Naomi lifted her gaze. "No," she said, softly.

The suit-liaison's smile tightened. "Dr. Park," he began, tone still polite.

Naomi didn't raise her voice. She didn't need to. "If I sign this," she said, "I sign a lie."

"It's standard language," he replied.

"It's intentionally vague language," Naomi countered. "Standard doesn't mean honest."

Drew shifted, uncomfortable. The room's exhaustion sharpened. People didn't like watching power struggle. It felt like extra risk.

The suit-liaison lowered his voice as if offering her a favor. "We need to keep public confidence," he said. "If this reads like panic, we invite shutdown."

Naomi's mouth went dry. She tasted the metallic edge of her own fatigue again.

She pushed the paper toward herself, picked up her pen, and drew a single line through the vague sentence. Then she wrote her own, block letters, unpretty:

PROCEEDING WITH NARROW WEATHER BREAK. ELEVATED LIGHTNING RISK. SAFETY MARGIN REDUCED. DECISION RECORDED WITH WITNESSES.

The suit-liaison's eyes widened slightly. Anger flickered—quick, controlled. "That's not necessary," he said.

Naomi didn't look up. "It is," she replied.

She slid the paper toward Drew. "Counter-sign," she said.

Drew stared at the sheet, at Naomi's added language, at the suit-liaison's face. His pen hovered.

The suit-liaison leaned in, voice low enough to be almost intimate. "Andrew," he said, and the use of Drew's full name was a quiet threat.

Naomi's gaze snapped up. She watched the suit-liaison's mouth, the way the word Andrew landed like leverage.

She spoke before Drew could decide. "Drew," she said, and her tone stayed gentle. "If you won't witness this, find someone who will."

A chair creaked behind them. The guidance specialist stepped forward, eyes burning with exhaustion and a kind of fury that had nowhere else to go. "I'll sign," she said.

Drew exhaled and finally set his pen to paper. His hand shook once, then steadied. "I'll sign," he said, voice rough.

The suit-liaison's face hardened. He didn't stop them. He couldn't without making a scene that would turn the story into something he couldn't control.

Naomi heard the rain roar, heard thunder roll farther away, heard the trailer's thin walls rattle with wind.

She held her breath. Then she signed.

Her name curved across the paper, familiar and suddenly heavy.

Drew signed beneath hers. The guidance specialist signed as a witness. Naomi watched the pen strokes, the way each line dried slowly in humid air.

The suit-liaison stared at the sheet as if it had betrayed him. "Fine," he said. "You've made your point."

Naomi didn't reply. She didn't offer him an exit line. She kept her fingers on the paper until it stopped sliding on the damp tabletop.

Then she spoke the decision aloud, clear, controlled. "We proceed if the break opens," she said. "We proceed under narrow margin. We acknowledge elevated risk."

Her voice didn't shake. Her stomach did.

The room absorbed it. The engineer at the end of the table swallowed hard, eyes fixed on the paper as if looking away would make it more real.

The suit-liaison turned and walked out. His shoes squeaked on the wet floor. The door shut behind him with a soft, final sound.

The decision sat on the table like a body.

A young team member in the corner—someone Naomi had seen dozing upright earlier—made a small sound. Naomi turned.

The team member's hands shook around a paper cup of coffee. Coffee sloshed over the rim and dripped onto his wrist. He didn't react. His eyes were fixed on Naomi like he wanted her to take the whole thing back.

Naomi stepped toward him slowly, not crowding. "Hey," she said, voice lower.

He swallowed. "My sister lives in Corpus," he said, words coming out too fast. "They're saying the corridor—"

"They're saying a lot," Naomi replied, careful. Not dismissive. "What do you need right now?"

He blinked hard, throat bobbing. "I need to know you're not... guessing," he whispered.

Naomi didn't lie. She leaned in slightly so her words didn't travel. "We're not guessing," she said. "We're working with ranges. We're working with a plan that changes probability, not fate."

His face tightened. "That's not—"

"It's not enough," Naomi finished for him. She kept her voice soft. "I know."

His eyes stung. He looked down at his cup like it had offended him. "Then why—" he started.

Naomi didn't let him spiral. "Because the alternative is doing nothing," she said. "And doing nothing isn't neutral."

His shoulders sagged. He looked like he wanted to be angry at her. The anger couldn't find a place to land, so it turned inward.

Naomi reached out and steadied the cup with two fingers, just long enough to stop the shaking. She didn't hold his hand. She didn't perform comfort. She just gave his body a moment to stop betraying him.

"Go sit," she said. "Two minutes. Drink water. Then come back."

He opened his mouth as if to argue. Then he nodded once, ashamed, and moved toward a chair.

Naomi watched him sit. Watched his shoulders slump. Watched the way exhaustion made people small.

She turned back to the table.

The paper authorization sat there with her added language. Her signature dried slowly. Drew stared at it as if it might burn through the table.

Naomi gathered the sheets carefully and slipped them into a folder. Not because folders mattered. Because order was the only shape she could give the chaos.

At her workstation, she pulled out a set of printed pages she had been building for weeks, adding to them after every pivot, every pressure point, every half-hidden decision.

The cover sheet read: MAXIMUM-BURN CONTINGENCY — FINAL WEEK ONLY.

She had written the words herself. She had chosen them because they were honest. Not heroic. Not pretty. Honest.

She added tonight's signed authorization copy behind the cover. She clipped the pages into place, then stapled the cover sheet at the corner so it couldn't slide free. The staple clicked loud in the quiet trailer, a small metallic snap that felt like sealing something alive inside paper.

Her wrist ached from gripping the pen too long. She rubbed the sore spot and kept going.

She labeled the folder in block letters and wrote the date and time: T–120, 23:58.

Then she slid it into a hard case beneath her workstation—an ugly, scuffed case with a latch that stuck. She forced the latch shut until it clicked, then wrote on a strip of tape across the seam: DO NOT OPEN UNTIL FINAL WEEK — PARK.

She didn't trust digital storage. She didn't trust that power would hold. She didn't trust that a file would still be there when the world started shaking.

Paper survived power failures. Paper survived lies, at least long enough to be found.

Drew came up behind her, voice low. "You didn't have to rewrite the authorization," he said.

Naomi didn't turn. "Yes," she replied. "I did."

He swallowed. "They're going to hate you for that."

Naomi finally looked at him. His face was tight, pulled between loyalty and fear. "Let them," she said quietly. "I won't sign a clean story when the truth is dirty."

Drew stared at her for a long beat. Then he nodded once, like he'd accepted something he didn't want to accept.

Outside, the rain shifted, easing slightly, then surging again. Thunder rolled, fainter now.

The weather liaison called out from across the trailer. "Lightning cells drifting south," he said. "We might get the break."

Might. Naomi's stomach flipped. She forced her breath steady.

Drew moved back to the radio. "Ben," he said, pressing the talk button. "Break may open. Stand by."

Static. Then Ben's voice, immediate. "Standing by," he said.

Naomi didn't speak into the radio this time. She couldn't afford to pour anything personal into a channel that could be overheard. She watched Drew's hands, the way his fingers tightened on the radio edge.

The break came with no ceremony. A small shift in the weather printout. A line on the lightning probability chart dipping just enough to meet criteria.

Drew's voice sharpened. "Go," he said into the radio, and the word carried everything: pressure, fear, commitment.

Ben's voice came back, clipped. "Copy," he said. "Moving."

Naomi watched the monitors. Watched the sequence steps turn from plan to action. She didn't narrate it. She didn't allow herself to romanticize it. She just tracked the numbers, the times, the narrowness of the gap they were pushing through.

A chair creaked behind her as someone stood. Another person whispered a prayer under their breath—so quiet it sounded like a habit, not a plea.

Naomi's fingers found the pen in her pocket. She hadn't realized she'd put it there. She held it anyway, like a tool and a weapon, like something small that kept her anchored to what she could control: clarity.

Hours blurred. Not because time moved fast. Because fatigue smeared it.

When the immediate rush eased into waiting again—waiting for confirmation, waiting for the next update—Naomi stepped out of the trailer one last time.

The rain had softened to a steady fall. Floodlights buzzed overhead, their hum sharp against the wet night. The mud clung to her boots as if it wanted to keep her here.

She walked along the short walkway, breathing in damp air that tasted like metal and dirt. The thunder had drifted farther away, its rumble muted.

In the distance, the crowd near the fence had thinned. A few poncho-covered figures remained, stubborn silhouettes under floodlights, their voices swallowed by rain.

Naomi stopped under the small overhang by the trailer steps. She pulled the pen from her pocket and clicked the cap on and off once, twice—just to feel something definite.

Inside, her signature dried on paper in a scuffed case under her workstation. A decision sealed by witnesses. A story she refused to let anyone clean up for her.

The sky didn't applaud. The sky didn't care.

Naomi watched the rain streak through the floodlight halos and felt her own body steady, not with relief, but with acceptance that had edges sharp enough to cut.

Chapter 14 - I-10 Contraflow Mile

Pink bled over a line of brake lights that didn't move.

The sunrise should have made the city look forgiving. Instead it turned exhaust into a pastel fog, hanging low in the cool air like something that didn't want to lift. Sirens wailed somewhere beyond the hospital's loading zone, then dulled as the sound hit the wall of idling cars and stalled engines and too many bodies awake at the wrong hour.

Malik stood under a flickering floodlight and watched a nurse wrestle a wheelchair over a cracked seam in the pavement. The chair bumped, the patient's head lolled, then steadied with a shallow breath. Oxygen hissed with each pull, a small steady sound that felt like a promise and a threat at the same time.

"Careful," Malik called, and kept his voice level because the patients could hear everything even when their eyes looked unfocused.

The nurse—Tanya, her hair pinned tight under a cap that had seen too many shifts—shot him a look that held a whole argument in it. Don't tell me careful. Give me space. Give me time. Give me things that don't exist.

He stepped in anyway, hands on the chair's handles for two seconds, taking the weight long enough to lift the front wheels over the seam. The wheelchair rolled, the patient's blanket slipping, the toes of hospital socks peeking out.

A diesel bus rumbled at the curb, its door open like a mouth. Behind it, two ambulances waited with engines running, their lights off to keep the scene from turning into a beacon. It still was. People saw motion and came toward it the way thirst pulled them toward water.

A man in a wrinkled polo paced near the bus's open luggage compartment, eyes darting between Malik and the nurses and the street. He held a set of keys in his fist like it was the last thing that still belonged to him.

"Darryl," Malik called.

The driver stopped pacing, shoulders tightening. "You got more than we planned," Darryl replied. The words came out flat, defensive.

"We got who we got," Malik answered. He kept his gaze on Darryl's hands. Hands told the truth before mouths did.

Behind Malik, another nurse snapped a glove on, latex popping in the damp air. A family member—Malik didn't catch the name—whispered a prayer into a paper bag of belongings, then pressed the bag to their chest like it was a shield.

A security officer in a vest stood near the loading bay doors, trying to look like control in a world that had stopped believing in it. His eyes skimmed the crowd forming at the far edge of the lot—neighbors, strangers, people with backpacks and pillowcases, people with nothing but their hands. Some held printed notices that had been photocopied so many times the ink had bled into gray smudges. EVACUATION PRIORITY. MEDICAL TRANSPORT. CURFEW ENFORCEMENT.

Paper didn't stop hunger. Paper didn't stop panic. Paper just told you who had the pen.

Malik turned slightly, scanning for the one face his mind kept circling back to like it was trying to keep it from slipping away.

Darius stood near the second bus, half in shadow, hood up even in the humidity. Too young to hide behind a uniform, too old to be carried. He held a small duffel and watched the loading with the strained stillness of someone trying to be useful without taking up space.

Malik caught his eye and lifted two fingers, the smallest gesture. Stay where I can see you.

Darius nodded once.

Malik's chest loosened for the briefest moment.

Then a woman in scrubs pushed through the loading bay doors with a clipboard held tight to her chest. Sweat darkened the collar of her scrub top already.

"Carter," she called.

Malik turned. "Yeah."

"We're missing two portable tanks," she said, voice clipped. "If we move without them, she won't make it to the drop."

She didn't point. She didn't have to. Malik knew which patient she meant—Mrs. Alvarez, the one whose breathing had sounded like wet paper tearing when Malik first walked into her room.

"Find them," Malik replied.

The woman stared at him like he'd told her to find water in a burned house. "They were in the staging closet," she said.

"Then they aren't now," Malik answered. He kept his voice calm and hated that he was good at sounding calm when his stomach was turning. "Check the second ambulance. Check the floor by the ramp. Ask the aides."

The woman's eyes flicked toward the crowd swelling at the lot's edge. "And if someone took them?"

Malik didn't answer directly. Answers turned into permission. He leaned in instead, low enough that the waiting patients couldn't hear. "Don't leave without them," he said. "Not on my call."

She swallowed, jaw working. "Okay," she whispered, and shoved back through the doors.

A shout rose from the street—someone arguing with a traffic officer. A baby cried. A car horn blared, long and angry, then cut off with a sputter.

Malik checked his watch. Dawn wasn't fully up and they were already late.

He moved down the line, tapping shoulders, giving short instructions. No speeches. No reassurance that wouldn't hold. He counted bodies the way some people counted beads.

"One, two, three," he murmured under his breath as the first stretcher rolled up the ramp into the bus. The stretcher jolted at the threshold. The patient groaned, a sound that turned into a cough.

Tanya steadied the frame. "Easy," she murmured, not to Malik. To the patient. To herself.

Malik's radio crackled. "Carter," a voice said, strained. "Checkpoint on the ramp is already backing up. They're doing wrist checks."

Wrist checks. Malik felt the phrase land like a bruise. "Copy," he replied, and kept his voice even. "Hold them. We're rolling in five."

He clicked the radio off and looked at Darryl. "I need you ready."

Darryl's eyes darted again. "I'm ready," he said, too fast.

That speed in his answer told Malik what his mouth wouldn't.

"You sure?" Malik asked, and didn't soften the question.

Darryl's throat bobbed. "I'm here," he said. "Ain't I?"

Malik held his gaze. "You're here," he repeated, and let the words hang between them like a line pulled tight.

Darryl's shoulders sank a fraction. "Let's just go," he muttered.

Malik didn't press. Not yet. He pushed motion instead, because motion was the only thing that kept the crowd from breaking its own rules.

They rolled out as the sun rose higher, turning windshields into bright panes that threw light back into eyes already raw from sleeplessness. The lead bus lurched forward, tires crunching grit. Malik drove an SUV ahead of the convoy, his hands gripping the wheel until his knuckles ached.

On the way to the ramp, the city looked peeled open. Stores with metal shutters down. Gas stations with handwritten signs taped to the pumps: NO FUEL. NO CASH. A line of cars wrapped around a grocery store where the doors were still closed.

At the first intersection, a police officer waved them through with a rigid, practiced motion. His face stayed blank, as if his mind had already stepped away.

The on-ramp to I-10 contraflow looked like an artery clogged with debris—cones, barriers, a line of cars that had been rerouted into the wrong lane and were now stuck like insects in syrup. A temporary checkpoint sat under a canopy that flapped in the wind, the fabric snapping with each gust.

Two officers and a National Guard member stood at the entry point, their reflective vests bright against the dim morning. A table had been set up with stacks of paper, a stamp pad, and a handwritten sign: MEDICAL CONVOY — WAIT FOR CLEARANCE.

Malik pulled up, rolled his window down, and immediately tasted exhaust.

An officer leaned toward him. His eyes flicked to Malik's badge, then to the buses behind him. "You're on the list?" the officer asked.

Malik held up a printed authorization letter with the hospital letterhead. The edges were curled from humidity and being clenched too hard.

The officer took it, glanced at it like he was reading a bedtime story to a child who wouldn't sleep. "We're checking everyone," he said.

"Everyone," Malik repeated. He kept his tone neutral. "These are patients."

The officer's mouth tightened. "You want them safe, you let us do our job."

Malik watched the officer's hands. Slight tremor. Stains under the fingernails. A ring of dried coffee on the cuff. A man who had been awake too long and was clinging to procedure because procedure was the last thing that made him feel like a person.

"Do it fast," Malik replied.

The officer's eyes sharpened as if Malik had challenged him. "We're doing it as fast as we can," he snapped.

Behind the officer, the Guard member lifted a hand, palm down, the subtle gesture of calm it down. The officer exhaled through his nose, then waved Malik's SUV forward with a short, irritated flick.

"Keep your convoy tight," he said. "No gaps. If you lose a vehicle, you lose it."

Lose it. Like it was a glove. Like it was a pen.

Malik nodded once and drove forward, easing into the contraflow lane that had been carved out by barriers and cones. On the other side of the barrier, the eastbound lanes sat empty, eerie, like a street abandoned after a parade.

The westbound lanes—the ones they were using—were full of slow-moving fear. Cars jammed bumper to bumper. Brake lights flashed in ripples like distress signals. People leaned out of windows with arms waving, voices rising.

A few miles in, the convoy slowed to a crawl. Malik's radio squawked with voices overlaid, drivers talking at once.

"Carter, there's a truck sideways—"

"Someone's on foot in the lane—"

"I got people banging on the side—"

Malik swallowed the surge of anger that rose first, because anger was easier than fear.

"Stay in line," he said into the radio. "Windows up. Doors locked. No one opens anything unless I tell you."

Static. Then Darryl's voice, tight. "They're coming up," he said. "They see the hospital logo."

Malik's stomach dropped.

He edged his SUV toward the shoulder, craning his neck to see. Up ahead, a knot of people pressed against the side of the lead bus. Hands slapped metal. Someone pounded with a fist, the sound hollow and frantic.

A man stepped into the lane, arm outstretched. In his other hand, something flashed—gunmetal, caught for a second by the early sun. He didn't raise it. He didn't have to. The sight of it changed the air.

Malik hit his hazard lights and stopped, heart thudding. He grabbed his radio and spoke with deliberate steadiness. "No one exits," he said. "No one engages."

"Carter," Tanya's voice cut in from the bus behind him. She sounded like she was trying not to let patients hear her panic. "They're saying they need seats. They're crying."

"I know," Malik replied, and hated how small those words were. "Stay inside."

He climbed out anyway, because there were moments when the only thing that worked was a body in the right place.

The moment his boots hit the asphalt, heat rose through the soles, the road already warming under the sun. The air smelled of gasoline, sweat, and hot rubber. He walked toward the lead bus with his hands visible, palms out.

"Back up," he called, voice carrying without yelling.

Faces turned. Eyes wide, red-rimmed. A woman held a toddler on her hip, the child's cheeks streaked with dried tears. An older man clutched a backpack like it contained his heart.

"We're sick," someone shouted. "We got meds! We got a grandma!"

A younger man stepped closer, jaw tight, eyes flicking to Malik's badge. "They got buses," he said. "They got space."

"They don't," Malik replied, keeping his voice low. "These are hospital transports. Patients on oxygen. People who'll die if they get left on the road."

"People die anyway," the younger man shot back.

The words landed hard because they were true in a way Malik didn't want to accept.

A hand slammed the bus's side panel again, a sharp bang that made the patients inside flinch. Malik saw a face pressed against the window, eyes blank with medication and fear.

He stepped closer to the younger man with the gunmetal in his hand. Not too close. Close enough to be heard.

"You're not animals," Malik said, quiet. "You're people scared and hungry and stuck behind cones."

The younger man's mouth twitched, like he hadn't expected that line. His grip didn't loosen.

Malik tilted his head slightly. "You point that thing, you turn this into something you can't undo," he said. "You don't want that."

A woman sobbed, "We just want—"

"I know what you want," Malik cut in gently. "I want it too. But this bus is full. These patients can't stand, can't run, can't fight. If you take this, you take their breath."

A beat of silence. Not calm. Calculation. People weighing one life against another like they had been forced into a math problem with no right answer.

From behind Malik, an officer's whistle shrieked. Two patrol cars in the distance started edging forward, not fast, not heroic. Slow enough to keep the tension from snapping.

The younger man's eyes flicked toward the approaching patrol cars. His shoulders rose, then fell. He swallowed.

"Move," he muttered, and shoved backward into the crowd.

The crowd shifted reluctantly, peeling away from the bus in small steps, hands still reaching. The toddler on the woman's hip started screaming, thin and sharp.

Malik backed up toward his SUV, keeping his hands visible until he was inside and the door clicked shut. He exhaled hard, chest tight, and wiped his palms on his pants because they wouldn't stop sweating.

He grabbed the radio. "Roll," he said. "Slow. Don't stop again unless you have to."

The convoy crept forward, brake lights pulsing. Malik kept his eyes on the mirrors, on the buses, on the way the cars around them inched close like they might swallow them.

A mile later, under an overpass where shade trapped heat and made the air feel thick, the convoy stalled again. A disabled sedan sat at an angle, hazard lights blinking weakly. People had gotten out of their cars and were standing in the lane, arguing, gesturing, pointing at the buses as if they were treasure.

Malik pulled under the overpass and cut his engine to listen. The sudden quiet made his ears ring. Above them, traffic thundered in the opposite contraflow direction, a continuous roar like the road was angry.

He stepped out and walked toward Darryl's bus. Darryl had cracked his window half an inch, just enough to breathe.

Darryl's eyes met Malik's and darted away.

"Talk to me," Malik said.

Darryl's jaw worked. He glanced toward the back of the bus where patients lay strapped on stretchers, nurses hovering with hands poised over oxygen valves and pulse monitors that beeped in tired rhythms.

"Not here," Darryl muttered.

"This is exactly where," Malik replied, and kept his voice controlled. "Why are you looking like you want to disappear?"

Darryl's shoulders sagged. He reached down and pulled a folded sheet from the dash, then held it out through the crack in the window.

Malik took it.

The paper was crisp, too crisp, like it had been printed yesterday for a future someone had already paid for. In bold letters at the top: ROUTE ASSIGNMENT. Underneath, a list of destinations with codes and times.

Malik's eyes snagged on one header: PRIVATE CONTINUITY TRANSPORT — PRIORITY CLIENTS.

Below it were locations that weren't hospitals, weren't shelters, weren't county staging lots. They were vague, sanitized phrases: INLAND FACILITY A. SECURE SITE 3. CLIENT ASSEMBLY POINT.

Darryl's voice came through the crack, strained. "They handed those out this morning," he whispered.

"Who," Malik asked.

Darryl's eyes flicked toward the far end of the overpass where another bus sat—one Malik hadn't contracted, its windows tinted darker. A man in a clean polo stood near it with a laminated placard hanging from his neck, talking into a radio with a calm that didn't belong on this road.

"The company," Darryl said. "Dispatch. They called last night. Said contracts got... revised."

Revised. Malik felt his mouth go dry.

Darryl kept talking, words spilling now that the seal was broken. "They offered bonus pay," he said. "Cash. Up front. For people with... papers. For people who got their names on lists."

"Lists," Malik echoed, and his throat tightened.

Darryl's eyes glistened. "They said if I didn't take it, I'd lose my route. Lose my job. They got drivers waiting."

"And you still came," Malik said, not a question.

Darryl's eyes flashed with something like shame. "I got a sister on dialysis," he whispered. "I got a kid. I got—" His voice caught. "I told them I was already assigned. I told them hospital was non-negotiable."

"And they let you," Malik said.

Darryl swallowed. "They didn't," he admitted. "They reassigned half the fleet. Took 'em off public. Told 'em this was the new priority. I'm here because I didn't answer my phone fast enough."

The words hit Malik like a shove.

He stared down at the printed route sheet. The paper trembled slightly in his hands, not from wind. From something inside him trying to break through his calm.

The warning from months ago surfaced, sharp as a splinter: The rich will buy the drivers. Malik had heard it then like rumor. Now it was a folded sheet in his fist.

He stepped back from Darryl's window and looked down the contraflow lane. Between cars, he saw it—two SUVs gliding along the shoulder, hazard lights blinking in sync, moving through the jam like they had permission from the road itself. A security vehicle in front, another behind. On the dashboard of the lead SUV, a placard caught the light, white paper with bold letters: CONTINUITY.

The road wasn't just traffic. It was a sorting machine.

Malik's radio crackled. "Carter," a driver called. "We got fuel readings dropping. We're losing time."

Malik swallowed hard, the sour taste of stress rising in his throat. He turned toward the convoy, eyes scanning.

"How many drivers left," he asked Darryl, voice tight.

Darryl's eyes flicked toward the other buses. "You got three," he said. "You were supposed to have six."

Malik felt the panic rise like heat under his skin. Three drivers. Three buses. Too many patients.

He forced his breath steady. "Who else got a sheet," he asked.

Darryl hesitated, then nodded toward the second bus. "Reggie," he said. "He got one too. He didn't show it."

Malik's jaw clenched. He took two steps toward the second bus, then stopped because he could feel his own anger begging to take over.

Anger would burn minutes. Minutes were oxygen now.

He turned back to Darryl. "You did the right thing," Malik said.

Darryl's eyes darted, disbelieving. "I didn't," he whispered. "I—"

"You did," Malik repeated, and made it sound like a fact. "Get ready. We're not staying in this lane."

Darryl's brow furrowed. "Where we going? They got barriers."

Malik looked at the overpass supports, at the frontage road signs beyond the concrete columns. Industrial district. Warehouses. Service roads. Places that didn't show up on any evacuation pamphlet.

"We're going sideways," Malik said.

Darryl's eyes widened. "That's not the route."

Malik leaned closer to the cracked window, keeping his voice low. "The route got bought," he said. "We're taking what's left."

Darryl's throat bobbed. "That's dangerous."

Malik's gaze flicked toward the tinted bus and the calm man with the placard. "So is staying," he replied.

He stepped back and clicked his radio on. "All units," he said. "Listen."

Static hissed. Then voices. "Go ahead." "Yeah." "What now?"

Malik kept his tone even, the kind of even that made people obey because it sounded like certainty. "We're rerouting off contraflow at the next frontage split," he said. "Industrial streets. Stay tight. No one breaks formation. If you lose sight of my vehicle, you stop."

A beat. Then Reggie's voice—wary. "We're not authorized for side streets."

Malik stared at the concrete column like it had personally offended him. "Authorized doesn't keep patients breathing," he replied. "We move or we get boxed in behind private convoys and dead engines."

Silence. Then Tanya's voice. "Do it," she said. No hesitation. She'd seen enough. She didn't need permission.

Malik's chest tightened. "Copy," he said, and clicked off.

The maneuver wasn't clean. Nothing was clean anymore.

At the next split, Malik swung his SUV toward the frontage road gap where a temporary barrier had been left half-open for emergency vehicles. A tired officer stood there, waving cars through with a lazy hand, not looking at faces, just managing flow like he was moving cattle.

Malik slowed and leaned out his window. "Medical convoy," he called.

The officer's eyes flicked to Malik's badge, then to the buses. His hand paused mid-wave. "You're not supposed to—"

Malik held up the hospital letter again, edges frayed. "We're out of drivers," he said. "We're out of fuel. If we sit, people die."

The officer stared at him, jaw working. His gaze drifted toward the contraflow lane where the tinted bus sat, where the placard man stood calm as a stone. The officer's eyes tightened, something like recognition flashing.

Then the officer waved Malik through, sharp and quick, like he didn't want anyone to see.

Malik didn't thank him. Gratitude turned into debt. He just drove.

The convoy peeled off the main artery and into the industrial district where the city looked stripped down to metal and concrete. Shuttered warehouses lined the street, their loading docks empty. A chain-link fence rattled in the wind. Somewhere, a metal door banged rhythmically, not from human hands—just a loose latch, catching gusts like a mouth trying to speak.

Dust hung in shafts of sunlight between buildings. The tires crunched gravel. The buses creaked as they took tight turns, suspension groaning under the weight of stretchers and oxygen tanks and fear.

Inside the SUV, Malik's hands cramped on the steering wheel. Sweat slicked his palms despite the morning cool.

His radio crackled. "Carter," Tanya's voice said. "We're bouncing. Alvarez is desatting."

Malik's stomach clenched. "Slow down," he said into the radio. "Keep the tanks steady. Tell her to breathe with you."

A pause. Then Tanya again, voice low. "We're doing it," she replied.

Malik glanced in the mirror. The second bus followed close behind, its hospital logo bright against grime. Through the windshield glare, Malik caught a glimpse of Darius's hooded head in the front passenger area—still there.

He swallowed, relief fleeting.

A pickup truck appeared in the side mirror, dark and dusty, trailing them at a distance that wasn't accidental. It kept pace when Malik slowed. When Malik accelerated, it closed the gap.

Malik's throat tightened. "We got a shadow," he said into the radio. "Don't engage. Don't make eye contact."

Reggie's voice came back. "I see it," he said. "Two guys in the cab."

"Keep moving," Malik replied.

The pickup edged closer, then fell back, as if testing. Malik felt the dread settle into his bones, heavy and cold. In the industrial district, there were no patrol cars idling on the shoulder. No cameras. No crowd—just space where anything could happen without witnesses.

Malik's mind flicked through options like cards thrown on a table. He didn't have a weapon. He had three buses of vulnerable patients and a few staff who were already stretched past breaking.

He tightened his grip on the wheel until pain steadied him.

At the next intersection, a delivery truck sat abandoned, half on the curb, blocking one lane. Malik swore under his breath and swung wide, tires scraping over gravel. The first bus followed, its rear wheels bouncing hard. Malik winced at the imagined jolt to the stretchers inside.

The pickup behind them hesitated at the abandoned truck, slowed—then rolled around it.

It was persistent.

Malik's radio crackled again. "We're losing distance," Reggie said, breath tight.

Malik scanned ahead. A ramp back toward a controlled route. A checkpoint visible in the distance—cones, officers, a line of vehicles merging from multiple directions.

A choke point. A risk. Also the only way back to a corridor with any protection.

"We re-enter at the next ramp," Malik said. "Stay close."

They climbed the ramp in a slow grind, engines laboring. As they approached the checkpoint, the pickup truck peeled off into a side street and disappeared behind a warehouse, as if it had only wanted to shepherd them toward the merge.

Malik's stomach dropped. He didn't like that it let go so easily.

The checkpoint was chaos wrapped in fluorescent vests.

Multiple convoys converged—county buses, private vans, a line of cars with hand-written signs taped inside their windshields. Families. Pets. People with everything they owned piled to the roof.

Officers shouted directions that contradicted each other. A whistle shrieked. Sunlight bounced off windshields so hard Malik had to squint, eyes burning.

Malik rolled his window down and leaned out. "Medical convoy!" he shouted. "We need priority passage!"

An officer turned, face flushed, sweat darkening the fabric under his vest. His eyes skimmed the buses behind Malik. "You can't cut!" he yelled back.

"I'm not cutting," Malik shouted. "These are patients!"

The officer's jaw tightened. He waved his hand in a sharp, impatient motion—left, left, then suddenly right.

Malik's brain tried to process the signal. The lane split in two around a barrier. The buses were too long to correct quickly.

"Left!" Malik yelled into the radio. "Left lane!"

Static. Then Tanya's voice, sharp. "Copy!"

Malik swung his SUV left, forcing his way between cones that rattled as he brushed them. The first bus followed, tires squealing slightly. Malik glanced in the mirror.

The second bus—Reggie's—hesitated.

The exhausted officer's hand shot out again, this time pointing right. His mouth moved, but Malik couldn't hear over engines and horns. The officer's eyes fixed on Reggie's bus as if it had offended him by existing.

Reggie's bus turned right.

"NO!" Malik shouted. The word tore out of him raw.

He slammed his hand on the radio. "Reggie—stay left! Stay left!"

Static swallowed the first half of his words. Reggie's voice came back, strained. "He's directing me right—barrier—"

Malik's heart pounded so hard it made his vision throb. He stared at the barrier between the lanes—a thick concrete divider, not cones. No crossing. No reversing. Cars packed in tight behind.

The physics of bodies and machines made the decision for them.

Malik threw his SUV forward, trying to reach the end of the divider where it might open. It didn't. The divider stretched on, a long, indifferent wall.

He leaned out the window, shouting into the open air. "Reggie!"

Reggie's bus rolled farther right, sucked into a stream of vehicles being funneled toward a different checkpoint booth. The crowd noise swallowed the engine's rumble. For a moment Malik saw through Reggie's windshield—Tanya's replacement nurse gripping a seatback, mouth open in a silent yell.

And then Malik saw Darius.

Darius's hood was still up, but his face had turned toward Malik's lane, eyes wide, hands pressed against the glass as if he could push through it.

Malik's chest seized.

"Darius!" Malik screamed.

Darius's mouth moved. Malik couldn't hear the words. The bus lurched forward with the wrong current, and the glass reflection swallowed Darius's face.

Malik slammed his hand against the steering wheel hard enough that pain shot up his arm. "Stop!" he yelled into the radio. "Stop, Reggie—stop!"

Static. Then Reggie's voice, ragged. "I can't! Cars behind—barrier—"

Malik's throat tightened until his breath came shallow. He tried to turn his SUV right, to chase. A car horn blared, someone shouted, an officer stepped into his path and waved him back with a furious face.

"You keep moving!" the officer yelled. "You stop, you block the lane!"

Malik's mouth opened to argue, to plead, to threaten. None of it mattered. The lane behind him was packed, cars pressed close like teeth. The buses behind him carried patients whose oxygen tanks didn't care about grief.

Tanya's voice crackled through the radio, sharp with controlled panic. "Carter, Alvarez is dropping. We need air steady. We need movement."

The words hit Malik like a slap.

He gripped the wheel so hard his hands shook, then forced them still. He swallowed the urge to jump out and run—run where? Into barriers and cars and guns and rules.

He drove forward.

It felt like tearing something out of his own chest and leaving it on the asphalt.

They cleared the checkpoint, the left lane finally smoothing into a controlled corridor. The convoy was smaller now—one bus missing, one line broken.

Malik kept checking the mirror as if Reggie's bus might suddenly appear behind them like a miracle. It didn't.

He tried his phone at the next slow patch, thumb trembling as he unlocked it. No bars. A dead little icon. Silence.

He called anyway.

The call didn't go through. The phone stayed quiet in his hand like a stone.

The drop location inland was a repurposed community college parking lot, sun-baked by afternoon. Pop-up tents flapped in the wind. Volunteers in mismatched vests moved with the frantic efficiency of people who had learned to stop asking why.

When Malik finally pulled in, his legs trembled as he stepped out. The heat hit him like a shove, thick and relentless. Asphalt shimmered. The air smelled of hot rubber and sweat and antiseptic wipes.

Nurses spilled out of the bus, faces drawn tight, moving on muscle memory. Stretchers rolled down ramps. Oxygen tanks clinked. A patient reached out a weak hand and caught Malik's sleeve.

"Thank you," the patient rasped, voice thin as paper.

Malik nodded, unable to speak. He squeezed the patient's hand once—just enough to be human—then pulled away because staying in that moment would break him open.

Tanya came down the ramp, face slick with sweat, eyes sharp. "Alvarez stabilized," she said, voice hoarse.

Malik exhaled a breath he didn't realize he'd been holding. Relief tried to bloom. It died fast.

"Where's Reggie?" Tanya asked.

Malik stared past her shoulder at the empty space where the second bus should have been. The absence looked wrong, like a missing tooth you couldn't stop touching with your tongue.

"Separated," Malik managed. The word tasted like failure.

Tanya's eyes narrowed. "Darius was on that bus."

Malik flinched at the name coming from someone else's mouth. It made the loss more real.

He turned away from Tanya and walked fast toward a volunteer station where a woman with a clipboard was directing arrivals. Her hair was plastered to her forehead with sweat. She looked up as Malik approached, eyes already tired of being begged.

"Medical convoy," Malik said, forcing his voice into a usable shape. "We had two buses. One got diverted at the checkpoint. I need reunification intake. Now."

The woman's gaze flicked over him, weighing. "What's the bus number?" she asked.

Malik swallowed. He hadn't looked. He had looked at Darius's face, not the bus's identifier.

Tanya stepped up beside him, saving him without making a show of it. "Unit four-seven," she said. "County contract."

The woman wrote it down fast. "We got a staging lot for diverted vehicles," she said. "They're sending them in waves."

"Where," Malik pressed.

She hesitated. Her eyes slid toward a cluster of private vans parked near a different tent, their drivers standing with arms crossed, watching. A man in a polo walked between them, calm as if this was just a traffic problem.

The woman lowered her voice. "East campus overflow," she said. "If they make it."

If they make it. Malik's stomach clenched.

He stepped away from the volunteer station and moved behind the bus where the noise dulled slightly. He tried his phone again. Still nothing. He pressed the device to his ear anyway, as if warmth could turn silence into sound.

His throat tightened. He forced air in through his nose, out through his mouth, counting—one, two, three—because if he didn't count, he would start shouting and never stop.

Tanya appeared beside him, her presence steady. She didn't touch him. She didn't offer a soft line that would feel like pity. She just stood close enough that he wasn't alone.

"You did the right thing," she said, quiet.

Malik stared at the empty seat visible through the bus's front windshield—a seat that had been filled when they left. The seat looked harmless. Plastic. Fabric. An ordinary piece of furniture. Now it looked like a wound.

"I drove," Malik replied. His voice came out rough. "I drove away."

"You drove patients to oxygen," Tanya said. "You didn't abandon them."

Malik's jaw clenched. "And what about the kid who was with us," he whispered, and the words scraped his throat. "What about the one person I told myself I could keep in my line of sight."

Tanya's eyes didn't flinch. "The road doesn't care what you promised," she replied, not cruel, just honest.

Malik's hands shook once. He pressed his thumb into his palm until the tremor stopped.

Across the lot, a private van started up, engine purring. A driver climbed in, door shutting with a confident thud. The van rolled out past a cone line that no one else was allowed to cross. A guard lifted a hand and waved them through like they were royalty.

Malik watched it, heat rising behind his eyes.

A man in a polo—clean, calm—caught Malik's gaze from across the lot. The man's expression was polite, almost sympathetic. A smile offered like a bandage.

Malik looked away first, not because he was ashamed, but because he didn't trust what he might do if he held that gaze too long.

He turned back to his phone. No signal. Just a black mirror reflecting his face—tight jaw, sweat at the temple, eyes that looked older than they had ninety days ago.

He dialed again anyway.

Silence.

In the distance, highway noise rose and fell, constant, swallowing everything—sirens, cries, commands—until it all sounded like one long breath the world couldn't catch.

Malik stepped toward the lot's edge where he could see the road beyond. He lifted his head and shouted the name anyway, because names were anchors even when no one answered.

"Darius!"

The sound went out into heat and engine roar and came back to him as nothing.

He lowered his phone slowly. The screen stayed dark. His hand stayed closed around it like he could squeeze a signal into existence.

Behind him, the bus doors hissed shut. Patients were inside a tent now, being triaged by overworked volunteers. They were alive.

A victory measured in breaths.

Malik stared at the empty seat again, the one that shouldn't have been empty, and felt the highway swallow his shouted name as if it had never existed at all.

Chapter 15 - Don't Take the Bridge

Hot metal sat in the air near the ship channel, the kind of smell that clung to the back of Darius's throat. The sun leaned low and mean, throwing light off guardrails and the roofs of stopped cars until everything looked like it had been plated in heat.

Grit worked into his sneakers with every step. His ankle kept time like a heartbeat that didn't belong there—throb, throb, throb—each pulse sharper when he tried to pretend he could walk normal.

He didn't let Manuel see the worst of it.

Manuel walked half a step ahead, not dragging him, not leaving him. Manuel kept checking the road the way people checked skies when storms came—eyes scanning, chin lifting, shoulders tight under a shirt that had gone dark with sweat along the spine. He carried a grocery bag looped around his wrist. The bag looked light, but Manuel held it like it mattered.

"Reunification point closes at curfew," Manuel said without looking back.

Darius nodded like that line didn't squeeze him.

"Give me two minutes," Darius said.

"You already took two minutes," Manuel answered, voice quiet.

Darius swallowed. "I mean—two more."

Manuel finally glanced at him. Not at his face first. At his feet.

Darius planted his bad foot harder than he should have. Pain shot up his leg and made his vision spark for a second. He didn't make a sound. He lifted his chin and kept going, jaw set like it could hold his bones together.

Manuel didn't call him out. That was what hurt the most—how Manuel let him have his lie without making him feel small.

Traffic sat thick on the frontage road. A line of cars crept forward in fits, then stopped. People stood outside their vehicles, arms folded, faces shiny with sweat. Someone pushed a stroller with a blanket thrown over it to keep the sun off. A dog barked from the backseat of a sedan, frantic and hoarse.

Darius tried not to look at the bridge yet. He could see it anyway. The ship channel crossing rose ahead like a spine. The obvious way through. The way everyone stared at because the human brain loved straight lines.

Manuel slowed when they reached a cluster of people near a chain-link fence. A handwritten sign hung from the fence with zip ties: CHECKPOINT AHEAD. HAVE PAPERS READY.

Darius's mouth went dry.

He wanted Malik. He wanted Malik's hands, Malik's voice that sounded calm even when everything shook. Malik would know what to say, how to hold his shoulders so no one read fear on him.

Malik wasn't here.

Manuel tapped Darius's elbow once. "Eyes up," he said, like it was a lesson and not a plea.

Darius forced his gaze forward.

The first checkpoint sat under a canopy stretched between two orange barricades. Two patrol vehicles idled nearby, lights off. The air hummed with engine heat. Boots crunched gravel. A radio murmured somewhere, the words too distorted to catch.

A tired patrol officer stood at the front of the line with a flashlight in one hand even though the sun still held the sky. He kept shining it at people's wrists, faces, bags. He didn't smile. He didn't threaten, either. He just looked like someone who had stopped believing his job could fix anything.

Manuel angled them toward the end of the line, keeping them behind a woman holding a toddler whose head lolled against her shoulder.

The officer lifted his chin. "Next."

The woman stepped forward. The toddler made a small sound, more breath than cry. The officer's flashlight skimmed the child's wrist, then the woman's face.

"Where you headed," the officer asked.

"Reunification," the woman said fast. "My husband's at the gym. I got the—" She fumbled for a folded paper in her pocket.

The officer waited, eyes flat.

The paper came out damp from sweat. The officer glanced, then waved them through without a word.

The woman hurried past like she'd been let out of a cage.

Manuel stepped up.

Darius stayed close enough to feel Manuel's heat.

The officer's flashlight hit Manuel's wrist, then jumped to Darius's.

His beam lingered.

Darius tried to keep his hand steady. He tried to keep his face blank. His ankle pulsed like it wanted to betray him.

The officer's eyes narrowed. "This one yours," he asked Manuel.

Manuel didn't flinch at the word.

"He's with me," Manuel said. Not defensive. Not begging. Just a statement, the way Malik would have said it.

The officer's flashlight moved to Darius's face. The light made everything harsh—sweat on his upper lip, dust along his jaw, the tightness around his eyes.

"How old," the officer asked.

Darius's throat tightened. He hated the question because it turned him into paperwork. A problem. A category.

Manuel answered before Darius could. "He's under my care," Manuel said.

The officer's jaw shifted. "That ain't an age."

Darius felt heat crawl up his neck. He wanted to spit something sharp. He wanted to say he wasn't a baby. He wanted to say his ankle hurt and he didn't have time for this.

He said nothing.

Manuel reached into his pocket and pulled out a folded slip of paper. It looked like it had been opened and closed too many times. The edges were soft, almost shredded.

The officer took it. Read. His eyes flicked once, quick, to Darius's ankle.

Darius hated that the officer noticed.

The officer handed the slip back. "Minors get processed at Station C," he said, already turning his head toward the next person. "You go there, you get your stamp."

Station C. The letter felt like a sentence.

Manuel's shoulders went stiff for a second. "Station C's across the bridge," he said, voice still respectful.

The officer shrugged with one shoulder like the bridge didn't belong to him. "Then you better move," he said. "Curfew in two hours. They start pulling kids after dark."

Pulling kids.

The words hit Darius in the chest. He imagined hands on his arms. A bus door shutting. Manuel's face behind glass.

"No," came out of Darius's mouth before he could stop it.

The officer looked at him like Darius had barked.

Manuel's hand settled on Darius's shoulder, light, quick. "We understand," Manuel said. Then, quieter, to Darius, "Not here."

Humiliation burned hot in Darius's stomach. He pressed his lips together until they hurt.

They stepped away from the checkpoint without being stopped, but Darius felt like he'd been marked anyway.

They moved down the frontage road, away from the canopy, away from the officer's flashlight. The sun slid lower, throwing long shadows from power poles and signage that no longer meant safety. The heat didn't drop. It just changed shape.

Darius tried to walk faster, like speed could erase what the officer had said.

Manuel didn't let him.

They ducked behind a concrete barrier where an abandoned billboard cast shade. Manuel knelt, eye level with Darius, and spoke like he was negotiating with something that could explode.

"Station C means separating you," Manuel said softly.

Darius stared at the road. He stared at the bridge. He stared at the cars that kept inching forward like they were being pulled by a rope.

"We gotta get to Malik," Darius said. His voice cracked on Malik's name. He hated that too.

"We gotta get to a reunification table," Manuel corrected, still gentle. "Malik will be there if he can be."

Darius didn't answer, because he didn't want to hear if Malik couldn't be.

Manuel stood. He reached into his bag and handed Darius a half-crushed granola bar. "Eat," he said.

Darius took it because his hands needed something to do. The bar tasted like cardboard and sugar. He chewed anyway, jaw working hard.

"I'm fine," Darius muttered around the bite.

Manuel's eyes went to Darius's ankle again. "You're stubborn," he said.

Darius tried to make it a joke. "You just noticed?"

Manuel's mouth twitched, almost a smile, but it didn't land. "Don't waste your jokes," Manuel said. "Save them for when they matter."

Darius swallowed the rest of the granola bar and wiped his palm on his shorts. His shirt stuck to his back. Sweat ran down his side and stung where fabric rubbed.

They moved again, detouring away from the main road. Manuel chose a narrower street lined with warehouses and chain-link fences topped with coiled wire. The air smelled like oil and sun-baked rubber.

A street sign hung crooked, as if someone had tried to rip it down. Darius stared at the empty bolt holes. He filed it away without meaning to. Little things changed when people got desperate. The city became something you couldn't trust by memory.

His ankle rolled slightly on uneven pavement. Pain flared bright. Darius bit the inside of his cheek hard enough to taste blood.

Manuel glanced back.

Darius widened his eyes like nothing happened.

Manuel didn't argue. He just slowed his pace to match Darius's.

That kindness made Darius want to scream.

They passed a convenience store with boarded windows. Someone had spray-painted NO MORE inside the plywood, letters thick and shaking. Darius didn't know if it meant no more food, no more gas, no more mercy.

Probably all of it.

As they approached the bridge area from the side, the noise thickened. Not traffic noise. People noise. Shouts, arguments, crying. A low roar like a crowd at a game, except there was no cheering in it.

Manuel stopped at the corner of a warehouse and leaned forward to look.

Darius stepped beside him, careful of his ankle, and peered around.

The bridge choke point sat ahead, a wide stretch of road funneled into narrow lanes by concrete dividers and metal barricades. A private security line had been set up near the entrance—men in dark uniforms, helmets, rifles slung across chests. They stood in a staggered row like they'd practiced it.

Behind the line, vehicles moved through. Not everyone's vehicles. The ones with placards in their windshields, white boards with bold letters that didn't care about shame.

On the near side of the line, people pressed forward, waving papers, raising hands, shouting names. A man lifted a small child onto his shoulders so the child could breathe above the crush. A woman held a grocery bag over her head like it was a flag.

Darius felt his stomach tighten.

"We can't go through that," Manuel said, voice low.

Darius swallowed. "We have to cross," he whispered.

Manuel's eyes stayed on the security line. "We don't take the obvious path," he said.

Darius stared. "Then what—"

A scream cut through the air.

Someone near the barricade shoved forward. The crowd surged as if pulled by the shove. The private security line stiffened, rifles coming up, not aimed at heads but aimed. The movement alone changed everything.

Darius felt his body go cold.

A security guard shouted something Darius couldn't make out. The crowd shouted back, louder.

Then a sharp crack split the air.

Darius's brain took a beat to understand it wasn't a car backfiring.

Another crack followed, and another.

Muzzle flash lit briefly at the end of a rifle, bright even in the evening light. The sound bounced off concrete and metal, making it feel like the whole bridge was snapping.

People screamed and dropped, not all hit, some just folding in fear. A woman stumbled backward, hands up, mouth open in a sound Darius couldn't hear anymore because his ears rang.

A bullet struck something metal and sent a spark. The spark flew and died.

Darius's legs moved before his brain did.

Manuel grabbed the back of his shirt and yanked him hard into the shadow of the warehouse.

Darius's ankle screamed as he stumbled. He nearly went down. Manuel caught him under the arm and shoved him farther back, out of sight.

"Run," Manuel said, voice harsh now, not gentle. "Move."

Darius tried. His ankle didn't cooperate. He stumbled, then forced weight on it anyway. Pain blasted up his leg, hot and white.

He didn't scream. He couldn't spare the air.

They cut down an alley between warehouses, the ground uneven with scattered gravel and broken glass. Darius's sneakers slipped once. Manuel shoved him forward, the pressure urgent.

Behind them, the cracks continued—fewer now, spaced out. Not a barrage. Just enough to keep people back. Just enough to prove a point.

Adults would shoot to protect access.

Darius's mouth went dry. He tasted dust and something else—fear so sharp it felt metallic.

They reached the far end of the alley and ducked behind a fence line where weeds had grown tall. Manuel crouched, pulling Darius down with him.

Darius's chest heaved. He pressed a hand over his mouth to keep any sound inside.

Manuel's breathing came tight, controlled. He looked past the fence at the bridge area like he wanted to burn the sight into memory and then erase it.

Darius's ankle throbbed violently. He pressed his palm against it like pressure could make it stop.

Manuel didn't ask if he was hurt. Manuel already knew.

They stayed crouched until the screaming dulled into a distant roar and the cracks stopped.

When Manuel finally moved, he didn't move toward the bridge. He moved away.

Warehouse rows stretched ahead, long blocks of metal doors and loading docks and dark gaps between buildings. The sun dipped lower, turning puddles in potholes orange. Shadows spilled across the street like something alive.

Manuel kept a hand on Darius's shoulder as they moved, guiding him without dragging.

Darius's anger rose, sudden and fierce.

At the bridge, Darius had been small. Something to be processed. Something to be pulled after dark.

Here, in the warehouses, no one cared what station letter he belonged to. That didn't make it safer. It just made it different.

They crossed a side street where abandoned pallets lay scattered like bones. Darius noticed a fresh tire track in the dust—deep, heavy, not from a normal car. He pointed without thinking.

Manuel followed his gesture, eyes narrowing. "Good catch," he murmured.

Darius's throat tightened. He didn't know why the praise hit him so hard. He wanted to be useful. He wanted to be more than a burden with a bad ankle.

They reached a corner where a chain-link fence had been cut and bent back. The opening looked recent. The wire ends gleamed bright, not rusted yet.

Manuel stopped. He leaned in, listened.

Darius listened too. All he heard at first was distant traffic and the low rumble of engines somewhere nearby.

Then he heard it—the heavier sound. Diesel. Multiple vehicles. Slow, steady, controlled.

Manuel pulled Darius back into shadow.

They crouched near a loading dock, tucked behind a stack of empty plastic crates. Darius's ankle throbbed so hard it made him dizzy, but he didn't move.

Headlights swept across a warehouse wall, bright and white. The light slid, then paused, then slid again.

A convoy rolled into view on the side street—SUVs and a box truck, all moving too clean for the chaos around them. Two security vehicles bracketed the line, one in front, one behind. Men in dark uniforms sat inside, heads forward, hands near radios.

On the side of the box truck, a stencil stood out in stark black: KLINE — UNIT 6B-17.

Darius's heart hammered. He stared so hard his eyes burned.

"Read it," Manuel whispered.

Darius's mouth opened. The words came out dry. "Kline," he breathed. "Unit... six... B... seventeen."

Manuel's fingers tightened lightly on Darius's shoulder. "Say it again."

"Kline—Unit 6B-17," Darius whispered.

The convoy slowed near the warehouse corner. One SUV had a windshield placard too—white board, block letters: CONTINUITY ACCESS.

A security guard stepped out of the lead vehicle and spoke to someone out of view. His posture stayed relaxed, as if he wasn't surrounded by a city ready to break.

The box truck's engine idled, steady. Diesel smell drifted toward Darius, thick and nauseating.

Manuel leaned closer to Darius's ear. "Keep it," he said. "Keep it in your mouth."

Darius swallowed. His tongue stuck to the roof of his mouth. He whispered the identifier again, softer, making it rhythm so it wouldn't slip.

"Kline—Unit 6B-17," he mouthed, over and over.

The convoy moved again, turning down another side street that led away from the bridge and toward whatever secure place waited inland. Their tires didn't hesitate over potholes. Their path had been cleared. Their path had been decided.

Darius watched until the last taillight vanished into warehouse shadow.

A rotor thumped overhead, distant but heavy. The sound made the air feel pressed down.

Manuel exhaled slowly. "We go," he said.

Darius tried to stand. His ankle buckled. Pain shot through him so fast his eyes watered.

He bit down hard, refusing to make the sound that wanted to come out.

Manuel's hand steadied him. "Don't lie to me," Manuel said, voice tight now.

Darius forced his voice. "I can walk," he said.

Manuel stared at him. Not angry. Not soft. Just tired.

"You can," Manuel said. "And we will. But you tell me when you can't."

Darius nodded, jaw trembling once, then steadying.

They moved deeper into the warehouse rows as night crept in. The city noise faded until all Darius could hear was their shoes on pavement, the distant hum of engines, and the rotor thump sliding away into smoky air.

They found a narrow gap between two warehouses where a fence line created a pocket of shadow. Manuel guided Darius down, and Darius sank onto cold concrete with a shaky breath.

The concrete chilled through his shorts. It felt good in a way he didn't want to admit.

Manuel sat beside him, close enough to block wind, far enough to keep Darius space. Manuel's breathing stayed careful, measured, like he was rationing it.

Somewhere in the distance, a siren rose and fell.

Darius closed his eyes for a second. When he opened them, warehouse shadows stretched long across the ground, reaching like hands.

He whispered the identifier again, barely moving his lips.

"Kline—Unit 6B-17."

Manuel nodded once in the dark. "One more," he said.

Darius obeyed.

"Kline—Unit 6B-17."

The numbers and letters sat in his mouth like something he couldn't swallow yet. He held them anyway, repeating them under his breath until they turned into a rhythm that kept his fear from taking over.

Above the warehouses, the rotor thump drifted, distant and indifferent, while Darius kept the string of characters alive like a song he refused to lose.

Chapter 16 - Hand-Crank Radio Hour

The basement air stuck to Lila's skin like wet cloth. Concrete held the day's heat and gave it back in a slow sweat, mixing with candle smoke, diaper funk, damp shoes, and the sour edge of coffee that had been warmed too many times on a camp stove.

Somebody turned the hand-crank radio on the folding table and the speaker squealed—high, thin, painful—before settling into a hiss of static. Heads lifted across the room the way animals looked up when a branch snapped.

Lila stood with her back against a pillar wrapped in chipped paint and paper notices. Her shoulders ached from holding herself small all day. She'd learned how to do it without looking like she was doing it. Blend. Breathe. Count exits. Don't move like a person with something to lose, even when the truth sat against her ribs like a bruise.

A baby cried behind a sheet someone had pinned as a curtain. A man near the stairs muttered a prayer that sounded more like bargaining. Two teenagers played a silent game with bottle caps, their hands quick, eyes too tired.

Lila scanned faces, not for comfort, for angles.

Malik. She hadn't met him. She only had the description people gave when they were trying to be helpful and ended up making a person into a rumor: tall, deliberate, moves like he's always late even when he's early. FEMA, or close enough that people said it like it meant "rescue." A name that, lately, traveled faster than supplies.

Manuel.

The room held too many bodies for her to check every corner without drawing attention. A few times she caught someone watching her like they'd recognized her from the piece she'd published months ago. The look wasn't admiration. It was accounting.

Lila slid along the pillar toward the volunteer table where handwritten notices had been taped up in crooked lines. The paper was wrinkled from humidity. Pencil marks smeared where hands had rubbed past. A small battery lantern on the table lit everything from below and made faces look hollow.

A woman with a lanyard stood behind the table, her hair pulled tight. She had the posture of someone who'd been put in charge without being given power. She looked up as Lila approached, eyes narrowing.

"We're not taking new intakes," the woman said.

"I'm not asking for a cot," Lila replied. She kept her voice low, steady. "I'm asking what's true."

The woman's expression twitched. "Everything's changing."

"That's why I'm asking." Lila leaned in, as if she was only another worried person. "Who's running the runner board tonight?"

The woman pointed with her chin at the far wall where a piece of plywood had been propped on two chairs. Papers were pinned there with thumbtacks, some already ripped down. People hovered in front of it like it was a shrine.

"Ask Pastor," the woman said. "Or ask—" Her gaze slid past Lila, toward the stairwell. "Ask the one with the radio."

Lila followed the line of her gaze.

The hand-crank radio sat on the table in the corner, surrounded by a loose half-circle of people leaning in. An older man with silver hair and a face worn smooth by years of not being surprised stood over it with both hands on the casing, as if he could steady the signal by touch.

The woman with the lanyard watched Lila too closely. Lila didn't like it.

"Who are you," the woman asked, too casual.

Lila let the question hang. The gap was a weapon. If she answered fast, she'd sound guilty. If she answered slow, she'd sound rehearsed.

"Someone who's tired of people getting hurt over bad directions," Lila said.

The woman's lips pressed thin. "You one of the press."

Not a question.

A few heads nearby turned. The room's noise softened for a beat, the way a crowd shifted when it sensed blood.

Lila kept her face still. She could feel her pulse in her throat, but she didn't let it reach her mouth.

"I'm someone with a pen," she said. "That's all."

"That's enough," a man at the edge of the table snapped. His voice was hoarse from talking too much, shouting too much, begging too much. "Y'all put words out and then we pay."

Lila didn't flinch. She made herself look at him like he was a person, not a threat.

"What's your name," she asked.

He blinked, thrown. "Does it matter?"

"It does if I'm going to repeat anything you say," Lila answered.

That landed. Not trust—never that. Something else. The shock of being treated like a source instead of a casualty.

The woman with the lanyard leaned closer. "We can't have you stirring anything up," she said, voice tight. "People already tried to rush a gate last night because of a rumor. Someone got trampled."

Lila's stomach tightened. She hadn't been here last night. She'd been somewhere else, listening to a different kind of scream.

"Where," Lila asked.

"Not here," the woman said, cutting her off. "Listen. If you're going to help, you help us keep them calm."

Lila nodded once. "That's what I'm doing."

The woman didn't believe her. She didn't have to.

Lila turned toward the notice board. She read fast—too fast, her brain hungry, trying to make order out of scraps.

CURFEW 8PM. NO EXCEPTIONS.

REUNIFICATION TABLE MOVED TO GYM (DOOR 3).

BUSES TO AUSTIN CANCELLED.

SHUTTLE PICKUP—PRIVATE—ASK AT DESK.

The last one made her eyes stop.

Private.

Ask at desk.

That sounded like a whisper disguised as a notice. Like a password dressed in pencil.

Lila looked back at the table. The woman's hand rested on a small stack of index cards. Names. Addresses. Something.

The woman caught Lila looking and shifted her arm, blocking the view.

Lila's jaw tightened. She swallowed it down.

If she confronted her, the room would become a stage. If the room became a stage, people would pick sides. If people picked sides, someone would bleed.

Truth could be a match. Lila had lit matches before. She'd told herself it was necessary.

Now she could hear the kindling breathe.

She moved away from the table, weaving between cots and blankets and exhausted bodies. A teenage boy lay on his back on a yoga mat, staring at the ceiling. A woman in scrubs sat with her head in her hands, forearms marked with faint bruises. Someone's phone screen flashed once, died, flashed again, then died for good.

Near the radio corner, the older man turned the crank with slow, practiced turns. The handle squeaked, a dry sound that somehow made the room feel quieter. Static hissed. Then a voice cut through, warped and thin, the kind of voice that had been recorded and re-recorded until it sounded like it belonged to nobody.

"...remain indoors...do not attempt bridge crossings...repeat, do not attempt—"

A ripple moved through the listeners. Someone gasped. Someone laughed, sharp and joyless, like the idea of "indoors" was a luxury.

The older man lifted a hand. "Quiet," he said.

His voice wasn't loud. It carried anyway.

Lila stepped into the edge of the circle. She kept her hands visible. She didn't push.

The older man glanced at her, eyes quick. He took her in in one sweep: dusty shoes, hair pulled back, the tightness around her mouth that came from deciding too much too fast for too long.

"You got something," he said, not a question.

"I've got ears," Lila replied. "And I don't trust what comes out of that speaker unless it matches what people on the ground are seeing."

That got a few looks. Annoyed looks. Curious looks. A woman with a toddler on her hip shifted her weight and watched Lila like she might either help or ruin them.

The older man's mouth twitched. "Good," he said. "I'm Raj. You?"

Lila hesitated. Names were handles. Names could be grabbed.

Someone behind her said it for her.

"That's Lila Reyes," a voice called out, too loud.

The circle tightened instantly. A few people leaned in. A few leaned back. The toddler's mother stiffened.

Lila turned.

A young woman stood near a column, arms folded. She had a shelter blanket draped over her shoulders like armor. Her eyes were bright with something that looked like hunger.

"You're the one who said they had seats," the young woman said.

Lila's stomach sank.

"I didn't say that," Lila replied.

"You wrote about it," the young woman pressed, voice rising. "You wrote and then everybody started moving. My cousin got stopped on the highway because of people moving. You did that."

It wasn't logic. It was pain looking for a face.

Lila let it land without flinching. She kept her voice low on purpose, forcing the room to lean in if it wanted to hear her. Volume was a weapon. She didn't want it.

"I wrote what I could defend," Lila said. "And I don't write routes."

"People died," the young woman shot back.

Raj's hand hovered over the radio like he was about to turn it off to stop the conversation.

Lila shook her head once, subtle. Not yet.

She looked at the young woman and let her own silence answer first. Let the gap do work.

"I'm not asking you to forgive me," Lila said. "I'm asking you to help me keep the next rumor from killing someone in this room."

A man in the circle scoffed. "Rumor already killed someone," he muttered.

Lila glanced at him. "Then let's stop feeding it."

The young woman's eyes narrowed. "How," she demanded. "They tell us stay indoors, but they close shelters. They tell us go to reunification, but they move it. They tell us bridges are safe, and then—"

Her voice cracked. She pressed her lips together and looked away like she hated that her body did that in public.

Lila held herself still. She could feel the room's attention on her like hands.

"By verifying like we're all we've got," Lila said.

Raj tilted his head. "That's what I've been saying," he murmured.

Lila nodded toward the volunteer table without pointing. "Someone has a notice about a private shuttle pickup," she said. "Does anybody here know where that came from?"

A few people exchanged looks. A woman in scrubs shook her head fast.

A teen boy said, "My uncle said if you got cash you can get on a van."

"Where," Lila asked, immediately.

The teen boy shrugged. "He heard it from a guy who heard it from—"

"Stop," Lila said, gentle but firm. "That's how people get crushed."

The teen boy's cheeks flushed. He looked down.

Lila softened her eyes. "It's not your fault," she said. "It's what your brain does when you're scared. It grabs any rope. But we don't pull ropes we can't see."

A breath moved through the circle. Some people eased. Some didn't.

Raj cranked again. The speaker hissed and popped. Then another voice came through, this one closer, like it had been recorded in a small room:

"...checkpoints will tighten at dusk...minors without a guardian will be processed separately...repeat..."

The young woman's face went gray.

Lila's throat tightened. She pictured Darius's face without meaning to. A boy with too much sharpness in his eyes. A boy who would hate being called a problem.

She forced her mind back into the basement.

"Who here saw a checkpoint today," Lila asked.

Hands rose. Not many. People were afraid to speak, afraid of being responsible for someone else's movement.

A truck driver in a stained cap said, "They're pulling folks off if they don't like your story."

"A nurse said Station C was taking minors," someone else added.

"Station C's across the bridge," the scrubs woman whispered.

The word bridge moved through the circle like a shadow.

Lila remembered the sound from two weeks ago when she'd driven past an overpass and heard distant cracks—too sharp to be fireworks, too spaced to be a celebration. She remembered ducking without thinking.

She didn't say it out loud. She didn't need to. The room already carried enough ghosts.

Raj looked at her. "You want to talk," he said softly.

Lila glanced toward the volunteer table again. The woman with the lanyard watched the radio circle like it was a threat to her authority.

Lila understood something then, clear and cold.

Control in a shelter was currency. Whoever spoke, whoever pinned the notices, whoever decided which messages got carried, that person held power people would trade anything for.

Including silence.

Lila stepped closer to the radio. She didn't touch it. She didn't claim it. She just positioned herself where her voice would reach without being shouted.

"I'm going to say one thing," Lila told the circle. "And then I'm going to shut up."

Someone laughed once, skeptical.

Lila ignored it. She kept her gaze on the scrubs woman, on the teen boy, on the young woman with the bright eyes.

"Do not go toward any bridge because someone says they have transport," Lila said. "If you have a reunification notice, bring it to this table, and we'll verify it with someone who's been there today—driver, nurse, pastor, runner. We don't move as a herd. We move as a line."

A murmur rose. Disappointment and relief tangled together. People wanted a miracle. She was offering a system.

The young woman's mouth tightened. "You don't get to tell us how to move," she snapped.

Lila met her gaze. "You're right," she said. "I don't."

The young woman blinked, thrown by the agreement.

"I'm not your boss," Lila continued. "I'm not your savior. I'm a person who learned—too late—that words can shove bodies. I'm trying not to shove you."

That landed. Not like comfort. Like gravity.

The room didn't calm. It listened.

The woman with the lanyard pushed through the circle then, face tight. "You can't do announcements," she said. "We have a process."

"What process," Raj asked, mild.

The lanyard woman's eyes snapped to him. "Don't start," she said.

Raj's brows lifted. "I'm old," he said. "Starting is all I've got left."

A few people let out a small breath that might have been a laugh. The tension shifted, angled away from Lila for a moment.

The lanyard woman pointed at Lila. "If you're press, you need to leave," she said.

Lila didn't move. She kept her tone polite. "On whose authority," she asked.

The lanyard woman's mouth opened, shut. She didn't have an answer that wasn't a confession.

A man near the stairs spoke up, voice worn. "She stays," he said. "We need someone who knows how to check."

The lanyard woman's face tightened. She looked at the room and realized it wasn't hers in the way she'd been pretending.

She swallowed her anger and forced a smile that didn't reach her eyes. "Fine," she said. "But if anything happens—"

"It will," Lila interrupted softly.

The lanyard woman stiffened.

"It will happen whether I speak or not," Lila continued. "The difference is whether it happens blind."

The lanyard woman stared at her for a long beat, then turned and walked back to the table, shoulders rigid.

Raj leaned toward Lila. "You make enemies fast," he murmured.

"I make them when I'm quiet too," Lila replied.

Raj's mouth twitched again. "Fair."

Lila's gaze drifted toward the stairwell. A draft slid down from upstairs, carrying a faint smell of rain and exhaust. Somewhere beyond the church walls, a siren rose and fell, the sound thin, distant, exhausted.

She still hadn't seen Manuel.

She forced herself to move. Staying in one spot meant being pinned.

She crossed to the runner board. Papers fluttered slightly when someone brushed past. A young boy with a pencil behind his ear stood on tiptoe, reading a note. His fingers trembled.

"What you looking for," Lila asked him.

He startled, then saw her face and froze. "My mom," he whispered. "They said she was at the clinic. But the clinic—" His voice broke.

Lila's chest tightened. She crouched so she was level with him. "What's her name," she asked.

He told her. Lila repeated it once, slowly, to lock it.

She scanned the pinned slips and the scribbles people had added along the edges. Names. Door numbers. "Saw him headed west." "She's with the pastor." "Don't go to the bridge."

Her eyes caught a familiar handwriting on a torn piece of notebook paper, the letters tight, slanted.

Lila's breath hitched.

Manuel. He didn't sign his name. He didn't have to. She knew his hand the way you knew the shape of someone's worry.

The note was short: BACK AFTER DARK. STAY LOW. —M

Her fingers pressed to the paper as if touch could pull him out of whatever street he'd been walking.

The boy beside her watched her face. "You found yours," he said.

Lila swallowed. "Not yet," she replied.

She stood and moved toward the stairwell, heart tight. If Manuel wrote he'd be back after dark, he wasn't here. Not yet. But he was close enough to send word through a runner, which meant the network still worked in scraps.

Close. Not safe. Not certain.

Lila stepped into the stairwell and leaned against the cool concrete wall. The air there was damp and quieter, muffling the basement's murmurs into a low, steady ocean.

She closed her eyes for one second.

She saw her apartment door in her mind, the way it looked last time she'd left it—bolt thrown, curtains drawn, the kitchen vent cover screwed back on like nothing had ever been hidden there. She pictured the papers inside, the tape, the notes, the evidence she'd collected piece by piece like it was a life raft.

Proof.

Proof didn't feed anyone. Proof didn't carry a child up stairs. Proof didn't stop a crowd from rushing a gate because someone whispered "private shuttle" like it was salvation.

Proof only mattered if it reached someone who could act.

Her phone sat dead in her pocket. No signal. No power.

She heard Raj's voice in the basement, gentle but firm, urging people to bring their slips for verification. She heard the lanyard woman's sharper tone, trying to keep control.

Lila's eyes opened.

She'd been treating the hard copies like a trophy. Like the story.

They weren't the story.

They were a lever.

But a lever was useless if you didn't put it under the right weight. Malik.

If Malik was building intake systems, if Malik was the one on the ground with an actual gate and actual bodies, then Malik needed to know what kind of pressure was coming. Malik needed to know whose convoys were moving while everyone else got trapped behind barricades.

Lila pushed off the wall and went back into the basement. She moved fast, not running, just cutting through people like a current.

At the volunteer table, the lanyard woman looked up with irritation already loaded. "What now," she said.

"I need a runner," Lila replied.

The lanyard woman's eyes narrowed. "For what."

"For Malik Carter," Lila said.

The lanyard woman blinked. Her control slipped for a beat. It was small, but Lila saw it.

"Who told you that name," the lanyard woman asked, too quickly.

Lila kept her face neutral. "People talk," she said.

The lanyard woman's hand tightened on the index cards. "We can't just send notes wherever," she snapped. "Runners get jumped. Notes get stolen."

"Then we fold it smaller," Lila answered.

A man at the table—older, with a pastor's collar loosened at his throat—stepped closer. His eyes were tired but clear.

"What does Malik have to do with this," he asked.

Lila held his gaze. "He's building lines," she said. "He needs to know what rumors do to lines."

The pastor looked at the lanyard woman, then back at Lila. "You want to send a message, you write it plain," he said. "No locations that turn into a stampede."

Lila nodded once. "Agreed."

The lanyard woman's mouth tightened. "You're making this shelter a newsroom," she muttered.

Lila leaned in, voice low enough that only the table heard. "You're making it a gate," she replied.

The lanyard woman's face flushed.

The pastor's gaze sharpened. "Gloria," he said, warning in his tone.

So that was her name. Gloria.

Gloria's jaw worked. She looked at the stack of index cards like they were her shield.

Lila glanced at the top card without making it obvious. A name. A number. A note in pencil: PRIVATE PICKUP CONFIRMED.

Lila's stomach tightened.

She looked up at Gloria. "Who confirmed it," she asked softly.

Gloria's eyes flashed. "Not your business."

"It becomes my business when somebody runs toward a bridge because you told them to ask at the desk," Lila said.

The pastor's eyes flicked to Gloria. "What did you post," he asked.

Gloria's mouth opened. Nothing came out fast enough.

Lila didn't press her in public. She didn't want the room to smell blood. She just said, "Take it down."

Gloria's nostrils flared. "I can't."

The pastor's voice dropped, quiet and steel. "Take it down," he repeated.

Gloria's eyes darted, calculating. Then she reached for the notice with stiff fingers and peeled it off the pillar. The tape tore, leaving a strip behind like a scar.

The room didn't erupt. Most people didn't even notice. A few did. A few watched Gloria with new suspicion.

Gloria shoved the torn notice under the stack of cards, as if hiding it made it disappear.

Lila wrote her message anyway. She borrowed a pencil tied to the table with a string. She wrote twice, because the first version sounded like a confession and the second sounded like a threat.

She chose the simpler one:

MALIK CARTER — I HAVE KLINE "CAPACITY" ON TAPE + PAPER PROOF OF CONTINUITY ROUTES. DO NOT ANNOUNCE ANY PRIVATE PICKUPS. VERIFY THROUGH RUNNERS. ASK RUNNER FOR PHRASE: RED WRISTBAND LINE. —LILA

She folded the note into a tight square and held it between her fingers like it could burn.

The pastor nodded at a teenage runner hovering nearby, a girl with a backpack and shoes worn thin at the toes. The runner's eyes flicked to Lila's face, then away, like she didn't want to get caught carrying something dangerous.

The pastor said, "You take this to the south intake board. You find Malik's people. You don't say names out loud."

The runner nodded once, jaw set.

Lila pressed the folded note into the runner's palm. Their fingers touched for a second—warm, damp, human.

"Thank you," Lila said.

The runner didn't answer. She tucked the note into her sock, under the cuff, and vanished into the stairwell.

Gloria watched her go with a look that wasn't relief.

Lila felt it like a hand on the back of her neck.

Someone else wanted control of the message.

Lila turned away before Gloria could speak again. She moved back toward Raj's corner. The radio's speaker hissed. Raj kept cranking in slow rhythm, eyes half-closed like he was listening for the shape of truth in the static.

Lila leaned close. "I need to borrow your corner," she said.

Raj's eyes opened. "It was never mine," he replied.

The circle formed again, drawn by the radio's heartbeat. People leaned in, faces lit by lantern glow, mouths tight.

Lila held her hands up, empty, then reached beneath her shirt and touched the spot where a bundle rested against her ribs.

Paper.

She hadn't retrieved it yet tonight. Not in this timeline.

Her mind jumped, quick, to the earlier hours.

She'd left the shelter that morning, before the sun burned the sidewalks into griddles. She'd watched the clock on the wall above the basement stairs—an old analog face with a second hand that jerked like it was angry.

If curfew was eight, she needed to be back before seven. Not because she believed in exceptions, but because she believed in how quickly a polite "hold on" became handcuffs now.

She'd done the math in her head like it was a prayer:

Leave at ten. Walk fast to the bus stop—twenty minutes if she didn't get stopped. Bus ride, if it came—forty. Walk to the building—ten. Get in, get out—five if her hands didn't shake. Back to the stop—ten. Back to the church—an hour if the bus ran. That gave her a thin margin, the kind that got people killed when they believed it was real.

She'd still gone.

Because the vent held more than her work. It held the only thing she trusted: paper that couldn't be erased by a blackout, tape that couldn't be "lost in transit" by somebody with money and a badge.

She'd kept Manuel out of it. She'd told him to stay at the church, to rest, to wait. He'd nodded and lied with his face, the way he always did when he was about to do the opposite.

Outside, the city sounded wrong—fewer cars, more engines idling in clusters, more shouting at intersections. She'd cut through side streets and kept her eyes on hands.

A patrol had stopped her once near an overpass, flashlight beam hitting her shoes, her bag, her face.

"Where you headed," the officer had asked.

"Church," Lila had said.

The officer's gaze had flicked to her hands. "You got papers," he'd asked.

Lila's throat had tightened. She'd forced a small, tired smile. "We all got papers," she'd replied, and held up her shelter wrist stamp—the faint ink mark on her skin already smudged from sweat and washing.

The officer had waved her through, bored or merciful or too tired to be cruel.

Her building had been quiet in the way places got when everyone who could leave had left. The stairwell smelled stale. Someone's door down the hall had been kicked in, splinters hanging from the frame. Lila hadn't stopped to look inside. She hadn't needed to.

Her own door opened with a reluctant groan. The air inside felt trapped.

She'd gone straight to the kitchen.

The vent cover sat above the stove, screws still in place. The room was dim, curtains pulled tight. She'd taken a screwdriver from the drawer and set it on the counter, hands shaking once before she forced them still.

The first screw had resisted, then turned. The metal squeaked. Dust puffed out when she loosened the last one. The smell hit her—old grease, stale air, the ghost of meals she'd cooked before the world decided to break.

She'd eased the cover off, careful. Inside the duct, she'd felt the bundle she'd wrapped weeks ago and shoved deep where a quick glance wouldn't find it.

Her fingers had closed around paper edges.

She'd pulled it out slowly, as if speed might tear it.

The bundle was wrapped in a dish towel she'd stolen from herself like she was her own burglar. She unrolled it on the counter, breath held.

Pages. Notes. A photocopy of a donor program with Gideon Kline's name printed clean. A handwritten timeline in her own hand. A list of continuity vendors and route changes she'd pieced together from phone calls and favors and people who'd whispered when they thought nobody listened. The microcassette was tucked between pages, the plastic warm from being trapped in a vent.

Lila counted the pages—one, two, three—making sure nothing was missing. She checked dates in the margins. She pressed her thumb to a sentence she remembered writing and felt the indentation where her pencil had bitten the paper months ago.

Real.

She wrapped it back up fast, tucked it under her shirt, and replaced the vent cover. Her screwdriver slipped once and clanged against the stove. The sound made her freeze, breath stuck, heart banging.

Nothing followed. No footsteps. No knock.

She'd left immediately.

Back on the street, she'd walked fast and kept her head down. A dark SUV had idled near the corner of her block, engine running. Two men sat inside, faces forward. Not cops. Not obviously anything. Just bodies in a car that didn't belong in a neighborhood that had run out of luxury.

As she passed, the passenger turned his head slightly.

Not enough to be a threat.

Enough to be a message.

She hadn't looked back.

By the time she reached the church again, sweat soaked her spine and her hands trembled from holding the bundle too tight under her shirt. She'd gotten through the basement doors and felt the room's damp air hit her like a wall. Safe, in the way caves were safe from storms until the roof collapsed.

Now, back in Raj's circle, the bundle rested against her ribs again, as if it had never left her.

The room pressed close.

Lila pulled the dish towel-wrapped packet out and set it on the edge of the radio table without opening it. Just letting people see that she wasn't making it up. That she carried weight.

A few eyes widened. A few people leaned in, hungry.

Lila lifted a finger. "No," she said softly.

The word stopped hands that were about to reach.

Raj watched her with a kind of respect that looked like recognition. He'd seen crowds. He'd seen how fast "help me" became "give me."

Gloria hovered at the edge of the circle, pretending she wasn't listening. The pastor stood behind her, silent.

Lila inhaled once. The air tasted of candle smoke and sweat and damp concrete.

"Listen," she said.

The room softened again. Not calm. Focused.

"This is not a headline," Lila continued. "This is not a route. This is not a promise."

Someone in the circle muttered, disappointed.

Lila kept going. "This is proof that private convoys are moving through checkpoints while families get turned away. Proof that people with money are buying silence and calling it 'capacity.'"

A ripple moved through the circle, anger rising like heat.

Lila lifted her hand again. "And if we turn that anger into a rush toward a gate, we will lose children," she said. "We will lose elders. We will lose the people who can't shove."

Silence tightened.

The young woman with the bright eyes stared at Lila. Her jaw worked like she was swallowing glass.

"So what," she demanded. "We just sit."

Lila looked at her and let the truth show in her face, not in words.

"No," she said. "We move smarter."

"How," a man snapped. "They got guns."

Lila nodded once. "That's why we don't fight them at their choke points," she replied. "We don't give them crowds to punish."

Gloria stepped forward, voice sharp. "You don't get to tell people to disobey," she said.

Lila turned her head slightly, eyes on Gloria. "I'm telling people not to die," she answered.

Gloria's face flushed. "You're trying to take over," she hissed.

The pastor's hand landed lightly on Gloria's elbow. "Stop," he murmured.

Gloria shrugged him off like his touch burned.

Lila saw it. The room saw it.

That was Gloria's scandal, small and ugly: control mattered to her more than safety. She'd been posting private pickup notices like bait, keeping a stack of names, treating the shelter like a guest list.

Lila could tear the whole thing open right now. Say it out loud. Point. Name.

The room's anger would do the rest.

And then someone would get dragged up those stairs and into the street and the church would become a crime scene instead of a shelter.

Lila kept her voice low. "If anyone offers you transport for money," she said to the circle, "you verify it with Pastor. You verify it with Raj. You verify it with a runner who has been to the pickup. You do not move because one person at a desk says so."

Gloria's mouth opened. The pastor cut her off with a look.

Raj nodded once. "Bring your slips," he said. "We check them."

The scrubs woman lifted her head. "How do we check," she asked, voice small.

Lila softened. "We ask three humans," she replied. "Not one. Not a speaker. Not a scrap of paper taped to a wall. Three humans who saw it."

The scrubs woman nodded, eyes wet.

Lila reached into the dish towel bundle and pulled out one page—a photocopy from the luncheon program, Gideon Kline's name printed in crisp black, sponsor list below it like a roster of people who'd paid to be safe. She held it up just long enough for eyes to catch, then tucked it back.

The room reacted the way rooms did when they saw a villain's name in clean print. People hissed. Someone whispered, "I knew it," like knowing made them less trapped.

Lila didn't let it grow.

"This stays with me," she said. "This goes to the right hands, not the loudest hands."

Someone in the back muttered, "Who's the right hands."

Lila swallowed. That was the question that kept her up in damp basements and stale apartments. Right hands didn't always exist. Sometimes it was just the least-wrong hands.

"I sent a note toward Malik Carter," she said. "He's building intake. He needs this to keep people alive when the lines tighten."

The young woman's bright eyes narrowed. "You trusting government," she scoffed.

Lila didn't bite. "I'm trusting a person who's been moving patients and kids and seniors while everyone else sells promises," she replied.

Raj's gaze flicked to her. He hadn't known Malik's name. Now he did. He filed it away.

Gloria's eyes flashed. "You don't even know if he'll get it," she said, sharp.

Lila's throat tightened. "I know," she said.

The admission hung there, raw. She didn't dress it up.

Then Lila did the thing she'd been avoiding.

She lowered her voice further. "If Manuel comes through those doors tonight," she said, "no one says his name out loud."

A few people blinked.

Raj nodded immediately, understanding more than she'd said.

Gloria's brows furrowed. "Why," she demanded.

"Because some people listen outside," Lila answered, and didn't look toward the stairs when she said it.

A hush fell, deeper than before. Fear moved through the room in a new shape—less chaotic, more focused.

The radio speaker hissed. Raj cranked. A voice came through, warped, distant:

"...stay off bridges...shelter capacity...please remain—"

Lila leaned toward the table, closer to the radio, and spoke into the space beside it, where voices carried in the curve of the basement.

"Here's what we do," she said, and kept her tone even. "We split into three checks. Raj hears the broadcast. Pastor verifies with a runner. Nurses verify with drivers. If it doesn't match, we don't move. We wait for the next check."

The young woman with bright eyes stared at her for a long beat. Then she nodded once, sharp, like it hurt.

"All right," she said. "All right."

The room didn't cheer. It didn't turn into a miracle.

It did something rarer.

It obeyed.

Footsteps sounded on the stairs—fast, uneven.

Lila's body went tight. Her hand slid unconsciously under her shirt, pressing the paper bundle against her ribs like armor.

A runner appeared at the bottom step, breathless. Not the teenage girl who'd taken Lila's note. A different one—a skinny boy with a cap pulled low.

He looked around, eyes wide, then spotted the pastor. "Message," he panted.

The pastor stepped forward. "From where," he asked.

The boy swallowed. "North side shelter," he said. "They said—" His gaze flicked toward Lila, recognized her, flinched. "They said the guy you're asking for—Malik—he's not there. He moved."

Lila's stomach dropped.

The room shifted. Murmurs rose.

Gloria's face tightened with satisfaction she tried to hide.

Lila forced her voice to stay calm. "Moved where," she asked.

The boy shook his head. "They don't know," he said. "They said the lines changed."

Lila nodded once, slow. That was the world now. Lines moved. Gates moved. Truth moved.

She didn't collapse. Not here. Not in front of people who needed her to be a spine.

"Okay," Lila said. "Then the note goes to the next board. We keep sending it until it finds him."

Gloria scoffed. "That's pointless."

Lila turned her head slightly. "Pointless is posting private pickup rumors on a pillar," she replied softly.

Gloria's face went red. The pastor's hand returned to her elbow, firmer this time. Gloria didn't shrug it off.

The room watched. The room learned who was trying to steer and who was trying to keep them breathing.

Lila didn't press further. She didn't need to.

She lifted her eyes to the circle again. "Radio hour continues," she said. "Bring your slips. Bring your questions. Bring your fear. But we don't sprint. We don't shove."

A woman near the back raised her hand like she was in school. "What about families," she asked. "What about reunification."

Lila's throat tightened. She thought of Malik again. She thought of Darius without knowing where he was. She thought of Manuel's handwritten note on the runner board.

She chose her words carefully, like placing glass on a crowded table.

"We verify reunification points the same way," she said. "We don't chase moving targets at night. We do daylight movement in small groups. We protect kids and elders first. We don't split guardians from minors unless someone with a badge forces it—and even then, we document names on paper and we send a runner."

Raj nodded. The pastor nodded. The scrubs woman nodded, eyes wet but steady.

The basement air didn't change. It stayed damp, crowded, hard.

But the room's sound changed.

Less roar. More murmur. Less panic. More planning.

Lila tucked the dish towel bundle back under her shirt. The paper edges rubbed her skin, worn from handling, real and finite and heavy.

She moved to the runner board again. She tore a small strip of paper and wrote one line in block letters, then pinned it where people could see:

NO PRIVATE PICKUPS VERIFIED. ASK PASTOR/RAJ BEFORE MOVING.

She didn't sign it.

She didn't need to.

When she stepped back, she heard a familiar cough at the top of the stairs—tight, controlled, the kind of cough someone tried to hide.

Her heart lurched.

She forced herself not to run.

Manuel descended slowly, one hand on the rail, face drawn. His eyes found hers immediately, not surprised, not relieved—just locked, like he'd been holding her in his mind as a fixed point.

Lila walked toward him, not fast, not slow. She met him at the bottom step.

"You're late," she said, voice low.

Manuel's mouth twitched, a ghost of a smile that didn't land. "I was busy not taking the bridge," he murmured.

Lila's breath caught.

She didn't ask questions in the open. She didn't need to. The words alone told her enough: gunfire, crowds, the obvious path turned into a trap.

Manuel's eyes flicked to her chest where the bundle sat under her shirt. "You went back," he said.

Lila held his gaze. "I did," she replied.

Manuel's shoulders sagged slightly, as if he'd expected it and still hated it.

"You shouldn't," he whispered.

Lila's hand hovered near his arm, not touching yet. "You shouldn't either," she returned.

Manuel's breath hitched once, tight in his chest, then he forced it smooth. He glanced past her at the room. "They listening," he asked.

Lila looked around.

The circle around the radio had grown, but it wasn't a crush. People stood in loose lines. A runner took a slip from a woman and carried it to the pastor. Raj cranked, steady as a metronome. The scrubs woman spoke to a driver near the door, checking a route with a face-to-face question instead of a prayer.

"They're listening," Lila said.

Manuel's eyes softened for a beat. "Good," he murmured.

Lila turned slightly, angling her body so Manuel was shielded from the room's attention. "I sent word to Malik," she said, low. "Not sure it reached."

Manuel nodded once. "Then you send again," he said.

Lila studied his face. There was dirt in the crease near his jaw. A faint scrape at his temple. He'd been close to something hard.

"Sit," she told him.

Manuel's mouth opened to argue. Lila lifted a brow. He stopped.

He sank onto a folding chair near the wall, exhaling through his nose. Lila crouched beside him and made her glance at his breathing look casual, like she was only checking whether he needed water.

Manuel's eyes closed for a second, then opened again. "I'm fine," he said.

Lila didn't answer. She handed him half a granola bar someone had left on the radio table. She'd already split it without thinking.

Manuel took it, chewed slowly.

Lila stood and returned to the radio circle.

Raj looked at her. "We got another broadcast in two minutes," he said.

Lila nodded. "Then we do another check," she replied.

She faced the room—faces lit from below, fear made visible, mouths tight with questions.

She lowered her voice instead of raising it.

"Radio hour," she said. "Bring your slips. Bring your questions. We don't move on whispers."

The room leaned in.

The radio speaker hissed, then steadied. Raj's hand turned the crank with slow patience. The basement's candlelight flickered. Somewhere above, thunder muttered far away like a warning that never stopped.

Lila's voice stayed steady in the dark, and for the first time in days, the room listened like survival was something they could build together, one verified sentence at a time.

Chapter 17 - Warheads in the Stratosphere

The briefing room air had been scrubbed too clean. It left Naomi's mouth dry and her lips tacky, like the building itself wanted every word to stick where it landed. Fluorescent panels washed everyone in the same pale light—no shadows to hide in, no corners to collapse into without an audience.

She set her water bottle down and watched the plastic tremble once against the table, a tiny shiver that didn't match her hands.

Across from her, paper packets sat in stacked piles, squared at the edges as if order could be manufactured by alignment alone. Someone's coffee breath carried across the table when they leaned forward. Someone else's uniform smelled faintly of sweat trapped under synthetic fabric. Chairs scraped as bodies rose and sat again, unable to settle.

They were six days out.

Time had stopped feeling like a number and started behaving like a pressure point.

Naomi kept her posture straight, shoulders back, chin level—her practiced shape of authority. She'd learned early that if she looked tired, someone would treat fatigue like permission.

The military liaison—Colonel Hastings, jaw like a clamp—stood at the head of the table beside a wheeled board where timelines had been clipped up with binder clips. He didn't look at the board as he spoke. He looked at faces, measuring compliance.

"We execute maximum-burn sequence per contingency," Hastings said. "We stay inside the boundary conditions authorized last week."

"Authorized," a deputy administrator echoed, eager, as if repeating the word made it true.

Naomi heard the way they all leaned on that word. How it could be used later as a shield.

She opened her packet anyway, not because she needed it, but because she wanted her hands doing something clean. The cover sheet was the one she'd labeled herself—FINAL WEEK ONLY in block letters so nobody could pretend they hadn't seen it. The corners were already softened from handling. The warning wasn't. She'd made sure of that.

"We also need to be explicit," Naomi said. Her voice came out even, slightly rough from dry air. "Authority boundaries. If anyone tries to insert an untested intervention into the burn window, you'll lose the corridor shift you keep asking me to guarantee."

A man in a suit—agency counsel, too smooth—smiled without warmth. "We're all aligned on the goal."

Naomi didn't return the smile. "Aligned is a word people use when they don't want to say what they're about to do."

A faint tension ripple moved down the table. Hastings's jaw flexed once.

An analyst at the far end cleared his throat. He looked young, cheeks hollowed by sleeplessness. He didn't speak until Naomi's gaze landed on him.

"The solar activity forecast has elevated," he said. "We're seeing potential for a storm that could degrade the array's stability."

Naomi nodded once. She'd read the brief. She'd read all of them. She'd read some twice because her brain didn't trust itself at this hour.

"How elevated," Hastings asked.

The analyst hesitated, searching for language that wouldn't get him punished. Naomi heard the gap between what he meant and what he was allowed to say.

"Enough to reduce our margin," the analyst said.

Naomi leaned forward slightly. "Don't say margin," she said. "Say what it costs."

The analyst swallowed. "It increases the drift risk. We'll have less tolerance for correction delays."

Naomi turned her head a fraction toward Hastings. "Less tolerance means we hold the burn longer to make the shift meaningful, which means the array stays hot longer," she said. "You can't have it both ways."

Hastings's gaze narrowed. "We have to have it both ways," he replied.

There it was. The confession dressed as necessity.

Naomi flattened her palm against the table. The cool laminate steadied her in a way breath couldn't.

"I can improve survival odds," she said, keeping her voice low. "I cannot make physics polite."

Someone laughed once—small, brittle—then stopped when nobody joined in.

Hastings lifted a hand, controlling the room with a gesture. "We execute," he said. "We keep external chatter out. Understood?"

Chairs scraped again. People moved like they were trying to outrun their own bodies.

Naomi stood with the packet under her arm. The paper stack felt heavier than it should have, like it carried the weight everyone was refusing to name.

In the corridor outside the briefing room, the air shifted—cooler, carrying faint disinfectant, stale recirculation, and something metallic that made her think of equipment racks and sealed doors. A muted alarm chirped somewhere distant, then fell quiet, as if it had been scolded.

The operations area hummed like a living thing.

Consoles stretched in rows, screens throwing soft light across tired faces. The low, steady sound of fans and power supplies filled the space. It wasn't loud, but it never stopped. Naomi felt it in her teeth.

She moved to her station, nodded at the ops lead, and slid the packet onto the desk. Her badge pulled at her collarbone when she leaned forward.

A warning light blinked on one panel—steady, patient, relentless.

"How's the drift," she asked.

The ops lead—Keller, eyes rimmed red—didn't look away from the display. "Within forecast. Solar interference is coming in pulses. We're compensating."

"Compensating isn't holding," Naomi said.

Keller's jaw tightened. "Holding is a fantasy. We're... keeping it inside the box."

Naomi watched the numbers shift, small changes stacking into something bigger. Every correction had a delay. Every delay was another chance for the system to slide past their grip.

She wrote the critical values down on a yellow pad anyway, not because she didn't trust the screens, but because her mind needed a second set of tracks. Pencil on paper had a friction the world was lacking.

Keller glanced at the pad. "You still do that," he said, a faint edge to it.

Naomi kept her eyes on the display. "I still need to be right," she replied.

Keller's throat bobbed. He didn't answer.

The analyst from the briefing room appeared behind them, breath shallow. He held a fresh sheet of printouts like they were fragile.

"Updated solar forecast," he said.

Naomi took it and scanned fast. The language was clinical, the implications not.

She felt her stomach clench, then release as she forced her breath to stay even.

"Okay," she said. "We keep moving."

A technician on the adjacent row swore under his breath when a warning chime sounded and a new message scrolled across his screen. He slapped the console lightly, like anger could intimidate software into obedience.

Keller leaned closer to Naomi. "They're already whispering," he murmured.

"Who," Naomi asked, though she knew.

Keller flicked his eyes toward the glassed-in walkway where liaison staff moved like ghosts. "Political," he said. "They want a spectacle. Something the public understands."

Naomi watched a staffer pause, glance toward the ops floor, then keep walking. She pictured headlines she wasn't allowed to read, crowds she wasn't allowed to see, the way every desperate person outside wanted one clean story: the plan worked, the threat is gone, go back to sleep.

She'd spent months learning to say the opposite in a way people could bear.

She leaned over the contingency packet and opened it to the first tabbed section. The pages were marked with her handwriting—checkpoints, sequence steps, the order she'd forced into existence when chaos tried to eat them.

"You have the burn schedule locked," she said to Keller.

"Locked," Keller echoed, but his voice wavered.

Naomi tapped the packet. "Then we treat it like law," she said.

A voice cut across the ops hum—too sharp, too urgent. "Dr. Park."

Naomi turned.

Hastings stood at the edge of the operations floor, a manila folder in his hand, another officer behind him. Hastings's face had the tightness of someone about to deliver damage without calling it that.

Naomi's stomach went hard.

She stood and walked to him, not rushing, not dragging her feet.

Hastings held out the folder. "Brief update," he said.

Naomi took it. The first sheet on top was stamped with a coalition header she didn't recognize. Not theirs. Not allied in any way that mattered.

"What is this," she asked.

Hastings's eyes stayed level. "A rogue coalition," he said, as if the word rogue was enough to absolve everyone else. "They've announced an intercept."

Naomi didn't blink. She looked down at the page again, reading the words like they were in a different language.

"Intercept with what," she asked, though the title already answered her.

Hastings's voice dropped. "They're launching a nuclear package. High altitude. Publicly framed as a last-ditch effort to shatter the body."

Naomi felt heat climb her throat. Her pulse thudded once, heavy.

Someone behind Hastings muttered, "They're calling it decisive."

Naomi lifted her gaze slowly. "Decisive is a euphemism," she said.

Hastings's jaw tightened. "They claim it buys time."

"It buys applause," Naomi replied. "And it burns our bandwidth."

Hastings held up a second sheet, already clipped to a board. "They've demanded tracking access," he said. "They're pulling analysts. They're pulling comm windows. It's happening with or without your approval."

Naomi's mouth went dry again.

"Where is the order coming from," she asked.

Hastings's eyes flickered, just once. "Not from this facility," he said.

That was another gap. Another omission that told her more than the sentence did.

Naomi turned toward the ops floor. The hum continued. People kept working. None of them knew yet that time was about to be stolen by a stunt.

Keller looked up, reading Naomi's face before she said a word.

Naomi stepped back into the operations area and raised her voice just enough to carry without becoming a shout.

"Eyes up," she said.

Heads lifted. Hands paused. The room tightened.

"A rogue intercept has been announced," she said. "It changes nothing about our mission. It will pull resources. We do not let it pull our discipline."

A technician laughed once, harsh. "A nuke," he said. "They think it's a movie."

Naomi looked at him. "Stop making jokes to hide terror," she said, not cruel, just plain. "We don't have time."

The technician's grin faded. He nodded once, chastened.

Hastings stepped forward. "Dr. Park," he warned.

Naomi turned to him. "If you want me to sit quietly while they waste time, you picked the wrong person," she said.

The words landed. Hastings's eyes hardened.

"You don't command this facility," he said.

Naomi held his gaze. "I command the burn sequence," she replied. "Or you can find someone else to sign their name to it."

Silence spread, thin and sharp.

Hastings's mouth tightened. He didn't like being cornered in front of witnesses.

"Proceed," he said, clipped. "But you will accommodate the tracking request."

Naomi nodded once. "We will give them what we can without breaking the sequence," she said. "No more."

Hastings stared at her for another beat, then turned and walked away, the folder tucked back under his arm like he owned it.

Keller leaned close again, voice low. "They're going to blame you when the nuke fails," he murmured.

Naomi kept her eyes forward. "Then they'll have to explain why they chose theater," she replied.

Keller's mouth twitched. "You think they'll explain?"

Naomi opened the contingency packet wider and ran her finger down the first checklist. "I think survivors will ask," she said.

Keller watched her hand. "You're really going to do it exactly as written," he said.

Naomi picked up her pen. The tip hovered over the first box.

"Yes," she said.

She read the first step aloud to the room—not because they couldn't read, but because speaking it made it real, a shared commitment instead of a private burden.

"Step one: verify array stability under interference," she said. "Call it."

Keller glanced at the analyst, who checked his figures and nodded once. "Verified," he said.

Naomi marked the box.

"Step two: initiate burn sequence at scheduled window," she said.

A clock on the wall ticked forward. The sound was almost nothing, but Naomi heard it anyway, each second a small shove.

Keller's fingers flew over controls. "Initiating," he said.

Naomi marked the box.

They moved through the list like that—Naomi reading, the room responding, her pen moving. The act of checking boxes by hand felt almost absurd inside a federal facility filled with screens and power, but it anchored the work to human bodies and human choices. No one could pretend later that the sequence had happened on its own.

Halfway through, a new printed timeline appeared on the wheeled board. Hastings had sent someone to post it. The sheet fluttered slightly as it was clipped in place, the corners lifting in the forced air.

Naomi saw the change without walking over.

A strip had been added in bold: NUCLEAR INTERCEPT WINDOW / TRACKING PRIORITY.

It sat on the schedule like a bruise.

The ops floor grew tense again. Naomi kept reading.

"Step seven: maintain burn through drift corrections," she said.

Keller's voice came tight. "Corrections lagging," he said.

Naomi's eyes snapped to the drift numbers. The deviation wasn't large yet, but it was changing faster than before.

"How long," she asked.

Keller's throat bobbed. "Minutes matter now," he said.

Naomi's hand tightened around her pen.

She forced her voice even. "Then we don't waste minutes," she replied.

A staffer approached from the liaison walkway, carrying another set of printouts. She held them out like an offering.

"Dr. Park, tracking demands—"

Naomi didn't take them. "Put them on the board," she said, without looking away from the drift. "We read them after we stabilize."

The staffer hesitated. "Colonel Hastings said—"

Naomi turned her head slowly. Her gaze was flat.

"I heard what he said," she replied. "If you want to interrupt the burn, you can do it with your own signature."

The staffer's cheeks flushed. She set the printouts on the edge of a desk and retreated.

Keller exhaled through his nose, a sound that might have been gratitude.

Naomi marked another box.

Then Keller's voice sharpened. "We've got an anomaly."

Naomi's stomach tightened.

"Where," she asked.

Keller pointed. A small indicator on the display shifted in a pattern Naomi had seen once before—in a different setting, on different hardware, with different stakes, but with the same ugly rhythm.

A failure signature that wasn't random.

Naomi stared at it until her eyes burned.

"Bring me the module," she said.

Keller blinked. "Which—"

"The one Ben Thorne flagged," Naomi said.

Keller's gaze flicked toward the equipment bay behind a partition. "It's here," he said, voice lower. "Sealed."

Naomi moved, the packet under her arm, her steps controlled. She didn't run. Running would invite panic.

Inside the equipment bay, the air smelled different—warm plastic, dust, the faint sharpness of overheated circuitry. A technician stood over a case on a workbench, hands gloved, face pale.

He opened the case carefully. Inside, foam held a compact module marked with serial numbers and QC stamps. A faint scorch smell clung to it, subtle but real.

Naomi leaned in. The technician looked at her like he expected blame. Like he expected her to make him the villain because it would be easier than naming the real one.

Naomi didn't.

"Print the readout," she said.

The technician nodded quickly and slid a narrow strip of output from a printer—black lines, figures, a signature pattern that made Naomi's mouth go dry.

She held the strip in her hand and compared it to the marks on the module casing. The QC stamp didn't match the expected batch. The serial alignment had a tiny irregularity, the kind a rushed replacement could produce.

"Say it," Naomi said softly.

The technician's lips parted. His voice shook. "This module wasn't the one that cleared QC," he said. "It's a swapped unit. The failure signature matches the attempted override pattern we're seeing on the array."

Keller stepped in behind Naomi, breath tight. "That means—"

Naomi held up her hand. "Don't fill the silence with guesses," she said.

She turned toward the liaison walkway where Hastings hovered at the edge, watching like he'd been waiting for something to go wrong so he could claim he'd predicted it.

Naomi walked toward him with the module strip in her hand.

Hastings's gaze went to the strip, then back to her face. "What is this," he asked, though he knew.

"Sabotage confirmation," Naomi said. "Physical. Not theory."

Hastings's eyes narrowed. "You're alleging—"

Naomi cut him off. "I'm stating what a technician said out loud with a printed readout and matching serial marks," she replied. "In this room. With witnesses."

A flicker moved across Hastings's face—annoyance, calculation.

"We can't chase ghosts right now," he said.

Naomi's mouth went dry again. "This isn't chasing," she replied. "This is naming what's already at our throat."

Hastings lowered his voice. "Dr. Park, careful," he warned. "Words carry consequences."

Naomi looked at him. "So do swapped modules," she said.

Hastings stared at her, then glanced away first. He didn't like losing.

"Document it," he said. "Quietly."

Naomi kept her voice low, but it carried. "No," she said.

Hastings's gaze snapped back.

"No more quietly," Naomi repeated. "Quiet is how we got here."

For a beat, the facility's hum seemed to pause around them, as if even the building was listening.

Then Keller's voice cut in, urgent. "Drift is worsening," he called.

Naomi turned on her heel and returned to the ops floor.

The drift numbers were climbing. The correction delays stacked. The solar interference pulses hit like invisible waves. Every time the system corrected, it corrected late.

Naomi opened the packet to the section she'd hoped she wouldn't touch.

Her pen hovered over a box she'd labeled with a blunt phrase she'd written when she'd still had the luxury of planning for disaster instead of living inside it.

CREWED SERVICING / LETHAL EXPOSURE RISK.

She heard someone exhale sharply behind her. She didn't turn. She didn't need to see faces to know what they looked like.

Keller swallowed hard. "We can't hold it," he said. "Not long enough. Not with this interference."

Naomi's throat tightened. She forced her breath into her lungs anyway.

"What are our options," Hastings called from the walkway, as if he hadn't already guessed.

Keller looked up at Naomi, eyes pleading without asking.

Naomi kept her voice steady. "The only way to hold alignment through this interference is physical servicing on station," she said. "Crewed."

A murmur rose—sharp, fearful, angry.

Hastings's voice turned clipped. "Define risk."

Naomi turned slightly so the whole ops floor could hear her, not just the liaisons.

"Radiation exposure likely fatal," she said. "Not guaranteed. Likely."

Silence slammed down.

Someone's chair creaked. A technician's hands trembled around a stylus. The warning light kept blinking.

Hastings stepped forward, voice too smooth. "We can't order people to die," he said.

Naomi looked at him. "Then stop asking me to pretend there's a clean choice," she replied.

Hastings's gaze hardened. "Is there another path," he demanded.

Naomi didn't soften it. "Not one that holds the corridor shift," she said.

Keller spoke, voice low. "We can pull back," he offered. "We can do a shorter burn, accept less shift."

Hastings seized it immediately. "We'll do that," he said. "We'll avoid—"

Naomi cut him off with a small motion of her hand. Not a slap. A stop sign.

"A shorter burn means the corridor shift becomes negligible," she said. "You'll still have a public-facing plan, but it won't protect the populations you keep citing when cameras are on."

Hastings's jaw worked. "You can't prove—"

Naomi pointed at the drift values, then at her packet. "The probability distribution is in your briefing packet," she replied. "If you want to choose comfort over outcomes, say it plainly."

The ops floor went still. People watched Hastings like prey watched a predator decide whether to pounce.

Hastings's eyes flicked, calculating. He didn't want to say it plainly. Plain words left fingerprints.

A voice came through a speaker near the liaison station—crackling, delayed. A calm voice, familiar from earlier coordination calls.

"Command, this is Servicing Craft Lead," it said. "We received preliminary advisory. We are standing by for confirmation."

Naomi's stomach tightened again.

The crew was already listening. Already present in the conversation. Not abstract.

She stepped closer to the speaker.

"Craft Lead," she said. "This is Dr. Park."

A pause. "Dr. Park," the voice replied. "We understand the exposure profile."

Naomi swallowed. Her mouth felt like paper.

"Do you have volunteers," Hastings interjected.

Naomi turned her head slightly toward him. "Don't ask it like that," she said quietly.

Hastings bristled. "We need—"

"We need consent," Naomi corrected, voice still low. "Not theater."

She faced the speaker again. "Craft Lead," she said. "If we authorize, you will be asked to hold station through a lethal exposure zone. You will not be forced. You can refuse."

The ops floor stayed silent, listening to her build a small bridge of honesty with words.

The voice on the speaker came back, steady. "Understood," it said. "We have crew who signed for risk. We did not sign for lies. Thank you for not lying."

Naomi's throat tightened. She felt her eyes sting and forced them open wider instead of letting them blur.

Hastings stepped forward, impatient. "Dr. Park, we need a decision."

Naomi lifted her packet and opened to the authorization sheet she'd printed in advance, the one she'd written plain language on after the last time someone tried to bury risk behind vague phrasing.

She placed it on the table beside her console. The paper slid slightly on the smooth surface.

She looked around the ops floor—at Keller, at the young analyst, at the technicians whose hands would carry the consequences of whatever she wrote next.

Then she looked at Hastings.

"You want to know what this does," she said. "It moves survival odds upward by sacrificing specific people."

Hastings's gaze flickered. "We don't have time for—"

Naomi pointed at the sheet. "Then stop wasting it with euphemisms," she replied.

She picked up her pen.

The room held its breath.

Naomi wrote her name on the line. The pen scratched across the page, a dry sound that seemed too loud in the silence. She signed, then slid the sheet toward Keller.

"Countersign," she said.

Keller's hands trembled once. He pressed his palms flat on the table for a beat, then picked up the pen and signed.

Naomi turned to the technician beside them. "Witness," she said.

The technician swallowed hard, then signed his name as witness, hand shaking, jaw clenched.

Naomi lifted her head and spoke into the room, voice steady, plain, impossible to misunderstand.

"At 16:42 facility time, I authorized crewed servicing to hold maximum burn through lethal exposure conditions," she said. "This decision is made to preserve the corridor shift toward open ocean. Risk is likely fatal. This decision is owned."

She stopped. She let the silence return.

No one clapped. No one spoke.

Hastings's face had gone tight, as if he'd expected her to flinch. As if he'd expected her to hide behind him.

Naomi didn't.

Keller leaned close, voice barely audible. "They'll hate you," he said.

Naomi didn't look away from the monitor. "They'll have the right," she replied.

The liaison walkway erupted in controlled motion—staffers moving, phones lifted, doors opening and closing. The building swallowed sound, but Naomi could still feel the current of panic and politics surging above the ops floor.

The nuclear intercept window approached on the posted schedule. Naomi didn't look at it. She refused to feed it attention.

A delayed cheer echoed faintly from somewhere down the corridor—someone reacting to news of the warhead launch like it was a victory.

Naomi's jaw tightened.

Keller watched the monitors. "Burn holding," he said, voice tight. "Drift stabilizing—barely."

Naomi's eyes burned. She blinked hard and kept watching.

On a large display wall, a live feed rendered the system as tiny points of light on a dark field. The object out there was too far to feel real, too vast to belong to human hands. Yet here they were, treating it like something that could be nudged, persuaded, bribed with sacrifice.

A few minutes later, a new indicator appeared: SERVICING CRAFT APPROACH INITIATED.

Naomi placed her palm flat on the table again. The laminate was cool. The coolness ran into her hand like a tether.

She watched the feed. Tiny lights moved—slow, deliberate, like insects crossing a black mirror.

Someone behind her whispered a prayer. Someone else whispered a curse.

Naomi didn't speak. If she spoke, she'd either sound like a leader or like a monster, and she didn't trust either role.

Her gaze flicked once to a side monitor where the nuclear intercept timeline ticked closer. A staffer had pinned another printed sheet to the board, the words bold: INTERCEPT CONFIRMED / PUBLIC STATEMENT DRAFTED.

Naomi's stomach turned. Public statement drafted while a crew moved toward likely death.

Keller's voice came low. "They're calling it hope," he murmured.

Naomi looked at the statement draft and felt heat rise behind her eyes. She forced it down.

"Hope doesn't come from fireworks," she said softly. "It comes from follow-through."

The servicing craft's tiny lights steadied near the comet on the display wall. The feed didn't show faces. It didn't show hands. It showed points in darkness, the kind of view that made sacrifice look clean.

Naomi hated that.

She looked away once, just for a second, toward the floor, toward her own shoes, toward the small human reality of scuffed leather and dust. Then she forced her gaze back to the display.

She stayed with it.

Hours later, when the burn held and the craft's lights still hovered, Naomi walked out of the ops area into a corridor that smelled like stale air and tired bodies. The building's quiet felt thicker at night, as if the walls absorbed sound until only footsteps remained.

Keller followed her, stopping at the vending machine that sat dark and useless. He leaned his head back against the wall for a beat.

Naomi's badge pulled at her collarbone like a weight. She adjusted it and felt how warm her skin was beneath it, how alive.

"They're going to write your name next to the deaths," Keller said.

Naomi looked at the blank wall across from them. "Then my name should be there," she replied.

Keller's throat bobbed. "You could've let Hastings do it," he said.

Naomi turned her head slightly. "He would've signed and called it 'mitigated exposure,'" she said. "He would've buried the cost in language. I'm done letting people die under softened words."

Keller stared at her for a long beat, then nodded once, slow.

Naomi walked to a small side desk where an administrative logbook sat—thick pages, pre-numbered, the kind of object that existed so future people could argue about past choices. A clerk had left it open, pen beside it.

Naomi took the pen and wrote one line in clear block letters, then closed the book.

She didn't linger. She didn't reread it. She didn't need to. The truth was there. It would outlive her.

When she returned to the ops floor, the display wall still showed tiny lights near the comet. The hum of the facility continued. The warning light still blinked, steady as a pulse.

Naomi slid her palm onto the table again and kept it there, flat, as if she could hold the world in place by refusing to lift her hand.

Chapter 18 - Concrete Air and Lullabies

The corridor kept breathing whether anyone in it could or not.

Ventilation pushed a steady stream of recycled air through slotted grates overhead, flattening the smell of disinfectant into something sharper—something that caught in Malik's throat when he swallowed. Fluorescent panels buzzed with a thin, insect sound. The light made every face look drawn and every patch of sweat shine like a confession.

Boots hit concrete in hard, measured steps. Somewhere behind him, a baby wailed until the sound went hoarse. Someone else laughed too loud, then stopped when nobody answered.

Malik stood near the intake choke point where the hallway narrowed and the rules became physical: stanchions, taped arrows, a mesh gate that swung open and shut like a mouth deciding who got to be swallowed.

The wristband station sat ten yards ahead under a sign that read INTAKE PROCESSING in block letters. The sign hung crooked, one corner tugging loose from its clip. Malik kept staring at it like he could straighten it with his eyes.

He had been staring at a lot of things like that lately.

A security supervisor paced on the far side of the gate. Stocky build, shaved head, a weapon on his hip that caught the light every time he turned. The man's name tag said RIVERA, and his face carried the confidence of someone who believed enforcement counted as morality.

Rivera's gaze kept sliding over Malik and stopping a beat too long, like he was tasting the shape of him: uniform, authority, a man who didn't look desperate enough.

Malik's badge still opened doors. It still got him waved past lines. It still made people step aside, even when they hated him for it.

That hate had a sound.

It rose and fell behind the mesh gate in a restless surge—voices folding into each other, pleading, bargaining, threatening. Malik caught fragments as they bounced off concrete.

"My kids—"

"They told us to come here—"

"You got room, you got room, I saw—"

"Don't touch me—"

He didn't look back. If he looked, he'd start counting faces he couldn't save. His mind would start doing what it did when it couldn't stop: building lists that never ended.

He pressed two fingers to the inside of his wrist where the skin was already rubbed raw from sweat and friction. The ache grounded him.

Darius. Lila. Manuel.

He didn't have time to say the names out loud. Names felt like invitations to grief.

A clipboard snapped shut at the intake desk. An intake worker—woman with her hair twisted tight, eyes bloodshot—kept peeling wristbands off a sheet that wouldn't separate cleanly. Her fingers stuck to the adhesive. She swore under her breath, then forced her mouth into a line and kept going.

A second worker stamped paper slips with a dull thud. The stamp pad looked too dry. Each hit left a faint, uneven mark.

This was the system now: paper, sweat, stiff hands, tired eyes. A machine made of people who were coming apart.

Malik moved closer to the desk, careful not to look like he was cutting. He had learned how to step forward without triggering the mob behind him, how to be present without becoming a spark.

Rivera watched him approach.

"You keep hovering like you lost something," Rivera said. His voice carried a casual edge that didn't match his hand near his weapon.

Malik didn't stop walking. "I did."

Rivera's mouth curled. "Everybody did."

Malik reached the desk and leaned in just enough to be heard over the roar.

"Any word from a runner," he asked the intake worker. "Female, dark hair, last name Reyes. Male with her. One minor."

The intake worker didn't look up right away. She kept peeling a band, fighting the adhesive. "You got a photo?"

"No," Malik said.

She huffed a humorless breath. "Then you got nothing."

A body shoved the mesh gate behind him and the whole line surged forward a half-step. The metal rattled. Rivera barked a command and two guards tightened their stance, shoulders squared, hands open like they were ready to shove people back into obedience.

Malik kept his voice low. "Someone was supposed to bring me a note."

The intake worker's eyes flicked up then, quick and sharp. "You Malik Carter," she asked.

He nodded once.

Her gaze slid sideways, checking Rivera without turning her head. Then she reached under the desk and pulled out a folded square of paper, creased so tight it looked like it had been clenched in someone's fist.

She slid it across the tabletop without ceremony.

Malik took it like it might tear.

The paper smelled faintly of old coffee and the shelter's damp air, like it had traveled through too many hands. The handwriting was small and plain.

Red wristband line. East door. Don't say my name. —L

His throat tightened. He didn't let his face move.

He folded the note again, smaller, and tucked it into his pocket.

Rivera leaned closer. "You passing notes now," he said. "This place turned into high school?"

Malik kept his eyes on the intake worker. "I'm doing my job."

Rivera's gaze sharpened. "Your job," he echoed, like it was a joke.

Malik didn't answer. Words were a trap here.

He stepped away from the desk and moved down the corridor, toward the east door lane marked by taped arrows and a strip of bright color on the floor—red bands hanging from a hook like a warning. The line for that lane was shorter, not because fewer people needed it, but because the rules for it were stricter. Anyone who couldn't prove status got bounced into the general crush.

Malik scanned faces as he walked, not looking for strangers, looking for a posture he knew: Lila's shoulders that never fully relaxed, her chin held level even when her body wanted to fold. Manuel's careful breathing, the way he guarded air like it was money.

He found none of it.

The corridor narrowed again near the east door. A guard stood there with a printed list clipped to a board. The guard's eyes moved down the list, then up at faces. Down. Up. Down. Like he was reading a future he had the power to deny.

Malik stepped into the guard's line of sight.

"Carter," the guard said, relieved. "Thank God. They've been trying to—"

A shout cut him off.

A woman in the crowd surged forward, arm outstretched toward the door, fingers clawing at air. "My mother's inside!" she screamed. "I got a paper—"

The guard pushed her back with an open hand that landed too hard. The woman stumbled into the bodies behind her. Someone grabbed her elbow before she fell.

The movement rippled through the crowd like a wave.

Malik felt his body tense, ready for a stampede that would crush the weakest first. He turned his shoulders sideways, making himself narrower, less of a target. He kept his hands visible.

"Back," Rivera shouted from down the hall. "Back or you're out."

The word out carried weight now. Out meant the doors, the night, the impact coming, the streets where private contractors and exhausted patrols shot first and asked questions later.

The crowd held, trembling.

Malik's gaze kept moving.

Then he saw her.

Lila stood near the wall in the east lane, half-shadowed beneath a flickering fluorescent panel. Her hair was pulled back tight. Her face looked smaller than he remembered, as if the last fourteen days had carved away everything that wasn't necessity. A bundle was pressed to her chest—papers wrapped in cloth, held close like warmth.

Manuel stood beside her, shoulders hunched. One hand rested on his own ribs as he pulled air in slow, controlled draws. His eyes were open wide, scanning the corridor the way hunted animals did.

A guard near them pointed down the lane. "Not here," he said. "General line."

Lila's head tilted slightly, just a fraction, like she was listening for the moment the guard's certainty cracked.

Malik moved without running. Running made people look. Running invited chaos.

He reached them and slid into their space, close enough that his body blocked the guard's view of Lila's bundle.

"East door," Malik said quietly.

Lila's eyes snapped to his. No relief showed on her face. Relief was dangerous. It made you sloppy.

"You got here," she said. Her voice stayed flat. The words meant more than they said.

Manuel's breath hitched once, then steadied again. "We almost didn't," he said. He didn't add the details. He didn't need to.

The guard leaned in. "Sir, they don't have—"

Malik held up his badge just enough to catch the guard's attention. "They're with me," he said.

The guard's eyes flicked over Malik, then over Lila and Manuel, measuring whether Malik's authority outweighed his own fear of getting blamed later.

The guard stepped aside. Not kindly. Just obediently.

Malik didn't touch Lila's arm. Touch felt like possession in a place where everyone was getting stripped of agency. Instead, he angled his body and moved, letting her and Manuel follow in his wake.

"Where's Darius," Lila asked, voice low, as if she was asking about weather.

Malik's jaw tightened. He kept walking. "Not here yet."

Manuel's breathing sharpened.

Lila didn't press. Her fingers tightened on the cloth bundle. Malik noticed the tendons in her hand stand out, pale against skin that had gone dry.

They reached the wristband station at the end of the lane.

The intake worker there looked worse than the one at the main desk. Her face was smeared with grime. Her eyes kept darting toward the crowd, then back to her clipboard as if the paper could protect her.

"You again," she said to Malik. "We're out of clean runs. We're tagging by hand now."

Malik leaned closer. "Three," he said. "Adult female. Adult male. Medical needs."

The worker's gaze slid over Lila's bundle, then to Manuel's careful breathing. She pursed her lips.

"Lane's locked," she said. "Supervisor says no exceptions."

Rivera's voice carried down the corridor. "No exceptions."

Malik felt the misprinted wristband spool against his hip where it sat in his pocket, heavy as a crime.

He'd taken it months ago during a rehearsal run, a mistake batch that would have been tossed. The numbers were slightly off. The color run was faint. The kind of thing that got rejected in a calm world.

In this world, rejection had a body count.

He kept his hand away from the pocket. Not yet.

He slid his badge across the desk. "Call Rivera," he said.

The worker's mouth tightened. "You want him here, he'll say no and make a show."

Malik glanced down the corridor. The crowd was getting louder. Bodies pressed closer to the mesh gate. A guard's weapon caught the fluorescent glare again.

"We don't have time for shows," Malik said.

The worker stared at him for a beat, then jabbed a finger toward a runner. "Go," she snapped. "Get Rivera."

The runner moved fast.

Lila shifted closer to Malik, still not touching him. She spoke without moving her lips much. "We can't stay in this lane," she said. "They'll notice."

"They already noticed," Malik replied.

Manuel's eyes lifted toward the ceiling vent. His chest rose and fell in controlled pulls. Malik caught the slight tremor in his hand.

Malik turned his head slightly. "Keep breathing," he murmured.

Manuel's gaze snapped to him, offended at the instruction, then softened when he realized Malik wasn't commanding him. Malik was watching. Malik was making room.

Rivera arrived with two guards at his shoulder. He moved like he owned the hallway.

"What," Rivera said, loud enough for the nearby crowd to hear. He looked at Malik's badge on the desk like it had insulted him.

Malik kept his voice low anyway. "They're coming in."

Rivera's gaze slid over Lila and Manuel and paused on Lila's bundle. His eyes narrowed like he had just smelled smoke.

"No," Rivera said. "Lane is locked."

Malik didn't raise his voice. "Then we put them in general and they get crushed," he said. "Or Manuel collapses and your people have to carry him while the crowd watches."

Rivera's mouth curled. "You threatening me with paperwork?"

Malik's throat tightened. He looked past Rivera, toward the mesh gate, toward faces pressed in desperation.

"Not paperwork," Malik said. "Physics."

Rivera stepped closer, lowering his voice so the crowd couldn't hear. His breath smelled like stale coffee and something sour.

"You been bending rules all month," Rivera said. "You think nobody sees?"

Malik met his gaze. "I think you see what benefits you."

Rivera's smile vanished. "Watch your mouth."

Lila's fingers tightened on the cloth. Malik saw her knuckles whiten.

Rivera's gaze flicked toward her bundle again. "What you got there," he asked.

Lila didn't answer. Her eyes stayed on Malik, waiting for him to decide whether he'd use her as a shield.

Malik didn't. "She's got nothing you need," he said.

Rivera's jaw flexed. "Everything's something now," he replied.

The corridor lights flickered once, a brief dimming that made the crowd's murmur spike. Someone shouted, "It's starting!" A few bodies surged forward before guards shoved them back.

Rivera's attention snapped to the noise. His shoulders tightened. Malik used the moment.

He leaned toward the intake worker and spoke fast, low. "When the lights go again, you look down," he said. "You act like your clipboard matters more than faces."

The intake worker's eyes widened. "Carter—"

"Do it," Malik said.

He reached into his pocket and pulled the misprinted spool halfway out, keeping it shielded by his body. The bands were a dull shade, the print slightly blurred. He could feel the tacky adhesive through the paper backing.

Lila's gaze dropped to it. Her mouth parted slightly, then closed.

Manuel's breathing hitched once.

Rivera turned back toward Malik. "What are you doing," he demanded.

Malik didn't answer. He waited.

The fluorescent panels buzzed, then dipped again—longer this time. A low tremor ran through the floor, subtle but real, like a heavy truck passing beneath the building. The sound arrived a beat later: a distant rolling that didn't belong to thunder.

The crowd reacted like one body. Voices rose. Someone screamed. A guard shouted.

The intake worker looked down, just as Malik had told her, hands tightening on her clipboard like it was a lifeline.

Malik peeled off three wristbands in one motion and snapped them around wrists.

Rubber met skin with a soft, decisive click.

Lila's wrist jerked when the band tightened. Manuel flinched as if the pressure hurt.

Malik didn't look at Rivera. He kept his focus on the task like that was the only reality.

Rivera saw it anyway.

His face changed. Not surprise—recognition. He understood what Malik had just done: stolen capacity, broken count, made himself vulnerable.

Rivera grabbed Malik's forearm hard enough to hurt.

"You just made yourself the problem," Rivera said through his teeth.

Malik didn't yank away. He kept his hands open. "Then arrest me after," he said. "Not before."

Rivera's grip tightened. "You don't get to decide after."

Malik leaned in close enough that Rivera had to hear him over the rising noise. "You're not going to shoot me in front of this crowd," Malik said. "You're not going to drag me out while the floor shakes. You'll lose control."

Rivera's eyes narrowed. His jaw worked like he was chewing on a choice.

The floor trembled again. The buzzing lights steadied, then flickered. Somewhere down the corridor, a metal door rattled.

Rivera released Malik's arm like it burned him.

"Get them through," Rivera snapped at the intake worker. "Now."

The intake worker didn't question it. She waved them toward the inner threshold where a heavy door waited, its seal visible like a thick black lip.

Malik stepped with Lila and Manuel, his body forming a buffer. He didn't touch them, but he stayed close enough that a shove would hit him first.

The inner door area was a second choke point, narrower, quieter in a way that felt wrong. The roar of the crowd stayed behind the mesh gate, but its pressure pushed through the concrete anyway.

A guard at the inner door checked bands and paper slips. His hand shook as he marked counts on a sheet.

"Three," the guard muttered, then looked up. "You can't—"

A shout cut him off.

A small figure limped into view from the general corridor, half-carried by Manuel's arm.

Darius.

His face was gray with dust. His hair stuck up in uneven clumps. One sneaker was scuffed so badly the toe fabric had split. His eyes found Malik and went wide, then narrowed like he was bracing for disappointment.

Malik's chest tightened hard enough he had to force a breath.

Darius took one step toward him, then stopped, like his body didn't trust the floor.

Malik moved fast, forgetting his own rules for one second. He reached out and gripped Darius's shoulder, firm, grounding.

Darius flinched at the touch, then leaned into it anyway, just a fraction.

"You're here," Malik said. His voice came out rough.

Darius's mouth moved like he wanted to speak, then stopped. He swallowed. He lifted his chin and made himself look older than he was.

"Don't take the bridge," Darius said, words clipped, like he was reporting, not confessing.

Malik's grip tightened once. He let go, forcing himself to keep Darius's body his own. "I didn't," Malik said.

Darius's gaze flicked to Lila. To Manuel. To the band on Lila's wrist.

"What is that," Darius asked.

"A ticket," Malik said.

Darius's eyes dropped to Malik's pocket, then back up. He didn't ask. He didn't need to. He had learned what adults did with rules.

The inner door guard looked at Darius and stiffened. "Unaccompanied minor line is—"

"He's not unaccompanied," Malik said.

The guard's eyes slid toward Rivera, who had moved closer again, face tight.

"Policy says—" the guard began.

"Policy can choke," Malik said, keeping his voice low. "Or it can breathe. Pick."

Rivera stepped in. "He stays with Carter," Rivera said, the words like a stone thrown.

Malik's gaze snapped to Rivera. The man's eyes held a warning: this isn't mercy, it's containment. Rivera wanted Malik inside the shelter where he could be punished quietly.

Malik understood.

He nodded once anyway.

He pulled another wristband from the misprinted spool and snapped it onto Darius's wrist. The rubber tightened over skin that felt cold under Malik's fingers.

Darius stared at the band like it might vanish.

Then the building shook hard enough that dust drifted down from the ceiling vent in a thin fall. The lights stuttered. A deep rolling sound surged through the concrete, closer now, like freight passing through the earth.

The crowd behind the mesh gate erupted.

Rivera shouted. Guards moved. The gate rattled under the pressure of bodies.

"Inside," Rivera barked.

The inner door guard fumbled with the latch. It resisted for a beat, then gave. The seal broke with a hiss that sounded like a lung releasing.

Malik shoved his people through—Lila first, Manuel close, Darius in the middle where Malik could see him.

The inner door slammed shut behind them.

The sound hit like finality.

For a second, everything went quieter. The roar became muffled, distant, as if the concrete had swallowed it.

Malik stood with his hand on the door, palm flat against cold metal, feeling the vibration of bodies on the other side. He could sense the crowd's desperation through the thickness.

Lila stood beside him, bundle pressed to her chest. Her breath came shallow, controlled. She didn't look at Malik's hand on the door. She looked down the corridor ahead, where more doors waited, where the shelter's interior stretched like a throat.

Darius stared at the door behind them. His fingers worked at the edge of his wristband like he wanted to peel it off and throw it back through the seal.

Manuel leaned against the wall and closed his eyes. His chest rose and fell in careful pulls. Malik watched him and adjusted his own posture, making himself smaller, less demanding of air.

A siren wailed somewhere deep inside the facility, then cut off.

A runner rushed toward them from farther down the interior corridor. He was out of breath, face slick. "Carter!" he shouted. "Secondary door—kids at secondary door—"

Rivera appeared on the interior side now, moving fast, weapon visible. "What kids," he snapped.

The runner swallowed. "Convoy got diverted," he said. "They're saying they had papers—contract lane—then the lane collapsed—"

Lila's head lifted at the word contract. Her eyes sharpened.

Malik's stomach clenched. He could picture it: an elite lifeboat promised safety, then abandoned when the physics didn't care about money. Children dragged along like baggage.

Rivera looked at Malik. "You already broke count," he said. "You want to keep going?"

The building trembled again. This time the vibration ran through Malik's bones and made his teeth click. A deep rolling sound surged, then faded into a long, drawn-out rumble that sat in the walls.

Impact. Not a clean moment, not one cinematic crash. A series of blows across the world, distant but felt.

Rivera's eyes flicked toward the ceiling, then back to Malik.

"You're not opening doors," Rivera said, voice low, urgent. "Not tonight."

Malik's mouth went dry. He reached into his pocket and pulled out the misprinted spool, holding it in his palm. There weren't many left. He could count them by feel.

He counted anyway. One. Two. Three. Four. Five.

Five thin loops of rubber that could decide who lived inside air that didn't freeze.

Lila's gaze dropped to the spool. Her grip tightened on her bundle.

Darius's eyes locked on it too.

"Those aren't for—" Rivera began.

Malik cut him off. "I know what they're for," he said.

Rivera's face hardened. "You gonna spend them on strangers while people outside—"

"Everybody outside is a stranger to somebody," Malik said.

Rivera stepped closer. "You want disease in here," he hissed. "You want a fight over rations—"

Malik held Rivera's gaze. "You already got fights," he said. "You just want them to happen where cameras don't exist."

Rivera's jaw flexed. "You think you're clean," he said. "You think this makes you clean."

Malik didn't answer that. Clean wasn't a word that belonged here.

He moved down the corridor toward the secondary door, body tight, ears ringing with the muffled roar from outside. Lila and Manuel followed, Darius limping behind them. Malik kept glancing back, counting steps like a prayer.

They reached a smaller threshold where another heavy door shuddered under pressure.

On the other side of the reinforced window, a cluster of children stood packed together, eyes huge, faces streaked with dirt. One clutched a torn backpack strap. Another held a younger one by the wrist so tightly the skin looked red.

An exhausted man in a uniform that wasn't federal pounded on the door. His mouth moved, shouting words Malik couldn't hear through the thickness.

A guard on this side shook his head hard, refusing.

The children's hands pressed to the glass. Their palms left smeared prints.

Rivera caught up behind Malik. "No," he said again.

Malik's throat tightened. He forced himself to look at the kids' faces, not the door, not Rivera's weapon, not the paper counts waiting to punish him later.

He spoke to the guard at the door. "How many," he asked.

The guard's eyes flicked over Malik's badge. "Too many," the guard said.

"How many," Malik repeated, voice low.

The guard swallowed. "Five," he admitted.

Five.

Malik's pocket felt heavy in a way that wasn't weight, just consequence.

Lila stepped closer. Her voice came low, tight. "If you do this," she said, "they'll come for you."

Malik didn't look at her yet. He watched a small boy outside the glass, maybe seven, mouth moving silently like he was trying to speak through a barrier that didn't care.

"They already are," Malik said.

Darius limped up beside him, jaw set. "Those kids," Darius said. He didn't finish the sentence. He didn't have to.

Malik took a breath that scraped his throat.

He peeled the first wristband off the spool and snapped it around his own thumb for a second—testing the adhesive, the stretch. It held.

Then he peeled it off and snapped it onto the first child's wrist as soon as the door cracked open a few inches under guard control.

"Inside," Malik said, voice hoarse but steady. "Single file. Hands visible."

The kids moved like they didn't trust the word inside. Like inside was another trap.

A small girl stepped first. Her eyes locked on Malik's face. She didn't blink.

Malik crouched to meet her at eye level, keeping his body between her and Rivera's weapon.

"What's your name," Malik asked.

The girl's mouth trembled. "Talia," she whispered.

"Okay," Malik said. "Talia, you hold your line. You keep your hands where I can see them. You don't run."

Talia nodded once, sharp.

Malik snapped the band around her wrist.

He did it again for the next child. And the next. Rubber clicking over skin. A rhythm.

Each click sounded like a door locking behind him.

Rivera's breath hit hard behind Malik's shoulder. "You're done," Rivera said, low. "You're done when this is over."

Malik didn't answer.

The fifth child stumbled through, smaller than the others, eyes glazed with exhaustion. Malik reached for the wrist and felt how thin it was under his fingers.

He snapped the band closed.

The door swung shut again, seal hissing.

The children stood inside the corridor now, blinking under fluorescent glare, shoulders hunched as if expecting a blow.

Outside the glass, the exhausted uniformed man slapped the window with his palm, then slid down the wall, head dropping. He didn't follow. He wasn't allowed. Or he didn't want to. Malik couldn't tell.

Rivera's hand grabbed Malik's forearm again, harder this time. "Move," he said.

Malik didn't jerk away. He let Rivera pull him back a step, then planted his feet.

The building trembled again—softer now, a lingering vibration like the world refusing to settle.

Somewhere deeper in the shelter, a child began to sing under their breath. Not words, just a humming line, thin and unsteady. Another voice joined, higher. The sound threaded down the corridor like something stubborn.

Malik felt his throat tighten.

He turned his head and looked at the children he'd just brought in. Their faces were blank with shock. Their eyes tracked Rivera's weapon, then Malik's badge, then Lila's bundle pressed to her chest like a heart outside the body.

Rivera's voice went cold. "You just made enemies," he said.

Malik nodded once. "I know."

Rivera's gaze sharpened. "You want to be a hero," he said. "You want to be seen."

Malik's mouth went dry. He thought of the crowd outside the mesh gate, their hands pressed to metal. He thought of the door seal hissing shut.

"I want to sleep without hearing the door," Malik said.

Rivera stared at him, then released his arm like he couldn't stand the contact.

"Carter," Rivera said, loud enough for the nearby guards to hear, "you're off intake after this shift. You'll be reassigned. You'll be watched."

There it was.

The cost, spoken plainly in a place built for quiet punishments.

Malik's jaw tightened. He nodded once again, accepting because arguing would turn into theater and theater fed the wrong people.

Lila stepped closer and, without looking at Rivera, slid a folded paper from her bundle into Malik's hand. No speech. No plea. Just weight transferred.

Malik didn't open it. He didn't need to yet. He closed his fingers around it, feeling the edge cut into his skin through sweat.

Darius's voice came soft beside Malik, almost lost under the ventilation sound. "I saw them," Darius said.

Malik turned his head slightly. "Who," he asked.

Darius's mouth tightened. He swallowed. Then he spoke the string he'd been carrying like a stone in his mouth.

"KCG—one-zero-nine-two," Darius said, careful, exact. "KCG one-zero-nine-two."

He said it again, like repetition could keep it from slipping away.

"KCG one-zero-nine-two."

Rivera's head snapped toward him. "What is that," Rivera demanded.

Darius flinched but held his chin level. He glanced at Malik once, quick, as if asking permission to be useful.

Malik nodded.

Darius's eyes shifted to the children they'd just brought in. "That convoy," he said. "I saw it on the trucks. I saw the sign. I saw the number. They had armed guys. They had papers. They said it was Kline."

The name hit the corridor like a dropped object. A few guards looked up. A staffer near a clipboard froze.

Lila's fingers tightened on her bundle. Her eyes went hard.

Rivera's mouth curled. "Kline," he said, dismissive. "Everybody got a story."

Lila spoke then, quiet but sharp. "Not a story," she said. "A contract."

Rivera's gaze snapped to her. "You don't speak unless asked," he said.

Lila didn't raise her voice. She didn't need to. "You don't get to tell me who speaks," she replied.

The air between them tightened.

Malik felt every guard in the corridor shift their attention, hungry for conflict. Conflict made them feel like the world still had rules.

Malik opened his hand and unfolded the paper Lila had given him. It wasn't long. It was a list of identifiers and a note in Lila's handwriting, tight and controlled.

Kline continuity lanes use blue-marked placards. "KCG 1092" reserved priority. Do not announce. Deliver to intake lead. —L

Malik's stomach clenched.

Blue-marked placards.

He flashed back to the earlier months: odd reroutes, privileged passages, the way certain convoys moved like they owned roads. He thought of Rivera's face when Malik challenged him. He thought of the printed list the outer guard had been reading like a fate.

He turned to the nearest staffer holding a clipboard. "Get me the convoy list," Malik said.

The staffer hesitated, eyes flicking to Rivera.

Malik didn't blink. "Now," he said.

The staffer moved, fast.

Rivera stepped toward Malik. "You're not doing this," Rivera said, low, warning.

Malik held up the folded note and kept his voice even. "You told me I'd be watched," he said. "Good. Watch this."

The staffer returned with a printed sheet—convoy manifests, stamped and clipped. The paper fluttered slightly in the forced air. Malik scanned down the columns until his eyes hit the string.

KCG 1092.

Beside it: PRIORITY INTAKE / CONTRACT LANE.

Under it: names. Not children's names. Adult names. Titles. A note: SILENCE AGREEMENT ON FILE.

The words made Malik's mouth go dry.

Rivera's hand shot out, trying to snatch the sheet.

Malik pulled it back, fast.

Lila stepped in beside him, her bundle pressed to her chest, her eyes locked on the paper like she'd been chasing it for months.

Rivera's voice went dangerous. "That list stays internal," he said.

Malik looked at him. "Internal to who," he asked.

Rivera's jaw flexed. "To the people keeping this place from becoming a slaughterhouse," he snapped.

Malik held up the list where the nearby guards could see it, where staff could see it, where witnesses could exist.

"You're keeping it from becoming a slaughterhouse by selling doorways," Malik said, voice steady. "You're letting a private company buy lanes while people outside get crushed."

Rivera's eyes went cold. "You don't know what you're saying," he said.

Lila's voice cut in, quiet, lethal. "I know exactly what he's saying," she replied. "They sold survival for silence. And you helped."

Rivera's face tightened. "You got proof," he challenged.

Lila didn't lift her bundle like a trophy. She didn't wave it. She didn't perform.

She just met Rivera's gaze and spoke in a tone that carried exhaustion and certainty.

"I have paper," she said. "I have dates. I have signatures. I have a witness who heard the offer."

Rivera's mouth tightened. "In a court, that's—"

"There is no court tonight," Malik said. "There is a door."

The building trembled again, a soft aftershock that made everyone sway. The corridor lights flickered and steadied.

The children huddled closer together, shoulders touching.

A staffer near the end of the hall began to cry silently, wiping her face with the heel of her hand and trying to hide it.

Rivera stared at Malik for a long beat. Malik could see the calculation in his eyes: how far he could push before he lost the guards, how much truth he could crush before it turned into a riot inside the shelter.

Rivera's gaze slid to the children Malik had brought in—dirty, shaking, alive.

Then Rivera looked back at the list. At KCG 1092. At the silence note.

He licked his lips once, a nervous tell.

"You think you did something," Rivera said quietly.

Malik's voice stayed low. "I did," he said.

Rivera leaned in close, close enough that Malik could smell the sour edge of his breath again. "You just made sure this place stays hungry," Rivera whispered.

Malik didn't flinch. "It was hungry already," he whispered back. "You were just deciding who got fed."

Rivera's eyes narrowed. He stepped back and raised his voice, making it official.

"Carter is removed from intake authority effective immediately," Rivera announced. "He is reassigned."

A guard shifted, uncertain.

Malik handed the printed list to the staffer with the clipboard. "Make a copy," Malik said, voice even. "Three copies. One for command. One for medical. One for the committee."

The staffer blinked. "What committee," she asked.

Malik looked at the children, at the exhausted faces, at the corridor built to swallow people whole.

"The one we're making," Malik said.

Rivera's mouth twitched like he wanted to laugh. "You're making committees during impact," he scoffed.

Malik didn't answer with words. He crouched again in front of the children and kept his voice low, gentle.

"You stay close," he told them. "You don't go anywhere alone. You hear me?"

Talia nodded, eyes fixed on him.

Darius stepped closer, limping, and stood beside the kids without being told. He didn't touch them. He just stood there, an extra body in their line, an unspoken shield.

Lila watched Malik, her expression unreadable. Then she shifted her bundle against her chest and, with careful hands, loosened the cloth just enough to show the edges of paper inside—thick, worn, handled too much.

She didn't offer it to Rivera. She didn't offer it to Malik either.

She held it like a promise she was choosing to keep.

Malik rose. The floor felt steadier now, or maybe his body had just adjusted to the shaking like it adjusted to everything.

Rivera stepped closer one last time. "You think you saved them," Rivera said, eyes cutting toward the children. "You think the door makes you righteous."

Malik looked at the heavy inner door farther down the corridor—the one they'd already passed, the seal hissing shut behind them like a lung. He pictured the crowd on the other side of the mesh gate.

He pictured the door sealing again and again.

"I don't need righteous," Malik said. "I need a line I can live with."

Rivera stared, then turned away sharply, barking orders at guards, reclaiming control with noise.

Malik stood still until Rivera moved far enough away that Malik could breathe again.

Lila stepped closer. Her shoulder brushed Malik's arm—accidental, brief. Still, the contact grounded him more than the concrete did.

"You're off intake," she said, voice flat.

Malik nodded once. "I know."

Lila's eyes flicked to Darius, then to the kids. "You'll be watched," she said.

Malik's mouth tightened. "I know."

Lila's gaze held his. The gap between what she meant and what she said widened. She wanted to thank him. She didn't. Gratitude felt like a debt, and she didn't barter with people she respected.

Instead, she asked, "What do you need."

Malik looked down the corridor where the interior hall stretched into the shelter's belly. He pictured rations, fights, sickness, resentment. He pictured Rivera's eyes on him, waiting for him to slip.

"I need you to keep your proof alive," Malik said.

Lila's fingers tightened on the bundle. "I will," she replied.

Manuel leaned against the wall, eyes half-lidded, breathing controlled. He opened his eyes and met Malik's gaze for a beat.

"Thank you," Manuel said. The words came out rough, reluctant.

Malik nodded once. He didn't respond with thank you back. He didn't have room for politeness.

The corridor lights flickered again, then steadied for good.

Somewhere deeper inside, that humming rose again—thin, persistent. A lullaby without words, carried by children who didn't know they were building a wall against the sound outside.

Thirty days later, the shelter still breathed in the same steady rhythm.

The ventilation never stopped. The concrete still held the faint scent of disinfectant, sweat, and cooked food that had been reheated too many times. The fluorescent lights had become softer in places where people taped makeshift shades over them, trying to carve out pockets of night.

Malik walked the interior hall with a mop bucket now, not a badge at the front of a line.

Rivera's reassignment hadn't been a bluff. Malik's uniform was gone, replaced by a plain shirt and work gloves. He cleaned spills, hauled trash, moved cots. He got shoved into corners of the shelter's life that most people ignored until they needed them.

He also learned names.

He learned who hid extra crackers under a sleeping mat. Who stole medicine. Who shared blankets. Who hummed when the tremors rolled through the concrete and made people flinch in their sleep.

He learned that survival wasn't one door. It was a thousand small decisions, repeated until they turned into culture.

Tonight, he pushed his bucket down the corridor and heard the lullaby before he saw the singer.

Talia sat cross-legged near a wall where cots lined up in tight rows. She rocked a younger child against her shoulder, humming under her breath. The child's fingers clutched her shirt.

Darius sat nearby, ankle healed enough that he didn't limp anymore, though Malik still saw him favor it when he thought nobody was watching. Darius was sorting a handful of plastic utensils into neat piles, eyes focused, jaw set. He glanced up when Malik approached, then looked down again as if he didn't want to admit he'd been waiting.

Lila sat on the edge of a cot a few feet away, papers spread on her lap—but not waved, not displayed. Her pen moved steadily across a sheet as she copied names and dates into a clean order, preparing a record that could survive rumor.

Manuel lay back on his cot, one arm behind his head, eyes half closed. His breathing was easier tonight. Malik noticed anyway.

Malik parked his bucket against the wall and leaned there for a beat, letting the lullaby wash the corridor smooth.

A low roll of distant thunder moved through the concrete—not sky thunder, something deeper, the earth settling after violence. The sound made a few heads lift, then lower again. People had learned which noises demanded panic and which demanded patience.

Lila looked up from her papers and met Malik's gaze.

No speeches. No promises. Just the quiet recognition that they had both crossed lines they couldn't uncross.

Malik stepped closer, careful not to jostle the children. He stopped beside Lila's cot and looked down at the paper in her lap. He didn't read it. He didn't need to. He trusted the shape of her focus.

Lila slid one sheet aside and folded it, neat, like she was sealing something.

"You still get watched," she said softly.

Malik's mouth tightened. He glanced down the corridor where guards moved at slow patrol, weapons still present, faces dull with routine.

"Let them," Malik said.

Lila's eyes flicked to his hands, rough now from work and chemicals. Then her gaze returned to his face.

Malik held still. He didn't reach first. He didn't take. He waited.

Lila's hand moved, quiet, and found his.

Her fingers closed around his with no ceremony, no performance, just pressure and warmth.

Down the hall, Talia's humming kept going, steady as breath, while the concrete held the sound like it was something worth saving.

The End.

If you enjoyed this book, a short review makes a real difference. Even a single sentence helps other readers find this story.

About the Author

Jobic Chakalisa is the bestselling author of The Diamond Curse, Target: Tehran, and North Korea's Secret Weapon. He currently lives in Chicago. He has always been a movie lover, and this certainly shines through in the way he writes his novels. You won't get lost in over-description, time will never be wasted on characters that have nothing to do with the story, and every single chapter has meaning. Jobic has only ever had one goal with his work, and that is to entertain. And he hopes your escape into his pages have at the very least done that.